RAZE VS RAZE

Raze vs Raze

*Book four in the Raze
Warfare series*

SHELLEY CASS

For those who are a work in progress.
For those who are willing to be Raze in their own way.
For those who know that love is love, and how greatly the world
needs it.

A trigger warning for readers:
There are emotional and sexual abuse scenes, mentions of sexual trauma and attempted suicide, as well as violent scenes in this novel. I promise, there's also an awful lot of sweetness and goodness.

Razes, Razes, snatched away.
Razes, Razes, break your chains …

| 1 |

One

Stars in his eyes.

Ragged breaths.

Kiddo half fell from his bike.

Heat scorched his cheeks as the helmet dropped from his fingertips.

Flames were lashing out from the top of Kid's Place to light the night, as if the diner had become a hellish birthday cake.

The glass windows had burst in their panes.

The building was creaking.

Sirens. Help was on the way.

There was yelling all around.

People running and then sinking down.

Patrons and diner staff gaped and panted out on the road.

"Police! We need the police!"

"Fire department! Call the fire department!"

Dead Raze recruits were strewn around the diner car park.

Silver Bullet and Hellion bodies littered the gravel among them.

Slain snatchers too. Freakish in their masks.

A bike skidded to a stop beside Kid. Its roar cut off.

"Shit."

Seethe's voice sounded distant in Kiddo's ears.

Seethe clutched his side and let his bike topple.

Hato caught up to them, hobbling off his own bike. Stiff all over.

Beneath fuzzy layers of shock, Kiddo could feel the distinct ache in the crook of his neck too, where Dom's fingers had struck. The odd sluggishness from the strike continued to weigh down his limbs, though stabbing bursts of tingles kept them from being totally numb.

"There's still a fight going on in there," Seethe hissed, eyes narrowed in the glare as his attention turned to the gang's base behind them.

It wasn't burning, but clubbers were fleeing from The Lair; snatchers on their heels ... and gangsters or Raze recruits were in turn on theirs.

The roller doors to the garage above the club had been stormed – broken inward by two crashed tank-like vehicles.

Over the raging of the blaze at Kid's Place there were sporadic cracks of sound. Like cars backfiring, or fireworks exploding.

Lights flashing in the windows of the warehouse and on the rooftop suggested the snatchers had resorted to a gun party.

"Sparks and Jingle might not be gone yet."

Seethe was off immediately, and Hato charged doggedly

toward the medical centre, trying to lift heavy feet filled with zapped nerves.

Frazzle and Daleeah would need help. If they hadn't been taken.

"Miss Dorris," a voice cried out in relief. "You're here! Get her to the ambulance ..."

A waitress was urgently lifting Miss Dorris' frail body up, struggling to support the stooped and wheezing lady toward where the first responders were racing down the street.

"We didn't think ... Miss Dorris made it out," a waiter coughed, his face creasing. "Rue ran back in ... before I could stop her."

For all the heat, Kiddo's blood ran cold.

Rue ran back in.

It was like a slap to the face – snapping him out of his fog.

A jolt to action.

Rue could not be gone too. Not like that.

"Kiddo?!"

A deep voice yelled after him as someone saw him take off.

In moments, they would have seen him disappear like a wraith – lost amongst the streaming shrouds of grey smoke that poured thickly from the gaping diner windows.

Blinking away pinpricks of light and particles of ash, Kiddo vaulted inside.

His shoes crunched down on crystals of glass and his hip slammed into a table. The tabletop scorched his palms before he pushed off – pulling up the neck of his t-shirt to cover his mouth and nose.

He stooped and tottered forward as the flames soared upward around him – eating up the walls to run across the roof as if in a backwards waterfall, with gravity reversed.

Huge sheets of plaster bulged overhead dramatically, and had fallen onto the tables in the middle of the room. The holes in the ceiling showed flames licking their way through the rafters.

He squinted through the amber haze, his eyes like burning coals, sweltering away in their sockets.

The vortex of whirling air inside the diner plucked at him as if trying to shove him off balance.

Kiddo ignored the rushing feeling of plaster crashing down behind him. The walls were groaning. Without the windows, the front of the diner was being consumed quickly.

He scanned under every table, tearing at scorched pieces of fallen ceiling, which glowed at the edges as he yanked each one away.

Nothing under that one.

She wasn't there.

Time was running out.

A new, odd hailing sound suddenly came from the front, and alarming booms resounded from the ceiling. Jets of water hitting protesting surfaces.

The fire department.

Likely they couldn't see any entry points to try a rescue.

The parts of the ceiling that hadn't already collapsed inward buckled and swelled in a sickening way.

Kiddo couldn't hear much over the impossible volume of the fire. But he did hear a child's piercing squeal when the front of the building finally caved in on itself in a thunderous crash.

The whole place shuddered and moaned then, visibly shifting and swaying slowly towards its doom. The diner's skeleton was breaking up.

The squeal came again as Kiddo desperately broke his way through a plaster pile over one of the tables near the counter, to finally reveal a tiny ghost, balled up in the dust.

Rue was all giant eyes and tear streaked cheeks as her arms reached for him desperately – her hands just little gloves of soot.

Kiddo didn't pause, scooping her up to cuddle into his body as he hurdled them both over the counter and toward the kitchen.

The swinging doors were half jammed under their sagging frame.

Gritting his teeth, Kiddo turned to barge his way through the door with a shoulder, only to collide with a fallen beam that had been blocking the other side.

The front of the diner had collapsed. The middle of the diner was about to follow suit. The back was an obstacle course of warping benches and destroyed ceiling.

"Hold tight," Kiddo rasped, and he felt Rue cling to him even harder.

He got down low, army crawling over rubble and under smouldering, hanging beams. Scraping along on his arms and toes to keep from dragging Rue against the wreckage on the floor.

He tensed as something heavy fell across his back, but forced his way out from under it, trying not to suffocate on the smoky dust that had rained down on them.

His forearms and elbows were as raw as his eyes and lungs felt by the time he reached the corner with the fridges.

Swallowing the taste of burnt metal on his tongue, and his core straining as he now held his and Rue's weight up with one arm, he reached for the crates between the fridges. He forced them aside, shoving them into a pile of broken wood and plaster that was walling them in on either side, so that at last he could see the square of floor that he needed.

Feeling for the hole he knew he would find, he fumbled the trapdoor open and slithered the two of them forward, into the darkness of the secret tunnel under the diner.

Dragging in the cooler underground air, Kiddo managed to turn painfully so that he wouldn't crush Rue beneath himself, before the starry lights that had been trying to obscure his sight for too long now, finally closed in on his vision.

He felt his frame jolting and juddering uncontrollably.

And then he was out.

| 2 |

Two

The world was growling and rumbling above.

Was he beneath an earthquake?

A shrill child's voice was squealing.

"I've hurt him too! I've hurt him too! I didn't shock him, I didn't mean it!"

The squealing was coming from a warm weight seated on his stomach – the panicked child tugging at his shoulders and pulling on his stinging arms.

"He chose to run in after you. He has epilepsy. This is not your fault," a deep voice reasoned.

Narkon?

Who else would sound so calm while the apocalypse was unfolding over their heads?

There were gulps from Rue.

"It's … it's not a shock?"

"He must have had a seizure. It's understandable." Definitely Narkon's tone. "I'm sure these concrete tunnels are safe, but shall we get out from underneath the diner?"

The weight on Kid's middle refused to budge for a moment.

Protective.

"I'll help you get him out," Narkon promised.

Kiddo groaned as he felt himself being hefted up to stand.

One of his throbbing arms was thrown over the taller chef's narrow shoulders, to be gripped at the wrist.

Narkon's firm hold also wrapped around Kid's waist, while a much smaller hand clasped a handful of Kiddo's t-shirt – as if Rue meant to stop Narkon from running off with Kiddo without her.

The night air next roused Kiddo enough that he registered the sirens and voices from the wreck as being more distant now.

Narkon had got them out to the street.

"The snatchers and any Hunters are going to get out of this area quick-smart as the cops come," Rue said in a frightened voice. "We've got to go before any duck out this way!"

"I need to call Kiddo an ambulance, or to get him to the clinic," Narkon disagreed.

"You keep him out in the open while he's weak and he'll get snatched too," Rue cried in exasperation. "The Razes are almost all snatched up now! You want that for him?"

"S'fine," Kiddo spoke up. "Sh'sright."

Narkon lowered Kiddo to the gutter, where Rue quickly pressed to his side to keep him from slumping sideways. Kid put his head in his hands.

"What are you doing?!" she demanded of the chef.

Narkon straightened. "My car is parked not too far from here. I'll get it. You try to find Kiddo's phone."

Kiddo's stomach roiled like the sea in a storm, and all he could do was take deep breaths with closed eyes until Narkon came to hoist him into a flashy car – laying him across the back seat.

Rue had managed to fish Kiddo's phone from his jeans pocket, but she tossed it to Narkon and scuttled into the car after Kid to cushion his head.

"Hurry up and drive," she insisted as the chef got into the driver's seat, his attention on the screen.

"There are twelve missed calls from Hato. He was the one I was intending to contact."

"He'll call back," she said urgently. "Hurry-hurry-hurry!"

Narkon pulled away from the curb, and Kiddo felt Rue's hands patting his hair and face more worriedly than comfortingly.

He lifted an arm so that he could take hold of her in support.

She sniffled.

She was hugging his hand when Hato apparently called again, with Narkon pulling over to answer the phone on speaker mode.

"Where *are* you?" Hato's voice rumbled. "Seethe and I thought they managed to snatch you as the fight was breaking up!"

There were heavy breaths over the speaker.

"Kid ... we're the only ones left."

No.

No ...

"Hato," Narkon interjected smoothly. "This is Narkon speaking. I have Rue and Kiddo in the car with me."

There was a pause. Noises and static.

"What's going on?"

Narkon pulled back out to keep on the move, and proceeded to explain how he had found the two of them.

"I'm headed toward the public hospital," Narkon went on. "But would you prefer me to bring him back to the clinic?"

"Don't do that," Hato stated quickly. Even though Hato would despise having Kiddo out of his reach right now.

"Did anyone see you take Kiddo out of there?" Hato asked gruffly then.

Rue was clinging on to Kiddo, hugging his hand to herself so tightly that he could feel her racing heart.

"Nobody saw us, we came out of the tunnels," Narkon assured Hato. "The last a number of people know, Kiddo disappeared into the fire and did not return."

"Then hide him with you to recover," Hato bit out begrudgingly. "The clinic has been locked down, and I don't want him traced to any hospital that he could easily disappear from while he's vulnerable."

"Hato …" Kiddo tried to project his voice from the back seat. He cleared his aching throat – sounding like a Hellion. "Fraz … and Dalee?"

There was messy background noise again on Hato's end as he paused once more.

"Frazzle and Daleeah weren't counted as Razes. Neither were the trainee Razes. Sparks and Jingle were taken. No sign of any of the others."

"You ... need to get out of there," Kiddo managed. "You, Seethe and I ... have targets on our backs."

"You are also welcome to stay with me," Narkon offered seriously. "I will send you the address."

"No," Hato negated. "Don't send your address. Get rid of this phone when you can. Kid, we'll be here. We're staying with the clinic, the community, and to patch up everyone who tried to stop Jingle and Sparks from being taken."

Rue wiped frantically at the moisture that Kiddo hadn't even registered gathering beneath his closed lashes.

"You got that, Kid?" Hato asked after a moment. His voice was heavy.

"Yeah," Kiddo sighed. "Yeah. I got it."

He understood that if one more attack went down tonight, he would be the only Raze left. The only one hidden enough to survive.

"Rue and I will take good care of him," Narkon promised before the call ended.

Kiddo squeezed Rue's hand again.

Done in.

"Don't be afraid, Rue. I'm not passing out right now. I'm just very tired. Need to sleep."

He felt like he was sinking in on himself.

Crushed.

Crashing.

"I'm sorry. Really sorry," she whimpered softly, and held onto him as he sank completely.

| 3 |

Three

Kiddo hissed and recoiled, flinching away from searing pain that shot up from his elbow.

"It hurts," he frowned. Eyes still closed.

This was the point when Dom would usually ask him where, and when Dom would begin one of his luxurious massages along helpful nerves and into tightened muscles after one of Kiddo's seizures.

"It will hurt for a while I'm afraid," a steady, thoughtful voice told him.

Not Dom's voice.

Kiddo blinked his eyes open blearily – his heart tripping over its last beat as a spike of memory hit him.

Kiddo hissed again as he lifted his head from where it had been rested back against a leather couch, in time to see Narkon dabbing at the abrasions stretching from Kiddo's wrist to elbow.

The room only spun for a moment, and Kiddo took in Rue – sleeping heavily, with her head crooked up against

Kiddo's hip, and with Narkon's beautiful jacket over her plaster covered form.

The room actually wasn't so much a room, as much as an expansive suite. It was warmly lit, with gleaming marble floors and creamy coloured rugs. Kiddo and Rue were probably the dirtiest things to have ever crossed the threshold.

"How'd we get here?" Kiddo frowned – wincing as Narkon continued to press at the wounds on his arm.

There were sooty marks all over Narkon from where he'd clearly supported Kiddo against himself.

Kid noticed that his own hands had been scrubbed clean already. A few cotton face washers that would never be white again were set beside a dish of soapy water. But the chef had moved on to using gauze patches for the raw abrasions and missing chunks of skin on Kid's arms.

"The elevator."

"Your place has an elevator?" Kid grimaced as he felt the gauze dabbing over embedded dirt and debris. "Where are we?"

The wounds already felt sticky from weeping, but Narkon tended them without issue, as unruffled as if he were cleaning the catch of the day for a fine meal in the kitchen.

"This is the penthouse of The Vire Hotel," Narkon replied. "Where I have been staying."

Kiddo let his head fall back again. "Well, The Hunt will definitely never think to find me here," he stated flatly.

The Vire was the most exclusive inner city hotel. And the most prestigious hotel in their whole region.

"Some patches on your arms are quite severe," Narkon told him. "Either missing a number of layers or containing splinters. These should be seen to. But for now, I'll just dis-infect and bandage them after you have rinsed away as much debris as possible in the shower."

Kiddo held still as Narkon went on in his work, method-ically and mercilessly. The chef resolutely clamped down on some particularly deep craters, which gradually slowed in their oozing under the pressure.

"Your room cleaning service won't be impressed by the filth your guests have brought in." Kid blankly observed the shadow-like imprints that he and Rue were leaving on the creamy leather of the couch.

"Rue refused to leave your side to wash up," Narkon an-swered, his voice dry with the fact that she hadn't been able to stay on guard by Kiddo's side anyway. "Though I have placed some comfortable clothing in the bathroom that you both may borrow."

Kiddo gingerly exchanged arms when Narkon prepared a new handful of gauze and motioned for the other one. Care-fully, Kid lowered his free hand to gently rest on Rue's mess of hair.

"I'm surprised you had a suit in Rue's size," he sighed, with no energy behind the jibe.

"One of my sleep shirts will be fine for a nightdress on her," Narkon returned, before squeezing Kid's wrist to fully draw his attention. "Is it alright that you have slept so much after experiencing a seizure?"

Kiddo shrugged, feeling the tension in his muscles and the bruising on his neck. "It's not the best if it's a struggle to stay awake after a fit. But I get tired out by them. It's normal enough for me."

"Tired out by rushing into burning buildings too, I suppose," Narkon remarked.

"Among other things that went on," Kiddo added in a monotone. "I'll pop the right pills and get myself on track back at the base tomorrow."

If Hato and Seethe made it through the night for the base to be worth returning to.

"Did you wreck my phone yet?"

Narkon angled Kiddo's arm so that he could deal with Kid's elbow with greater ease.

"Rue was adamant that it had to be done before we got here," the chef answered. "And with force. She smashed it on the road so thoroughly that no chips could have survived and no new battery could ever revive it. I also placed it in a puddle of water to be sure."

If Kid had had the energy to snort out a laugh, that image of the very distinctive styles of Rue and Narkon would have done it.

"However," Narkon went on. "I noticed that Hato had emailed you a prescription. Before Rue destroyed the device, I forwarded it to my private account, and then to our night service here at the front desk. They are taking care of it as we speak."

Kiddo did half puff, half cough incredulously at that.

Despite everything, Hato had still made sure Kid would get his meds.

Here he was, waiting for a prescription to be filled. Not even queuing up in some late night pharmacy to do it himself – instead with a helpful front desk employee in a top hotel doing the work for him. All while the other Razes were ...

"Thank you," Kiddo said tiredly. "You've got to be the best volunteer I've ever taken on."

Narkon discarded his used gauze to begin besmirching another handful.

"I've had many great students," the chef countered matter-of-factly. "But none that I respect and admire quite so deeply. I am honoured to help."

Kiddo caught his breath and bit the inside of his lip.

Shaking his head to himself.

Compliments and kind words were about as dangerous as a hug would be to someone on the brink of tears.

"Everything this student has worked for has just gone up in smoke," Kiddo uttered bleakly. "I can't even comprehend what I've lost."

It felt like something more than skin had been carved away from him.

Narkon could also tell he wasn't just talking in a literal sense about the diner.

The chef tapped Kiddo's knee to still its jumping.

"Do you want to discuss what happened?" Narkon asked, and Kiddo's stomach bunched sickly.

He released a breath that had nothing to do with the physical pain of his injuries.

"The Wolf saw his moment to split us up, and he took it."

He took everything.

Narkon regarded him grimly. "Why do you think you were all hit in such a way tonight? You are often separate, doing your different duties. What made this time special?"

Rue shifted against Kiddo, making a sad noise in her sleep. He stroked her forehead.

"The Wolf had his baby spy to tell him exactly when Dom would be ready for snatching," Kid swallowed thickly. "But we didn't know that Rue was being forced to be more than just a spy."

Narkon closed his eyes momentarily to collect himself. "And what was she being forced to do?"

He finally set aside his cloths, and released Kiddo's arm.

"Jingle was sent footage of the Wolf using shock torture, and some kind of snatcher mental conditioning, on Dom."

He felt sick all over again.

"Yorak also revealed that he had been threatening to kill Rue if she didn't take every opportunity to shock Dom too. And Dom kept telling her it was fine."

Kid pressed his fingers into the corners of his prickling eyes.

Narkon's shoulders dipped. He was likely remembering how devastated Rue had been in the diner when Teddy had pointed out that Rue and Dom were not meant to care about each other. That snatchers normally hurt Razes.

Rue had been so excited to read that book, 'My Big Family,' with Dom. Before she'd been reminded that she couldn't actually have such happiness herself. That she was playing a role in destroying it.

"So, Raze's gaps in memory, and poor health ..." Narkon began.

"Were Yorak's latest, most concerted efforts to physically weaken and mentally hijack Dom," Kiddo answered. "I think it was happening regularly, for as long as the poisonings had been going on."

He held his head, feeling as though it was weighted.

"The Wolf seems to have the ability to use hypnosis with the shocks. Dom had no memory of what was happening to him, but he was becoming more and more addled with time."

Kiddo was still in disbelief. He stared down at the ring on his thumb – put there by Dom so recently.

"And now, after today's final shock, Dom has no memory of ever coming home. Of the Raze gang. Or of me. He thinks *we* snatched him from Japan, and that Yorak is the only one who has been trying to help him."

Narkon's brow was furrowed. "Rue reported that the damage was done, and Yorak set the last parts of his plan in motion then?"

"He just had to captivate our group with his footage, while waiting for Dom to wander away in confusion, and for the rest of us to react. The Wolf would have watched some Razes going off to try to keep others safe, some chasing Dom, some staying behind. Even the international Razes were distracted enough to be hit right then."

Kiddo stopped himself from rubbing at his eyes again. He didn't need to smudge ash into them.

He wanted to burst up off the couch and hunt Dom down. He wanted to find out if Teddy was alright. He wanted to charge away to back up Seethe and Hato. To find Sparks, and his entire family.

He wanted to curl up and escape everything.

"What can be done?" Narkon asked solemnly. "Is there any way to take the power back? To get an advantage?"

Kiddo puffed a dark, humourless laugh.

"Yorak will be moving on with whatever his next long

term plans are now. Who knows where the Razes have been taken to? Or where they'll be by tomorrow. He'll have buyers lined up ready to go."

Narkon rubbed at his brow. "Seethe and Hato have their minds on what they can do here, now, to reclaim order. Perhaps you can think further ahead, like the Wolf. And consider what needs to happen next. What is the most important thing you can do, that might help you to move forward?"

Kiddo tried not to be hopeless. He thought it through, and then exhaled slowly.

"We need to find the cleverest of the Razes, or we'll never find the rest of them."

That meant not wallowing in helplessness.

"And what needs to happen, in order for you to find the cleverest of the Razes?" Narkon prompted.

"We're going to need to avoid being snatched ourselves. And we're going to need help from the system," Kiddo answered.

It was time that the Razes weren't left to fight alone, on behalf of secret benefactors.

"How would you get the system on board?" the chef pondered.

Narkon knew enough to see that world leadership and organisations had long been well aware of such a widespread underground issue, and yet had not directly involved themselves in a war on the corrupt underworld before.

"I'll have to think on how to make this a thing of public interest," Kiddo sat up a little straighter. Still drained, but with a glimmer of energy to prop himself up now. "And use what contacts we have to get the message out to the right, influential parties."

Narkon was nodding. "Good. This is proactive. We can't control much right now, but we can control how we proceed. And …"

"And?" Kiddo asked warily.

"We can control infection and hygiene," the chef told him. "I'll show you to the bathroom."

| 4 |

Four

Rue woke up like a feral cat when Kiddo stood and tried to slip away from her.

Her fingers were claws that dug into his forearm, and she was up like a shot after him – her face red with sudden anger that he'd tried to leave.

Then in an instant, she saw the pain that had crossed Kid's face at her grip on his arm, and her anger dissolved into heartbreak.

Kiddo was startled as she shifted abruptly to cling onto his waist, wrapping her arms around his middle like a tight belt, and wailing into his stomach.

Narkon was stunned to silence himself for a moment; stupefied by how attached and turbulent the usually abrasive Rue had suddenly been in a series of seconds.

"Ah, Rue," Kiddo said tentatively; gently patting her scrawny shoulders. "I'm sorry that I scared you awake. I was just going to shower."

"Nooo," she wailed. "I h-h-urt you and you're lea-leaving. I'm sorrrrry. Please don't g-go."

Her frame heaved under Kiddo's hand, and he quickly knelt down to be on the same level as her.

At once she swapped to grab onto his neck and to bury her face against the bruises Dom had given him. He could feel her tears dampening his skin.

"You couldn't do anything that would make me want to abandon you," Kiddo told her firmly. "Narkon's cleaning hurt my arms much more than you could hurt me anyway," he cocked an eyebrow at the chef.

"I-I'm … thereasonyou … lost them alllll," she sobbed, struggling to regulate her breaths. "D-Dom and Sparks are l-lost. M-my fault. And they c-cared about meee."

Even Narkon's cool demeanour had become anguished on this devastated child's behalf.

"None of this is your fault," the chef assured her in a sombre tone. "It's all the Wolf."

Rue shook her head against Kid. "I didn't have to … p-put my own skin first. But I d-did. I h-helped him to h-hurt people I liiiike." The last word drew out, becoming a howl.

"Rue, Dom chose to put your life first too. He preferred you do whatever you had to do to stay alive. And he chose exactly as I would have," Kiddo tried to speak levelly. "We have forgiven you. You need to be more forgiving of yourself."

"F-forgive mys-self?!" she spluttered, tightening her hold so that Kiddo winced over her shoulder. "I-I'm a traitor! I *hate* traitors! *You* should hate me!" she was half strangling him, and he had to lever her a little to catch his breath.

"The Wolf told Dom what he'd had you do, and Dom still said he would choose your safety every time. I knew everything you'd done, and I decided I would go into a burning building after you," Kiddo tried to put her at ease. "There's no hate for you here."

"You knew I was bad ... and you still saved me," she choked. "Th-then you got hurt. Just like anyone ... else who cared."

Her small form was radiating alarmingly with heat and anxiety.

"Even if it hurts, I'll always save you," Kid answered. "It would hurt more not to save you, or to give up on you."

Narkon sat slowly on one of the sofas so that he wasn't hovering over them. "Kiddo is right. You should be more understanding of why you acted as you did. You knew what the Wolf was capable of, and you were trapped into doing things you did not want to do."

"Betraying ... the only ... people who ... ever felt like ... my own big family," she howled. "I d-don't want to be a traitor anymore. N-no matter what. I want to get a family."

Kiddo held her securely. "You've got me. I'll be your family, while we try to get the rest of them back."

She took in big gasps of air against him, her breaths hot and shuddery against his neck.

"I w-wanted you to say that," she managed, though she still sounded heightened rather than consoled. "And now I c-can't let anything ha-happen to you."

"We'll try not to let anything bad happen to each other," Kiddo promised. "But bad things do happen. And in that case, we'll try to get through them together."

There was just the sound of her trying to get in enough breaths for a few moments. But finally he felt a begrudging nod, even if her fingers were still digging into him; unwilling to let go as she gulped in more air.

"Will … Hato and S-Seethe be happy that you have me?" she asked, at last a little less hysterically. She was trying to rein in the wildness of her tone.

Kid managed a slight smile. "Hato will surely love being a grandfather," he mused. "And Seethe will be Seethe."

She gave a wet sort of snort that bubbled against his neck.

This truly had to be a parental type of love for that not to be any sort of bother to him. He leaned his temple against her head.

"Hato's Raze profile said he's not even thirty," she protested half-heartedly. "H-He's not a grandpa."

Kid shrugged, jostling her face. "You wait. He'll act like one without meaning to."

Narkon coughed lightly. "In the scheme of things, I'm old enough to be Hato's parent. But I don't think I'm ready for great-grandfather status. If you can make do with a distant uncle, I would be glad to fill that role."

Kiddo felt Rue's mouth moving in a reluctant smile.

Her wiry frame lost some of its tautness.

"Yes," she sniffed. "I need one of those."

Narkon nodded in satisfaction. "Well, as the authority figure here, I had suggested Kiddo wash up. Are you ready to release him so that he may use the bathroom?"

At once every bit of tension that had relaxed out of Rue burst back out of her again. "Nooo," she said, gripping Kiddo hard once more. "He's not leaving me."

Kiddo tried to loosen the pressure of her bony forearm against his Adam's Apple.

"It's alright, I'll just be in another room," Kiddo forced the words out past her strangulation as placatingly as possible. "I don't feel like another fit is coming on. I can't drown in the shower. And from penthouse height, nobody will be snatching me from any bathroom windows."

"No," she repeated, and he could feel her heart starting to race her back toward another outburst.

"I'm going to need my privacy," Kiddo tried. "Just like I'll be giving you yours."

Her breathing was speeding up once more.

"Perhaps," Narkon suggested, "while Rue is so concerned tonight, she and I could take seats to guard the bathroom door."

Kiddo grimaced at the chef.

"Door open," Rue insisted.

"Door closed," Kiddo negated at once. No way was that happening.

"Door ajar," Narkon reasoned.

Kiddo gave the other man an accusatory glare.

Rue considered it.

"Alright."

"Ugh," Kiddo uttered. Hoisting both of them up.

She clung to Kiddo's neck so that he had to carry her while Narkon fetched two chairs to set down outside the bathroom.

She only finally disentangled herself from him and stayed in her seat when Kiddo grumbled and left the door open by the tiniest of slivers.

The chef immediately distracted her by telling her how nice it was going to be to act as an uncle. He had no siblings, and had never found the time to settle down with a wife or to have children of his own.

"I'll be able to spoil you with so many nice new things of your own. You'll have to think of your favourite colour," he was saying. "We can teach you to cook. We can take you for bike rides ... We can hear *you* cursing in there," Narkon paused to call through the door when Kiddo reacted to the jets of water hitting his arms.

Now the man was taking his uncle gig much too seriously.

"Nasty language is not suitable around children," Narkon chided, using the same kind of shark tone that he used for scolding trainees in his kitchens.

"Nothing I haven't heard," Rue announced in return.

"This is the world's most awkward shower!" Kiddo griped back. But he gritted his teeth silently as he tried to let the shower wash away some of the stuck fragments of grit and dirt.

He was grateful for Narkon's selection of relaxation-wear as he gingerly dressed. His own clothing looked like it should have stayed behind at the diner – consigned to the fire. But, far from relaxing as the new clothes encouraged, Kid tensed in the middle of pulling on a soft, short sleeved shirt.

The doorbell had chimed.

Narkon gasped outside the door.

"Rue –"

Kiddo quickly crossed to find Narkon clutching Rue's hand, which clasped a little sheathed knife.

They both blinked at Kid – one wild eyed and the other incredulous.

"She carries a knife in her pocket," Narkon stated.

"She's lived on the streets," Kiddo answered.

She probably still had her mini taser too.

Rue scowled, and lowered her hand.

"It's just room service, Rue," Narkon gathered himself. "Bringing Kiddo's medication and some dressings. Please don't stab anyone when I open the door."

She tensed as Narkon left to attend to the delivery, watching the exchange carefully until he closed and locked the door again.

"No Hunter would announce themselves so politely," Kiddo reminded her. "Your turn in the bathroom. Narkon's sleep shirt will have to do for you tonight."

Rue sulkily got up when Narkon returned with a glass of water and his paper bag of pharmacy supplies. She pushed Narkon back into his chair, and then hustled Kiddo down onto the one that had been hers.

"Do you need help with getting the water temperature right?" Kiddo asked her uncertainly. He'd scolded his own arms just before.

"I've used public ones, I know how," she huffed, closing the door over like Kiddo had.

But they both noticed her eye quickly peeping at them to make sure they weren't going anywhere.

Narkon passed Kiddo the glass of water and his medication, and Rue deigned to move off to turn the shower on.

"I'm sure this is just a phase after such a traumatic time," Narkon commented discreetly, taking one of Kiddo's arms so that he could tap ointment over the open sores and begin bandaging them.

"She'll be back to kicking me and running off in no time," Kiddo grimaced.

The chef got to work winding his roll of bandages patiently. He was finishing the second arm when Rue re-emerged, looking like a scrubbed pink wraith from the turn of the century in such an oversized white shirt.

"I have some spare toothbrushes in the top drawer," Narkon informed them, "and a hairbrush, so that your hair doesn't dry in knots," he added for Rue.

Her surprise stopped her short. "Really?"

"Hato was always a big advocate for brushing teeth twice a day when he took me in," Kiddo agreed. "Best to start good habits now."

She seemed incredibly gratified to do her teeth beside Kiddo at the basin, and to let him try to tame her wet hair with a comb and hotel dryer before the curls dried into tangles.

She didn't complain at the pulling and clumsy fussing.

She did complain when Narkon suggested she sleep in the other available bedroom in the penthouse. The chef proposed that she could make herself at home there for as long as she wanted, even if Kiddo had to leave for the base. But she immediately went back to tearfully attaching herself like a belt that was two sizes too small for Kid's hips.

After cajoling and reassurances, Kiddo and Rue both wound up taking a sofa each in the main room. Narkon gave them bedding before switching off the lights and retiring, and Rue at last settled down in a quiet ball on her couch ...

Leaving just silence and stillness.

Why was that worse than disinfectant, burning arms and mournful tears?

Kiddo stared up at the dark ceiling, rubbing at his sternum absently.

An ache was growing there.

And a constricted feeling in his throat and lungs. As if his ribs had started to pull inward.

Maybe he'd taken in too much smoke.

What a small, selfish thing to worry over, when the other Razes might be …

Could a diaphragm get too tight or damaged with smoke inhalation?

It had become a taut band in his chest.

It could be asthma.

It could be heartburn.

It could be panic.

Kid sucked in an unsteady, slow breath.

Grief.

It was grief.

It was as if someone had dropped a loaded barbell across his middle, winding him with a heavy blow that threatened to cave in his whole core.

He understood how wretched Rue had felt through her own dramatic gasps while she'd cried so violently.

It started to feel awfully hard to get oxygen in.

His airways felt like they were becoming too narrow to be of any use.

But then he started as he felt Rue plonking herself down on his couch to sleep beside him.

She squirmed around, elbowed and kneed long limbs in her way, and then settled again.

He became aware of the warmth that came from her bundle of blankets against his side.

And he focused intently on the rise and fall of her breaths, until he was able to fall into a sleep of his own.

| 5 |

Five

Kiddo froze.

Rue had cracked one cranky eye open as he'd started to edge out from between her and the couch.

Throughout the night she'd sprawled out like a starfish to take up most of the room, so it had been near impossible to avoid jostling her when he woke.

"I'll be right back," he whispered.

She scrunched her face up and wiped at her mouth with the back of her hand.

"Promise," she said testily.

"Of course. Promise."

Kiddo was relieved that she relaxed again, rather than going into a meltdown as he backed toward the bathroom.

It was Kiddo who came rushing right out to check on her when he heard her squeal from the main room not long after.

"What?!" he burst out, and then drew up short.

Rue was holding up a bright yellow shirt, with a glittery flower printed on the chest. The flower was smiling.

"What?" Kiddo asked again, taking it in with a frown.

Narkon had apparently headed out while they'd still been sleeping. And he'd now surrounded the child in a number of shopping bags.

"These are really for me to keep?" Rue gushed, awestruck.

"I was worried you wouldn't like them," Narkon commented. "They are age appropriate. But, you have always worn … a different style."

"I love them," Rue cried ecstatically. She hugged the shirt to herself. "They're the nicest things I've ever owned!"

Kiddo pulled a little denim jacket from a bag. "Lots of pockets," Kiddo commended the choice. "Rue loves pockets."

"I asked her not to stab me with the thing that lives in her pockets before I opened the door," Narkon admitted wryly.

In her excitement, Rue rummaged through Narkon's shopping to find the day's ensemble, and didn't think twice about rushing out of Kiddo's sight to change.

"You are generous. And brilliant," Kiddo told the chef. "You gave her something positive to start with, and snapped her out of her clinginess before it could become a habit."

"I doubt it has been dealt with quite so quickly as that," Narkon warned. "Though the rate she has bounced back this morning is impressive."

He pointed out another bag to Kiddo.

"I didn't go overboard for you, considering you already own a wardrobe of your own," he stated. "However, should you wish to stay here and play dead until it's safe, I will gladly keep you supplied."

Kiddo gave the chef a warm, sad smile. "I don't think 'safe' will happen any time soon. But I appreciate the offer."

Narkon gave a slight nod, with a touch of disappointment.

"I was sure that would be your answer. I take it you'll be heading back to your base after breakfast?"

Kiddo grinned, though with a twist in his stomach at the thought of facing the base and the Raze gang's reality.

"We would certainly never skip breakfast, when it's on offer from a famous chef."

Kiddo and Rue both looked fresh and uncharacteristically stylish as they sat down to eat with Narkon. Rue was even thoughtful enough to insist on doing the dishes herself; industriously slopping sudsy water about, and scratching the bottom of a pan.

Her mood only dipped slightly when Kiddo told her to put on one of her new jackets with a hood, because it was time they left.

"I will have all of your new clothes sent to you," Narkon vowed. "And I shall see you again soon. I intend to oversee the re-building of Kid's Place, if Kiddo will allow it."

Kiddo gaped. He couldn't find the words to reply to that. Though Rue had some special words that she'd thought of.

"I'm going to need a handbag, if I've got more than one set of pockets now," she told the chef solemnly. "I'm thinking pink. With a rose at the front."

"Right," Narkon coughed with a laugh. "I will make it my first priority, even ahead of the diner."

She nodded appreciatively, reaching out to take the kitchen shark's hand, and shaking it as if he worked for her now – and she had every faith in his abilities.

"So, you have your medication," the chef said, with a small touch of amusement still in his voice as he turned to Kid. "I have asked for the front desk to have a driver waiting for

you." He straightened his blazer. "I want you both to take notice of your trip, so that you remember how to get back here
if you need to. Reception have been informed of your names
and of your permanent welcome here during my stay."

"Thank you," Kiddo told him sincerely. He gripped the
kitchen shark's hand firmly in both of his own, with as much
faith, and gratitude, as Rue had shown in her hand shake.

"Thank you," Rue echoed just as earnestly.

And she slipped her little hand into Kiddo's as they left the
safety of the penthouse.

Just as her presence had helped when the dread and grief
had begun to settle over him the night before, her tight, small
hold kept Kid steady for the ride.

He pulled up her hood as they got closer to the base, covering her bright cloud of curls.

He'd noticed that there were a surprising number of Dires
circulating on the roads leading up to the base. And one had
followed their car for a while.

"Stay sharp," he murmured to Rue out of the driver's
earshot. "Who knows if the Wolf still has eyes on the area."

She gave a small, determined nod; the tough hoodlum
gleam coming back into her eyes as they pulled up and she
scanned the street.

She uttered a foul expletive that was not at all right in
coming from the mouth of a babe when she saw the wreckage
that remained of the diner.

"Language," he admonished, as he quickly led her to the
busted doors of Sparks' garage.

They skirted between the crashed Hunt vehicles.

"I've said worse," she answered grumpily, but then quietened.

Because the moment they'd entered, four figures had stepped forward to surround them.

Rue's hackles rose immediately, but Kid put a hand on her head and steered her back to stand against him.

"Good to see you," he told the four people grimly. "Wasn't sure I'd be seeing anyone."

The group loosened up in relief. "Kiddo."

There were two battered Raze recruits, a Hellion and a Bullet.

"Kid, we thought you were dead in the fire. Or snatched," a recruit rubbed her eyes wearily. "It's good you got the girl out of there."

"Please don't tell me you four are it?" Kiddo asked in a low voice.

There was a distinct lack of activity in the whole lower level.

And obvious signs of blast marks, blood spatters, and ammunition shells.

"No, no," the Hellion rasped. "Anyone who's able has been helping the housekeepers to try to upright the base again. They haven't made it down here yet."

"The clinic beds are full up with everyone else," a Raze recruit added soberly. "Our team had thirteen losses."

There were eighteen recruits left of Dom's team.

"Even four of Sparks' apprentices went down in the fight," the other recruit informed him.

Kiddo flicked his eyes to the gang members.

"Fifteen Bullet casualties," the Bullet answered his unasked question unhappily.

"Ten Hellions," the woman added. "So far."

Both gangs would still be formidable in size, despite those losses. But they had only recently had to mourn the deaths of their own from when they'd been hit by The Hunt themselves.

"To their credit, the Dires have stepped up," the first Raze recruit informed him. "They showed up as soon as they heard. Got people to the clinic, chased down any snatchers who hadn't got out quick enough. Now they're patrolling, watching the base like it's their own."

They were returning the aid that the Raze gang had so recently granted them.

At least the Raze gang base was still standing.

"Did …" Kiddo took a deep breath. "Did any of you four see what happened with Sparks or Jingle?"

They shifted in front of him, and Rue held Kid's bandaged arm.

"Yeah," the Bullet answered uncomfortably. "I was down here when The Hunt started hurling fire bombs onto the diner's roof," he said darkly. "I know now that they were just trying to draw everyone out of the base and Kid's Place. That's what Hato's lady cop said."

Kiddo nodded curtly.

If they emptied all the other people out, it would make it easier to find their key targets inside.

The casualties last night were just people who'd got in the way of the ones that The Hunt wanted alive.

"When the garage doors were broken in, Sparks and Sora

tossed out c-gars like she was arming us up for a war. And we went to war for her, Kid. We tried."

Kiddo couldn't reply. He angled himself to lean against the wrecked vehicle beside him. Rue pressed close like a protective shadow.

"Their numbers were crazy," the Hellion cut in with her grizzled voice. "They weren't taking any chances. We were swamped, and they carried Sparks off in the middle of it all. They didn't care that she was shooting them down – enough of them kept coming that she was inundated and subdued. Then they got all through the base while we were busy down here. Jingle didn't stand a chance. They had that many eyes and ears trained on finding her, and they were willing to rip everything apart until they did."

"A bunch ransacked the club too," the female recruit said. "Seeing if they could carry away any extra scores to be marketed off for smaller money."

Kiddo kneaded Rue's thin shoulder blades absentmindedly. She kept herself positioned right in front of him.

"Thanks," he managed at last. "For telling me. And for sticking around." He took a breath despite that aching diaphragm. "Thanks for trying to stop them."

The four others shuffled around, abashed now, and almost pitying as they gazed at him.

"Course, Kid. We're still in this."

"The Dires have sworn to watch out for the last Razes now, to keep the rebellion against Yorak's dictatorship alive."

"The Raze gang's battle is more important than ever."

They parted for him and there were reassuring pats on his back as he and Rue filed past.

Kiddo's expression hardened as he observed bullet holes, rusty smears, overturned benches, bullet riddled cars and wrecked training equipment.

Rue's eyes flicked from the mess of the fight to Kiddo's face, but he stonily led her to the stairs.

There was no point even letting his brain play its usual tricks of racking up a mental to-do list, which usually started with the stairway.

There were too many chips in the stairs, and too many marks on the walls.

"I need alcohol."

Seethe's voice carried to them from the kitchen above.

There was the sound of the fridge door clanking, and then of a beer being cracked open.

Nobody would begrudge him the drink in this climate. And nobody in their right mind would deny him anything on a normal day.

A chair scraped back as Seethe threw himself down into it.

"Kid?" Hato's exhausted voice came from the lounge area.

He'd been sealing up a broken window; a few cleaners sweeping up the glass and straightening the room around him. But he dropped his tape at once.

Seethe was out of his chair instantly, and Hato crossed the space in big, purposeful strides.

Kiddo was taken aback as Rue decided to step away to give them room, and as Seethe quickly eyed Kiddo for damage, before gripping him hard in what could be called an embrace.

Hato wasn't far behind him.

Now Kiddo couldn't restrain it any longer.

He sagged into them.

And sobbed against their hold.

| 6 |

Six

The cleaners had tactically withdrawn to help with whatever work was still going on to fix the upper levels.

When Kiddo disentangled himself, raking his fingers over his scalp shakily, he took in Seethe's very bruised face, and Hato's strapped shoulder and hands.

"You two ok?" Kid asked gruffly, stepping back and pulling himself together.

Seethe snarled. He dropped into his seat again.

"Dom did a number on my ribs. Some Hunter smashed up my nose. And Hato got sliced up keeping the hordes from charging into the medical centre. But it was nearly over by the time we got here."

Hato regarded Kiddo as Rue quickly resumed her place, hovering by Kid as he moved to lean against the bench.

She scrambled up to sit by the sink, where Duncan Jr. was as unbothered as ever, cruising in his bowl on the windowsill as if nothing out of the ordinary had unfolded in the base around him.

Kid tried not to think about Rue and Dom concocting stories together about that fish.

"It's just a bunch of scrapes. It's nothing," Kiddo responded to Hato's questioning gaze over his bandages. "Narkon did his best with them."

"Hm." Hato sank into a seat at the table across from Seethe. "That chef has definitely proven his worth."

Seethe's icy blue eyes were critical as he jutted his chin at Rue. "And you? You with us now?"

Rue folded her arms defiantly. "I'm not gonna be a traitor anymore. I'm going to be part of your family."

That got a glimmer of a despondent smile from Hato.

It got a desolate tsk from Seethe.

"Good luck," he uttered, and then tipped back his beer. "We can hardly keep ourselves safe, let alone a pipsqueak."

"I'll help keep *you* safe," Rue said earnestly. "I'll do my best to help here too. You'll be glad I'm around."

Hato grunted. "We can use any help." He shifted in his chair with a wince.

As if he'd just made a grand overture of acceptance and welcome, Rue glowed with a returning smile that matched the beaming flower on her shirt.

"We're coming up," a voice announced then. "Don't shoot."

Hato straightened at the sound of that voice, and winced again.

Officer Koa ascended to the kitchen level, with Madam Hellion, Jeffrey, Sora and Beef Cake trailing her.

Madam Hellion and Sora took seats at the table with Hato

and Seethe, while the usually cheerful Raze recruit, Jeffrey, made the quietest entry of his life. Downcast, he and Beef Cake leaned against the back of one of the couches.

Kiddo blanched as he noticed how the stuffing had burst from multiple slashes and bullet holes in that couch.

The TV screen had also been shattered behind the recruit and the gangster.

"I come with gifts," Koa told Hato, and Kid saw how her stoic face softened a fraction as she observed the careworn man.

She opened an orange envelope, and tipped a stash of phones out across the tabletop.

"As protected as we could get them," Koa informed Hato, pushing a specific one toward him. Possibly the one she'd already saved her number in.

"I appreciate it," Hato told her, and Seethe even offered the cop one of his beers – while neglecting to ask any of the others.

"Any news?" Sora asked the officer gruffly.

He truly did appear battered enough to have gone to war for his once brightest protégé, Sparks.

Koa took a seat close to Hato. "My helpers haven't heard anything yet," she answered regretfully. "Even the Dire boss says he hasn't seen any under-web ads of Razes for sale."

Seethe's lip curled. "In his perverted little torture movie, Yorak sounded like he'd worked out his wealthiest, most obedient buyers already. It might all be private sales. Near impossible to trace until the buyers brag to their friends."

Koa leaned back in her chair thoughtfully. "One of my analyst buddies said that Yorak's car headed off to the east in the first part of that footage, and that the group also retreated east when they left the carpark attack. Not much to go on. But it could at least give a direction toward Yorak's location."

Kiddo gripped the benchtop behind him as his remembered Dom's struggle against his captors in the clip, and Yorak's sensual delight in subduing him.

"When Yorak left with Dominic last night, the car did head eastward," Hato admitted heavily.

"Your friend Teddy's description also suits the east theory," Koa went on. "The street she thinks the snatcher vans disappeared down is headed away from the docklands too. Upper class, inner city."

The last Kid had heard of Teddy, Quicklips had messaged to say that their car had been ploughed off the road. Pash, Teddy and Quicklips had been too hurt to get out.

"Was Teddy alright when you questioned her?" Hato asked with a hollowness about him.

Koa put a stout hand on his, patting his bruised knuckles for a brief moment that none of them missed.

"She was distraught when she woke in the hospital. But in mostly one piece, and more angry than traumatised," Koa answered honestly. "She broke her arm, has a few sore burns and got some nasty whiplash. Though her major focus was on how very wicked the snatchers are, to have taken her friends from her."

Rue's cherubic mouth had become a hard, thin line.

Poor Teddy.

"Based on what she said," Koa went on clinically. "We're either going to have a harder time trying to track down Pash and Quicklips, because they won't be able to be brought out for sale right away. Or an easier time, because they'll need to be somewhere that can treat serious injuries. Sounded like severe burns and breaks from the crash."

Kiddo felt himself scowling alongside Rue.

"The hardest will be to track down the international Razes," Seethe stated gruffly. Then sculled the rest of his beer. "You've got no jurisdiction outside your city to work with overseas cops."

"There are so many Razes to track down," Jeffrey announced hopelessly. "They'll all slip through the cracks and be scattered soon."

"Shouldn't you try to find the girl Razes first?" Rue asked hotly. "It's worse for a girl to be sold, than for a boy. I've heard what things can happen."

There were cringes all around.

It was Madam Hellion who found the words to answer the child.

"It's not good for *anyone* to be sold to a power player," the wizened boss told Rue carefully. "We've got to hope they aren't after that kind of power over your friends."

Seethe muttered bleakly. "Any gender can be used and abused."

He got up stormily, holding his ribs, and revisited the fridge.

"We have to get them back *now*," Jeffrey said brokenly. "Of course that's the kind of power a buyer would be after. I heard how Yorak himself acted in that clip."

"The Wolf posted the torture clip as a temporary story on the under-web last night," Beef Cake admitted. "He added some new, live footage of Raze passed out in the car against him." The gangster rubbed his brow. "It was captioned something like, 'mine now'."

Seethe slammed the fridge door so that its contents rattled and stomped back to the table.

"We need to be less reactive, and more calculated," Kiddo spoke up hollowly then, his voice low. "We need to put our resources into finding one Raze in particular, and go from there."

Rue drew her legs up to hug them. "How can you focus on only one Raze? Don't you want to save them all?"

Kiddo dipped his head. "I most definitely do," he said quietly. "But if we thoughtlessly rush around trying to find everyone without a clear plan, we'll stay weak. The rest of us might be taken in the process too."

Hato sat forward painfully. "Then, when you say we need one Raze and a plan, you mean ..."

"We need to focus on finding Start first," Kiddo asserted. "He can work out the best way to get help from higher up, where the Razes might be, and how we can take on our real problem."

"The Wolf," Koa agreed.

"If we don't work out how to combat the Wolf's increasing influence," Kiddo sighed. "We'll just keep finding ourselves in this same position, and unable to really do anything about our true goal of taking down the snatcher system."

"How would you find Start?" Beef Cake questioned uncertainly. "Without Jingle or her contacts?"

Kid flicked his gaze toward Rue. "You once said to me that

the snatchers would talk about who they would buy if they could."

"Yeah," she shrugged. "I wanted Velvet. Or Sparks or Trix," she sounded a bit dubious to be saying it again now. "My favourites."

"You wanted them because they are tough women, who would make you feel strong," Kiddo said gently. "But most other people wanted Jingle or Start, because –"

"They are clever and could help you get rich or powerful real fast," Rue replied as she recalled what she'd said to Kiddo.

"So we need to work out what kinds of underworlders, or surface players, might benefit most from owning Start," Koa surmised. "Take note of who might be making ripples or solidifying their position at the moment."

"Who *isn't* doing that?" Sora asked dully. "Below or on the surface, there are so many leaders trying to further themselves all the time."

"We could focus on who might be an appealing ally to the Wolf," Jeffrey stated. "Or who makes a sudden move that improves their standing now."

Koa grimaced. "This all sounds like a me job. I'm limited in who I can ask to help with unofficial extra work, so it won't be quick. But at least my superiors are being supportive in their own way."

"The system is being supportive of you working with us?" Sora asked sceptically. "What does 'in their own way' mean?"

Koa smirked. "As of last night, my usual rounds were cleared from the roster. I've been listed as active, but on special, independent duties. It's their unspoken way of giving permission for me to be involved, without seeming to be involved themselves."

Sora crossed his arms. "So they gave us one ordinary cop. Against the entire underworld."

Koa crossed her arms too. Somehow exuding even more steel than the biker gang boss.

"Do you think one of your allies on the force could reach out to a contact of Jingle's for extra help?" Kiddo asked Koa, before a battle of retorts began.

Koa turned her unimpressed gaze from Sora to listen to Kid.

"General Wolder?" he asked her.

Seethe bristled. "He's the one who recommended Raff. Where this whole mess started with Dom getting poisoned."

"The retired general was Chief of the Defence Force," Hato said slowly. "He could still hold enough sway that he can make up for that mistake. He respects Jingle, and she respects him."

"I'll reach out," Koa answered. "See what happens."

There were brisk footsteps on the stairs then, and everyone stiffened, despite no alarm having been raised from the four on guard duty below.

Kiddo relaxed as soon as he saw the soft tones of a hijab, and the smart neatness of the medical centre uniform.

The others remained less relaxed however, as Daleeah held a kit, ready for action.

She had the commanding air of a scornful matriarch right now.

Eyeing the tense room for a moment, Daleeah then set her sights on Kiddo.

"I had to find out from your chef, that you had made it back?" she asked Kid sternly. "He has the time to call our clinic to see how your injuries are, but you don't have the time to walk next door?"

Kiddo held an arm out to her, and though she pursed her lips; unimpressed, she swept in under it as if he had extended an olive branch, and wrapped him in a relieved hug.

"Your turn," Seethe told Kiddo evilly.

He had strategically let go of his second empty beer bottle, pushing it away as if it had never been his.

Dalee tutted as she carefully unwrapped, and in some places peeled free, Kid's bandages to survey the damage.

"It's fortunate I brought a dose of tetanus up with me," she remarked clinically. "Just in case. And I'm going to need my tweezers too."

"That's my cue," Beef Cake announced – paling as Daleeah started picking at the sticky, raw skin on Kiddo's right arm.

All but Seethe, Hato and Rue also went out in sympathy or got back to work at that point, and Kiddo was glad to have less of an audience.

"Which hospital is Teddy staying in?" Kid asked the others, focusing through the sting as Daleeah worked on some grit caught under the skin at his wrist.

"You shouldn't go galivanting around the city," Hato replied tiredly. "Just call her. Use one of our new phones."

However Kiddo shook his head. "I was thinking about it this morning. The Wolf could have let Dom cut us down and then brought Hunters along to take the three of us in. Yet he didn't. He wanted to turn you two into Dom's focus – as adversaries, so that he can be Dom's ally himself. But he wants me to come willingly, and to stay for Dom, like Raff said."

Seethe sneered. "You get one, the other will follow. Dom's his hostage."

Daleeah made a disgruntled sound in her throat. "Animal."

"What's the difference in calling Teddy compared to visiting?" Hato argued. "There's plenty to do here. All of the bedrooms and the library were ransacked as they searched for –" he swallowed.

Jingle.

"I want to see her face to face," Kid answered slowly. "Because she deserves that. And because I know she can work with us on something. She'll want to."

Seethe cocked an eyebrow. "I take it you don't mean cleaning up the diner ruins. It's all police tape and char now."

"I mean," Kiddo paused, liking the idea as it formed. "Teddy can get us more help from where it matters most."

"Now I take it you don't mean with world leaders?" Seethe stretched, and then cradled his side, his face at once turning mean.

Kiddo regarded him patiently. "Teddy can get a social movement happening. I'm sure she can. She knows more about Pash's work and fans than Pash does."

Hato rose with an effort. "Rue should stay here then. She can help me put the library books back on the shelves and the rooftop plants back into pots."

Rue actually appeared to love that Hato wanted to spend time with her – even if it was an obvious ploy to keep her out of harm's way.

"I promise I'll do that when we get back," she said decidedly. "But I go where Kiddo goes."

| 7 |

Seven

Teddy's eyes watered and her face crumpled when she saw Rue and Kiddo in the ward doorway.

She wore a neck brace. One arm was plastered and hugged to herself. Some of her hair had been burned away to leave a bald, red, leathery patch on the side of her scalp and down a cheek.

Kiddo bit his lip and Rue gasped – dashing to Teddy's bedside.

"I am so glad you are both alright," Teddy declared tearfully, as Rue clambered onto the bed to clutch Teddy's unharmed hand.

"You poor thing," Rue lamented, almost crooning in sympathy.

Though Rue and Teddy hadn't known each other long, they had developed a strong affinity for each other. Something about the bond forged between ladies in a women's toilet always seemed powerful and secret.

Kiddo cleared his throat, perching on the edge of a visitor's chair. "Are you in much pain, Teddy?"

Teddy reached for a tissue box and blotted at her nose. "Not really Kiddo," Teddy told him bravely. "Just in my heart."

His stomach wrenched.

"But some medicine got rid of the rest of the soreness, and it's actually a good thing that my nerves aren't all numb on my burns," she explained. "The nurses are keeping up a steady flow of jelly cups and sandwiches that make me feel better, too."

"Do you remember much?" Rue asked Teddy intently, her little face contorted with a scowl as she shuffled closer on the bed.

"Mhmm," Teddy nodded with a shiver, patting her cast wrapped wrist glumly. "I remember they hit us by purpose, but I think it was harder than they meant to," she sighed despairingly. "Our car crumpled so far into a barrier, like we were in a soft drink can being crushed up for the bin. The car even caught fire." She shivered forlornly again. "Quicklips was driving us, and he got stuck in the mashed up front. Pash was beside me, and her window was down. She … she got really hurt when the fire sucked in."

Kiddo sank back fully into the chair.

More fat tears rolled down Teddy's cheeks again. This time Rue blotted at them for her.

"Those snatchers came quick and yanked us all out and away," Teddy went on. "I think they weren't careful enough with Quicklips, because they argued pretty loudly over what they might have done by accident. Then there was a huge, boiling boom from our car."

Teddy pulled a face at the memory, struggling for a few seconds to continue.

"They dropped me when they saw I wasn't a Raze. But they ... they took Quicklips, and they took Pash ... and their van drove off fast."

Teddy's breath shuddered in her chest when she tried to draw it in, and her bottom lip formed a miserable bell curve as her mouth drew downward. Her chin was bunching against the neck cuff.

"I'm just so sad," Teddy admitted. "Those snatchers are such bad people. And my friends were being the best people. All they wanted was to take me home safely."

Rue glowered. "I want to kill all those snatchers for you," she said fiercely. "I might be able to get a few."

Kiddo stiffened.

"Thanks for the offer," Teddy told the child dolefully, as if it were a perfectly reasonable and valid one. "But I don't want to take a chance. We could lose you, too. I know about all the rest of the Razes." She turned her baleful, watery eyes on Kiddo. "And I'm scared we won't get to see our friends ever again."

Rue bunched her fists. "It sure was a lot easier when I didn't care about anybody but me," she said flatly. "But now you have me as your friend, and I didn't disappear. I'm still here 'cos Kid saved me."

Teddy gave a tearful laugh. "I like that. It makes me a bit less sad."

Kiddo sat up straighter and regarded Teddy seriously.

"I wanted to offer you a job that may also make you feel better. And it might help our Razes."

Teddy stilled, her face becoming hopeful.

"What will I be able to do? I want to help."

Of course she would want to do what she could for others, no matter what she'd just gone through herself. Her heart was enormous.

Kiddo nodded. "It involves you breaking our pinkie promise about never telling anyone what you know of the snatchers or Razes."

"Oh …" Teddy gave him a sideways, guilty glance. "I did break that already. To Hato's girlfriend this morning. I forgot. And I really was so sad."

Koa.

Kiddo couldn't help but smile. Teddy always sapped the darkest of moods out of him.

"It's alright," he assured her. "But I mean *really* break that promise. Telling as many people the truth as you possibly can, as quickly as you can, so that there's no point in anyone coming to silence you. The public awareness would actually keep you safe."

Teddy was confused for a moment. "I just told you most of my friends are gone, Kiddo. I can really only tell you two and the shelter workers. But they already know, and so do you."

Kiddo gestured to where her phone – which was worse for wear – sat on the wheelie table beside a brown water jug and a tray of empty jelly cups.

"Pash said her friends and followers love you even more than they love her," Kiddo explained.

"Ahuh," Teddy nodded. "They really do."

Then her face brightened with realisation.

"They would be glad to hear from me."

Kiddo agreed. "Pash's supporters are devoted. They deserve to know exactly what cause Pash has been fighting for, and exactly what has happened to Pash, and to you, because of that."

Teddy considered it thoughtfully. "I must look just right for making an upsetting clip right now. With my hair melted and my face puffed from crying."

Kiddo grimaced at that choice of phrasing, but she wasn't wrong.

"You know, Pash made me an administrator of her social accounts, because I was even better than Pash's own agent," Teddy went on pragmatically. "I posted things for her on the ride home all the time. So I can spread messages straight to Pash's fabulous-fanaticals so easily."

She reached for her phone, already showing more enthusiasm than despondence now.

"That's great Teddy," Kiddo said encouragingly. "I think you could get the word out, and open everyone's eyes to what's happening to vulnerable people all around them, as well as to people like Pash who have tried to fight back."

"Yup," Teddy said keenly, eyes on her screen. "Leave it to me Kiddo. Everyone will know. And I'll have the whole world crying in no time."

Now she was grinning like a Cheshire cat as she imagined it, mentally plotting out her course. She sank back against her pillows contentedly.

"Want us to film you?" Rue asked curiously. "Or are you tired?"

Teddy shook her head. "My mum is coming in soon. She's

furious enough to take on all the snatchers by herself! She'll make a great socials team mate."

Kiddo stood slowly. "I'm sorry you've been hurt just because you know us Teddy," he told her remorsefully. "I understand how your mum feels."

Teddy gave him a stern glare. "I am glad I know you. And I am glad that I can be a Raze in my own way now. Thanks Kiddo."

| 8 |

Eight

"I'm going to head out tonight," Rue informed Kiddo breezily.

He accidentally let the drill skid away to leave a mark on the inner wardrobe wall, the screw half dangling from its hole.

"Careful," she reprimanded him.

Rue was on a chair, holding up the clothing rod that had been torn out of the plaster by hasty snatchers hunting for Jingle.

Kiddo managed to correct his mistake, drilling his final screw in so that Rue could hop down.

She handed him some hangers that held his formal shirts.

"*Why* are you heading out tonight?" he asked as smoothly as he could, dutifully hanging the garments up so she could pass him another bundle.

She hadn't left his side from the time of the diner rescue.

Every other night since they'd got back to the base she had insisted on staying with him. He had a stiff back from four nights of taking the floor beside his own bed, so that she could have the mattress.

"I can fish around for information from the snatchers," she explained, as if it was nothing.

He choked.

She pulled an impatient face as he held up the clothes-hanging production line.

"Up 'til last week I was around snatchers every day, idiot," she said, but almost gently.

That had been her insult, turned term of endearment, for Dom.

The next shirt she handed Kiddo was one of Dom's.

"I'll ask about Yorak, and where he might be," she went on decidedly.

Kiddo crossed his arms, feeling the tightness in the healing skin.

"And what if I don't agree that you should go?"

Rue snorted. She seemed to feel that that was enough said.

"I'll go with you then," he asserted. "I'm sure many snatchers would be aware that you're with us now, and it's not safe for you to just wander between the two worlds anymore."

She frowned at him in disbelief. "You turning up to watch over me would prove it," she retorted. "And I wouldn't exactly get anything juicy out of them if they're busy focusing on you."

"I'll be inconspicuous," Kiddo promised. "Unnoticeable."

Most real parents had to do this kind of bargaining over their child attending first dates or going out with friends at the cinemas. But *his* child had recently offered to go off and kill some snatchers for Teddy.

Rue rolled her eyes. "Oh, the Wolf's now most wanted Raze. One of the last few left. Under the radar?" she quipped sarcastically. "Don't think so."

Again, unlike other children, she wasn't worried he'd embarrass her in front of all the snatchers. She was worried he would be snatched, no matter the Wolf's long game.

"How do you plan to make it out of there yourself, then?" Kiddo asked in exasperation.

The idea of letting her go off alone – let alone into a den of snatchers – was intolerable, even though that had been the exact arrangement between them until about a week ago.

She handed him a hoodie, trying to force him to get moving again. "I'll tell 'em I'm still on assignment. Special orders from the Wolf to make you love me. His power's through the roof now, and they won't touch me."

It wasn't unbelievable. Something along those lines had gone on with Dom.

"What happened to you saying wherever I go, you'll go?" Kid asked queasily. "Now you want to split up?"

Rue pulled a face. "What happened to you saying just the other day that I can't tag along everywhere with you?"

"I was going to the *toilet*," he argued, thrusting the hanger onto the rod brusquely.

"Well a snatcher's den is basically one big toilet. And you can't come with me everywhere either," she informed him emphatically.

"That is nowhere near the same thing."

"Fine. It's not. But I'm telling you I'm going." She was becoming surly now. "And you are not invited."

He abandoned the wardrobe and sank down onto the end of the bed. "I guess I should be grateful you're even telling me first. It's considerate of you," he said unhappily.

Rue scuffed her shoe against the carpet awkwardly.

"Well, I know you have trouble sleeping," she muttered. "Didn't want to make it worse by making you worry about where I was."

As if he would sleep a wink with her out on the streets either way.

He felt a pang over the fact that she'd noticed his insomnia. Was she staying so close to comfort *him*?

He pinched the bridge of his nose. "I'm new to this whole guardian type of role. But this sure doesn't feel like what a good one would allow."

She fidgeted with one of her hangers. "I'm new to this whole adopted daughter thing. Never much bothered with getting permission before."

Kiddo twisted Dom's spinner ring on his finger.

"Are you even asking for permission?"

Rue smirked then. "Not really. But I wanted you to know that I'm gone on purpose, and will be back."

"Officer Koa has got the ex-general, Wolder, on board. He and Koa are doing their own fishing," Kiddo told her. "Teddy's galvanising the public; making them be more vigilant. Why do you have to go out looking for trouble?"

He realised he was sounding very Hato-esque. Although, when he'd been younger Hato would have outright forbidden it, and Kiddo would have gone anyway – if he'd even have bothered to mention it to anyone else at all.

Rue picked up a jacket from the pile on the floor.

A leather jacket.

Dom's trademark jacket.

"The general and the cop are searching for Start, because that's a good idea. The public are on the lookout for Pash, because that's the Raze they know," she said quietly. "What if I can help to find Dom, by finding the Wolf first?"

Kiddo's insides twisted.

"Firstly, it's not your responsibility to make sure I can get to sleep," he told her. "And it's not your responsibility to save anyone. In this arrangement, the adults are the ones who are meant to take care of the child."

Rue stepped closer to him, and laid the leather jacket across his legs.

"This isn't a normal set up," she said. "I can take care of you guys too. And I told you I was going to be useful. Nobody will have any excuse not to want me around. Ever."

"If anyone ever made you feel that way, they'd have me to deal with," Kiddo said sourly. "You never have to prove yourself or earn your welcome here."

She shrugged. "It's not other people that I'm proving myself to. It's me."

That stumped him.

How was he having one of the deepest conversations of his life with a child who wasn't sure if she was eight years old yet?

"If ..." he swallowed. "If I said I'd let you go this time ..."

She made a disapproving scoffing sound. "If I acted like I really needed your consent," she corrected.

"And I promised not to follow you," he went on. "Would you do something for me in return?"

"What? Say thanks?"

She was coming to learn how adults loved youngsters to say their magic words. She found it fascinating how important manners apparently were.

He smoothed the jacket, tracing its creases and lines of wear.

"Would you consider carrying a phone?"

She huffed, as if he'd just yelled out 'love you, honey!' across a full school yard.

"Police issue, with a tracker app?" she asked, unimpressed.

"Yes. But it looks just like a normal phone," he answered with a small grin. "None of the other kids will know."

"Pft. Fine then."

Kiddo chose his next words carefully. "And –"

"There's an 'and'?!"

"Yes. *And* … would you think about working on this whole 'good daughter, good stand-in parent' scenario?"

Rue was more hesitant this time, apprehensive about what she would have to commit to.

"I'm eating those foods on Frazzle's diet plan. I've been brushing my teeth two times a day. I'm doing baths. It's pretty good I didn't just leave and do what I wanted tonight, too," she reminded him.

"Oh, it certainly is *great* that you are doing all that," he was quick to tell her. "… But I was wondering how you would feel about … home schooling?"

"Home schooling?" she repeated the words slowly.

He wasn't sure if hitting her with so many new things in her first week with them was too much. Putting his focus into her was definitely more valuable than falling into despair while he waited for progress on the Start front, but he had to be careful not to push her too far.

"Jingle isn't here to sort you out an identity for a surface school yet," he explained tentatively. "But one of our housekeepers could tutor you. Catch you up on some skills you'd need. Anushi understands a lot about our way of life," he went on encouragingly.

Rue was listening, but wary.

"We saved her from an organ farm a few years back, and back then Hato helped her to get into night school. She's nearly finished an education course. When I spoke to her, she said she'd love to do some intervention work with you, so you didn't feel behind when you join in with other kids your age …"

Kiddo's voice trailed off.

He was struggling to gauge the expression on Rue's pinched little face.

She was staring at him so intensely, he wondered if he'd somehow just pushed her back toward outburst territory.

"When would it start?" she asked with narrowed eyes.

"Ahh, well, as soon as you'd be able to," he said. "Though if you're going to be up late, it doesn't have to be tomorrow," he admitted.

"And she wants to make me the same as normal kids, huh?"

Kiddo winced. "Just to help you to feel confident in your learning, so you can join in with a classroom without any problems."

"You said learning was hard for you when you did it," she recalled.

An understatement.

"I started later than you, without teachers who had been through similar things," Kiddo tried. "And it'll be tough. But you've been through worse, and this would be to get to your goals."

"To get clever. To have my own life," she said almost to herself.

Kiddo paused. He might have misread her reaction.

"Yes … exactly."

"I won't be embarrassed. I won't be stupid."

Her gaze was fierce, but he could see now that it was with the right kind of ferocity.

Before he could register his relief, she had launched herself at him.

This time her arms didn't strangle him with frenzied hysteria. But with gratitude.

"I want to learn," she insisted. "Tomorrow. I want to be as smart and tough as Sparks, so I'll try my hardest," she promised. "And you can be like a proud dad one day."

He hooked his chin over her shoulder and smiled.

"Rue … I already am."

She hugged him harder.

"I'm still leaving after dinner, though."

He sighed.

"I know."

"But I'll be back."

"Yes. I know. You'll be back."

| 9 |

Nine

They hurt me. They took Pash away. And they have been taking people away for a long time...

Kiddo caught the last parts of Teddy's now familiar declaration as he meandered down the stairs listlessly.

The living room was dark, apart from the light spilling from the new TV screen fixed to the wall.

Seethe had passed out on a taped up couch, and Hato was flicking through news channels from the dining table.

Teddy's lacerated, imploring face, and echoes of different sections of her heart-wrenching speech came from most channels.

"You couldn't have found a better spokesperson," Hato commended Kiddo quietly. He muted the TV and set the remote down. "She makes me want to blubber every time I see this."

Some of Pash's most liked photos started to play across the screen then. Lady Pash, man Pash, and from when Pash became something in between.

There was a newspaper folded on the tabletop, with

Teddy's pleading face also pictured on the front of that. A huge title asked: 'Where is Pash?' and a subtitle demanded: 'Justice for Teddy.'

Kiddo grabbed a glass of water, and slumped into a chair across from the big man.

"You haven't seen half of it," Kid admitted. "The hashtag 'pashwatch' is trending. And 'catchasnatch' isn't far behind. As soon as the story had over a million shares, the media got on board." He clinked Dom's ring against his glass lightly. "A large group of schoolgirls even performed a citizen's arrest on a masked thug trying to rob a servo today."

Hato made an amused sound. "Ordinary thief?"

"Ahuh," Kiddo told him. "Dangerous for them to have done it, but tells you what the current attitude is."

"It's incredible how quickly Teddy has been able to inflame so many people," Hato remarked. "It's good that everyone's talking about it."

Kiddo's gaze flicked to the stairway, thinking he'd heard someone ascending.

It must have been movement from the guard group in the garage below.

"Why'd you ever think acting like my parent was a good idea when you were this age?" Kiddo groaned. "This is beyond stressful for a twenty year old to handle."

Hato shrugged and adjusted his weight in the seat so that it creaked. "You are doing well. Your patience is impressive."

Kiddo managed a slight smile at that. Hato had had to be so strict to rein Kid in, that it had taken Kiddo a long while to see the love that went into the tough love.

"She can be an angry little mite," Kiddo sighed. "But I

think she's making things easier on me than I did for you, because she wants to be cared for."

"Mmm." Hato reached to move Kiddo's glass away from the light, rhythmical tapping of his ring, which had been tinkling in the quiet of the room.

It wouldn't do to piss Seethe off.

"She's going to adapt faster, because she's younger than you were. But think about the progress you made in just a few years with us floundering around trying to give you some kind of stability," Hato reasoned in Kiddo's defence.

"You were due to start high school when we took you in. On the edge of puberty. You had to detox, to learn a completely different lifestyle, to get new medications right. You had to settle in, when you were at the least settled stage of your life."

Kiddo shook his head at the awful cloud that had hovered over him at that time.

Once the real wildness of addiction had begun to pass, he'd been resentful from the cravings, hyper and rebellious. Or as doctors tried new things, he'd been half asleep, withdrawn and jittery.

"I regret how harsh we were on you," Hato reflected honestly, thinking back. "We must have seemed cruel."

Kiddo grimaced. "I deserved it. Unlovable hood."

Hato, Seethe, Tiny, Flip – when he was around, and Jingle had seen the absolute worst of him.

He wasn't sure that he would have saved himself, or stuck with it, if he'd come across such a vicious, hateful creature.

Yet they had brought him into their midst, and had forced the best of him to start coming through instead. They'd earned his hard won, begrudging respect, and had been the first people he had wanted respect from in turn.

Marko, Velvet's brother, had visited often – drawing him out with cooking lessons and helping him to find his niche in the gang. Then when Sparks had joined them, he'd started to become less selfishly inward. Taking notice of someone who treated him as an equal from the start.

Once he could truly see one other person, it was easier to properly recognise the value in the rest. To surface out of his own haze.

"We saw a kid worth saving. Our Kid," Hato negated. "And we had no idea what we were doing. But I learned that you can trust yourself to work out such a tough new role, because at the end of the day, your intentions are good ones."

"I guess when I mess up, Rue will have you, Dalee and Fraz. Seethe as well," Kiddo tagged on dryly.

Hato nodded, his expression illuminated by the distant TV glow as he reminisced. "When she's too much, you have a buddy system so you can subtly tap out. I used to do it to the others with you. All the time."

Kiddo snorted. That was how he'd wound up being taught to shoot, punch and stab with Flip. And how he'd wound up being caught on his way out to search for a hit – half hanging out of windows – by Seethe. Tiny had first shown him how to shave. Hato had shouldered the driving lessons. Jingle had got him through homework at a time when he could hardly keep from crawling up the walls or sleeping at the desk.

"I messed up at different points too," Hato sighed. "But you were on a journey that was bigger than any little mistakes I could make. And look how well you did getting to this point."

"You were flawless," Kiddo assured him. Knowing full well he'd be dead if Hato hadn't intervened. "Nobody could have asked for a better father figure."

"Well," Hato examined the bandages across one of his massive palms. "I let Duncan Jr. die," he stated gruffly, as if confessing to the most grievous of crimes.

The fish was calmly blubbing away in his bowl on the sill.

Now Hato scratched the back of his head, eyeing the innocent fish. "That's not the first Duncan Jr."

Kiddo rubbed his lips to hide his smile, and Hato cleared his throat.

"When Marko had just died, and Velvet was moving in, I knew you were a mess," Hato admitted. "You were at risk of slipping right backward. I should have made sure someone was feeding that fish while you got back on track."

Poor original Duncan Jr.

"I didn't want you to deal with another death. Even the death of a fish." Hato explained quietly. "I couldn't tell you and break your little kid heart, when you'd been trying to take responsibility for a pet. So Seethe snuck out to get you a new one before you saw the empty bowl."

Kiddo let out a gust of breath.

"While we're confessing," he replied. "I was so hell bent on keeping that fish alive after Marko's death, I think I actually overfed it. I noticed there was a different Duncan Jr. because the first one had a white patch on its tail. But I couldn't tell you that I knew, and break your big heart when you were trying so hard to take responsibility for a kid."

Hato stared at him for a moment.

Then the expanse of his shoulders shifted with a suppressed laugh.

"Sometimes fish just don't last," the big man muttered – excusing them both. "But I'm glad *you* did. I'd have even more regrets if we'd over or underfed you to death."

Kiddo grinned at him affectionately. "You're going to make the greatest father of your own children someday."

That drew the big man up short.

When Hato was silent for a moment, eyes on the tabletop, Kiddo grew concerned.

"Uh, sorry," Kiddo fumbled. "I shouldn't have presumed …"

"You are my only kid," Hato answered haltingly at last. "Frazzle helped me do some tests a while back, and," he hunched in his chair with an air of resignation. "When our owners pumped me full of their untried steroids as a teen, it had more of an affect than increasing my muscle mass. We'd thought it was reversible. But …"

Kiddo's heart fell and his face hardened.

Hato couldn't have kids of his own.

"Watching Dominic and Seethe take down our drug boss in Japan," Hato continued thoughtfully. "It was horrific. And gratifying."

They both straightened at the sounds of footsteps on the stairway then.

Not just the tired footsteps of an underweight youth.

"I'd unofficially say that that would have been justice served," Koa's resolute voice announced that she was accompanying Rue. She sounded deadly serious.

Rue trudged up into sight first, rubbing her eyes and yawning extravagantly.

Koa wasn't far behind – in uniform, and her gaze softer than ever as it fell on Hato.

"Oh my lord," Seethe hissed from the couch. "You might as well turn all the lights on at this point."

His sharp features were even sharper with irritation as he rose from the couch and flicked the switch so that the living space lit up.

"I've heard about Teddy's groupies, Kiddo's insecurities, a dead fish, and Hato's infertility," Seethe uttered darkly, holding his side. "Now what are you two going to add?" he demanded of the newcomers.

Rue seemed to brighten a little from her own tiredness at how incredibly poisonous Seethe was as he glared at them.

"I have three important things to say," Rue announced in a pleased tone. "The first thing is that I got a ride home in a cop car, without being arrested." She was really quite chuffed at that.

"The second?" Seethe growled.

"The second is my tooth!"

She opened her mouth to show them the bloody, gummy gap that used to house her front tooth.

Kiddo gaped in outrage, yanking her closer to himself. "Who hit you?" he demanded hotly. He reached for his glass of water and pushed it into her hands. "Here, rinse it out. Something similar happened to Quicklips once. A dentist will be able to work something out, I'm sure it'll be alright," he promised her adamantly.

Rue snickered. "I *lost* the tooth. It was wobbly."

Kiddo froze.

Children did that.

They lost teeth all the time.

"I'm just annoyed it dropped somewhere," she sighed. And she didn't pull away – instead leaning against Kiddo.

He relaxed sheepishly.

"Bet she's gonna tell us she believes in the tooth fairy now," Seethe drawled accusingly. "Well if there ain't no tooth, there ain't no money."

"The third thing was the most important thing," Koa cut in.

She had come to stand beside Hato, her hand on his broad shoulder, as if to reassure him of her support after she had overheard such sensitive personal information.

"After I spotted Rue on her way back here, she told me what was going on," the officer prompted.

"I had to make sure the system didn't think my new guardian let me run away already," Rue assured Kiddo. "I explained that you gave me *permission* to go out alone at night with the snatchers."

She winked at him exuberantly, and he died on the spot.

"Spit it out," Seethe grunted. "Along with any other loose teeth."

Rue swilled a mouthful of Kid's water. "I found out," she said enthusiastically. "That the Wolf has a fancy, guarded mansion set up in the middle of the city, away from all the snatcher dens. So that Raze doesn't find out Yorak's the biggest snatcher of them all."

She clanked the glass down on the table.

"He only lets unmasked snatchers or really careful Hunters go there. But they said it's where the rich and famous stay. Real nice. And near the best hotel in the city," Rue said pointedly.

Kiddo felt the blood drain from his face. Had he and Rue been that close to Dom when they'd stayed with Narkon in The Vire?

"Keeping Dom locked up in a mansion won't stop him from eventually coming across the truth," Seethe glowered. He flicked irritably at the newspaper on the table.

"Aaaand," Rue said, before she yawned again. "Yorak and Dom aren't even in the mansion at the moment."

"What?" Kid asked with a frown, confused.

Koa explained. "My helpers and I worked out that Yorak must've swept Raze straight onto a private flight before he could recover his senses. Seems like they had a trip to India."

Hato swivelled to face the officer. "India?" he asked in surprise.

"Is the Wolf trying to honeymoon Dom?" Seethe scowled in consternation, folding his arms.

Dom had stayed for the greatest amounts of time in Delhi and Tokyo when he'd been the only Raze. India would seem fresh and familiar in his mind.

Koa shook her head. "I heard from the Dire boss that something big went down in India just a few hours ago. The under-web is abuzz with reports that a snatcher base was destroyed in Mumbai."

There was silence around the table then.

It was one of the biggest and most influential bases remaining in the world.

"He's using Dominic to solidify his control," Hato stated flatly.

The Wolf wanted to eliminate any especially strong bases and Top Two leaders left who might challenge him. He wanted the rest of the underworld to be intimidated.

"Mumbai news is reporting that a private enterprise has fallen. They're assuming that there must have been a gas-line issue," Koa told them. "Not enough was left of the site to find any snatcher survivors, but there is confusion over how an influx of homeless youths suddenly poured out into the city just before the explosion."

Kiddo closed his eyes with the tiniest flutter of relief. "The Wolf didn't care that Dom would insist on saving a whole heap of snatched kids first."

No matter how confused Dom was right now – he was still hell bent on his true goal. He just believed that Yorak Wolf was working with him to take down the human traffickers.

"Maybe keeping up a charade for Dominic and gaining his trust is more important to Yorak, than the money the underworld just lost," Hato rumbled. "The underworld he's making himself king of, with Dominic as his weapon."

"Yeah," Rue pulled a face. "So that's what we found out."

She tugged on Kiddo's shirt.

"Anyway. We have to do our teeth before we sleep."

| 10 |

Ten

"What do you think?"

Rue did a twirl in front of Kiddo as he blinked drowsily from the end of the bed.

Daleeah was changing his dressings.

"You look lovely," Dalee answered on Kiddo's behalf, as he squinted with bleary eyes. "You are ready for your first day of study."

Once Rue had fallen asleep, Kid had been too tense to unwind. Especially from his position on the floor.

He'd spent the rest of the night clearing out Raff's old room down the hall. Each day Narkon had been dropping off helpful new items for Rue to rejoice in, including a shiny pink handbag with a plastic rose at the front. And Kiddo had decided it was time she had a bedroom for herself that she could put it all in.

"I chose this dress because it's exactly like the little uniforms I've seen other girls wear to school," Rue told the doctor happily. "Narkon said the pattern is called plaid."

Then she pointed to the purple cover over the bed, which

was getting rumpled by Kiddo. "Narkon has got to be the best fake uncle. He chose that for me, the pretty fairy lamp, and I have a hairbrush. And two lovely bottles of perfume! I also have my own pencil case, all filled up for today. He's so sweet."

"Yes, that's right," Dalee agreed. "You are just like the other school children. You are lucky to have such a kind uncle. And how fortunate that your new teacher agreed to start today."

"Well, she's finished wiping the place down for blood and bullets," Rue shrugged. "I didn't realise she was the housekeeper who gave Dom and I crayons to draw Duncan Jr. that time. I'm going to like her. I'll call her Miss Anushi."

"You need to have breakfast to get your brain working for a day of thinking," Kiddo managed. Though his was the slower acting brain right now. "Frazzle's diet plan says you're having oats with honey this morning."

Rue beamed delightedly with her gappy smile.

"Ahuh, healthy habits for healthy minds," she declared, tugging Kiddo up as Dalee finished with him. "I read that on yesterday's cereal box. By myself. I think it sounds smart. I'll tell Miss Anushi that I read it."

Kiddo prepared them both their bowls of porridge with fruit, rubbing at his face.

Anushi had said they would take it slow and wouldn't start with full days of learning, but Kiddo wondered who out of the tutor and Rue would run out of zeal first.

"Remember, you promised you would tell me before you leave to go anywhere," Rue prompted him, when they'd eaten. She dutifully took their empty bowls and placed them haphazardly in the dishwasher. "We'll be in the library, or in the rooftop garden. Miss Anushi will probably be waiting for me soon," she added with importance.

"Got it," Kiddo agreed. "I won't forget."

She made an excited, high pitched squealing noise then, and stunned him with a fast peck on his cheek, before she hurried up the stairs again in delight.

Kiddo blinked after her, eyebrows raised.

"Poor Teddy – she's such a trooper," Jeffrey's voice announced from the couch beside Beef Cake.

The two of them were on their break.

We've been hearing a lot about the disappearance of the young beauty idol known only as Pash. Pash was your personal friend, wasn't he?

Kiddo's attention switched to the TV.

"Pash *is* my dear friend," Teddy's voice corrected as Kiddo crossed to lean against the back of Beef Cake's couch.

Two morning show hosts were nodding sympathetically from a sofa of their own. The scrolling banner beneath the story read: 'Have you seen our queen? #pashwatch' and 'Teddy speaks out. #catchasnatch.'

"You, yourself were injured when Pash was abducted," one host prompted then. "And you saw that these 'snatcher' people are real?"

"They are real," Teddy insisted emphatically. "Pash was standing up to them to help people who can't stand up for themselves. That's why Pash is gone now."

"We've been getting footage from Pash's fabulous-fanaticals," the second host tapped his tablet, as if the evidence was all there, and it was damning.

"They've been sharing what they say are 'snatcher sightings,' all over social media."

The picture on the screen changed to show grainy, phone reel footage of a group of friends, messing around on their walk home from a big night. They were cackling and posing as they walked obliviously by a homeless woman – who eyed them warily from her spot outside a darkened shop front.

But as the group passed a shadowy alley just a little further along, Kiddo caught a fast glimpse of movement from the darkness.

Three masked figures slinking out of the lane. Fanged faces.

Another clip followed this one immediately, and it was from the surveillance camera of one of the front shop windows from the previous reel. One moment the young homeless woman was sitting on her pile of blankets, surrounded in her few meagre belongings. The next, she was being yanked out of view – kicking and struggling – by those same masked figures.

"Is this them? These are snatchers?" the host asked gravely.

"That's them," Teddy affirmed. "They're everywhere around the world. They are hiding in the shadows, picking on people they don't think will be missed."

The fact that none of the party goers had given the woman on the street a backward glance was a painful confirmation of Teddy's words.

"Isn't the question then," the female host asked dramatically: "why can't our leaders comment on where people like Pash have disappeared to?"

"Absolutely," her co-host agreed. "If they can't comment, is it because they did not know that 'snatchers' exist? Or because they knew, and never did anything?"

Jeffrey switched the program off. "Ugh." He threw the remote at Beef Cake.

But then the Raze recruit paused when Beef Cake didn't react to a remote bouncing off his middle.

Beef Cake was staring at the under-web feed on his phone, wide eyed.

"What is it, man?" Jeffrey asked.

Beef Cake glanced up at Kiddo.

"You should see this."

The Silver Bullet turned up the brightness on his screen, and there was Dom.

Dom came hurtling out of a grand building, on an isolated estate – sprinting toward the person filming. He expertly launched himself toward the person, who was waiting in a helicopter that had already started to lift off.

Floods of scared youths were scrambling away across the lawns, still terrified in their very recent liberation. Snatchers laid with twisted necks at the front entrance.

The helicopter rose as the grand building exploded upward – one level detonating at a time.

"Wow," Jeffrey breathed from where he'd hurried to peer over Beef Cake's shoulder.

Beef Cake scrolled to read through anonymous comments that were already appearing beneath the new post.

"People are saying they think this one's a base in Jakarta."

"Wealthy," Jeffrey guessed. "Maybe their wealth made them a threat to the Wolf."

Kiddo stared at them blankly.

Then the stairway rattled as Seethe made his way up in a rush.

"Get your smarts down here," he told Kid.

He was already turning back around to descend.

"Hato's cop and old Wolder think they've found Start. And he's no longer such an international Raze. He's close."

| 11 |

Eleven

"It's so cute that Rue's going to dedicate all her learning to you today," Beef Cake commented nervously beside Kiddo. "So that you aren't distracted worrying about her."

"Mm," Kiddo agreed.

She'd said that; all moodiness and concern, after he'd sworn to come back in one piece.

Just as he'd had to let her go alone the other night, she'd had to accept him going without her.

Right now Kiddo's attention was fixed on the sprawling luxury house ahead of them. What it didn't have in height and levels, it made up for in extensive spread. There were a number of cars in the long driveway. But nobody had come in or out in the short time they'd been there.

"Did…" Beef Cake swallowed. "Did you know Narkon was going to speak out to the media like Teddy did?"

"Nope."

The chef had made an appearance on a prime time news channel the evening before, calmly attesting to what he'd witnessed of the snatchers while working with struggling members of the community himself. Supporting everything Teddy had been saying, and asking for world leaders to acknowledge the problem – or be revealed as corrupt and involved themselves.

His level of celebrity had already reignited any conversations that had started to dwindle since the start of the week.

Many of Narkon's famous friends were commenting on his upright nature and trustworthiness – declaring that they now believed in the issue wholeheartedly, as Narkon had never been an unnecessarily outspoken person before.

Kiddo guessed that Narkon's more silent circles had either chosen to distance themselves from controversy, or had known.

"Such a risk. Good guy that one," Beef Cake glanced around uncertainly. "Real good."

There were five other young Silver Bullets with Kiddo and Beef Cake, and they all kept readjusting their c-gar grips and shifting their weight.

Seethe had some Hellions and Bullets with him, and Hato had a group of Raze recruits. Their teams were heading around to the back of the property.

Koa was going to plead ignorance of their whole unlawful siege, but she was waiting for them to create a reason for her to bring in her own legitimate one.

She was counting on them to make enough noise in that house for concerned neighbours to call for a police check in. Or for frightened staff to ring for aid. Then she could sweep in and conveniently discover what Start's buyer had been up to.

It had to be that way – punishment by the justice system.

Because it had turned out that Start's owner was the current Commissioner of the Federal Police.

If they took down Start's owner themselves, it would look like the Commissioner was just an innocent victim of gang violence, and the facts would become murky after that.

The truth of how far the corruption was spreading in even the surface world would be lost.

"Don't worry too much," Beef Cake told his comrades a little shakily. "Remember this guy has security, but they're not Hunters or snatchers. It's a typical security team, following a patterned roster."

Kiddo's eyes narrowed as he saw movement at one of the sheer curtains from the front of the house.

Then the curtain rod was torn down – ripped out of the wall by whoever had been holding the curtain as they crashed to the ground.

"Maybe worry a little," Kiddo stated quietly. "That's not normal."

He pulled out his phone.

Kiddo: something's not right. Odd movement inside.

There had been no reaction to the disturbance in the house from the sentry box in the front yard. It seemed to be empty of sentries.

Seethe: yup. There's a security guard floating face down in the pool back here. Bunch of others taking permanent naps on the lawn.

Seethe: ooh, and a cleaner and two kitchen staff just charged out screaming.

The call to the cops might already be imminent.

Koa had made sure she and a few trusted others were the closest cars.

Seethe: there goes the innocent secretary that Wolder warned us to leave alone. The one who came up clean. Run, run, run.

"Oh geeze," Beef Cake uttered, glancing over Kiddo's shoulder.

Hato: stick to the plan. Be inside in ten. But be aware there's a third party here. A dangerous one.

Beef Cake swallowed. "Ok, let's recap that plan," he said, glancing at Kid and wiping one palm at a time on his trousers – swapping his c-gar from hand to hand.

Kiddo tucked his phone away.

"Don't think we'll need a costume change or tools for show. Just the ladder." Kid jutted his chin at two Silver Bullets, who quickly scuttled back to their 'work' van to fetch it.

"Our focus is the front of the house. And, remember, the floor plan showed that the grand entrance is a very open space, so we've got to hurry. Cut straight across to the main hallway, and keep your eyes peeled for the attic access. If a gun fight breaks out, run low and fast along the walls."

Seethe and Hato's groups were going to take care of keeping the rest of the household busy with a ruckus while Kiddo's team checked out the roof. It had seemed like the best place to stow a Raze away from prying eyes.

"If you see security pointing a weapon at you, shoot to kill," Kiddo went on soberly. "They were hired at the same time as Start's arrival, and likely know exactly what their employer is involved in."

Kiddo glanced back down the driveway.

"Beef Cake and I will check out the sentry box first. Watch for our signal."

Beef Cake slithered along beside Kiddo, keeping close to the hedges that lined the driveway.

"That's definitely dodgy," Beef Cake whispered coarsely as they peered into the booth.

The surveillance screens all showed a 'disconnected' message, and the security guard on duty was slumped over the desk. His neck at an awkward angle, and blood that had dribbled from his mouth now coagulating stickily between the keys of the keyboard.

"This has Raze all over it, Kid," Beef Cake added – not sure whether to be pleased about Dom possibly being there or not. "And he doesn't seem jetlagged."

Kiddo gave a curt nod, scanning the front windows and gardens again before motioning for the others to hustle to the entrance.

Beef Cake worked some magic on the lock at the stately door – clicking it quietly open after some picking.

"Oh so dodgy," Beef Cake reiterated when he peered inside.

He swung the door open to reveal two more limp guards already, in just the first few metres of the entryway.

"Quick," Kiddo reminded the Bullets. "For now, this situation is good for us."

They stole in with their ladder as soundlessly as possible, rounding a large sculpture in the centre of the grand opening.

The ethereal woman's marble arms were supposed to be reaching out in supplication. But right now they were full. A guard had been draped over each smooth stone wrist like a couple of tea towels on the arms of a waiter.

"Here," Kiddo breathed, halting his team's progress as he peered up at the ceiling of the main hallway.

That was the exact removable square hatch they needed.

"Find somewhere close-by to take cover while we're up there," Kiddo instructed the others. "Make sure the ladder's ready for a fast exit."

Kiddo scaled the ladder as fast as he could without rattling it, while Beef Cake followed. Kid carefully pressed his fingertips against the manhole cover, and eased it up and over into the ceiling.

"Easy does it," he muttered.

The whole place was too hushed.

"See anything?" Beef Cake uttered tensely.

"Nope. Too low. We'll have to go in."

Kiddo stretched himself up, and with protesting new skin along his arms, he hoisted himself into the room within the roof.

His pulse quickened as he spent a moment taking in the layout, before turning hurriedly to help Beef Cake to scramble up.

"That's a good sign!" Beef Cake breathed to him.

Monitors were hooked up along the sloping underside of the roof. Computer towers flashed as if they'd just climbed into a set for a spy film.

On the opposite side of the expansive roof there was a mini fridge, a privacy corner behind a screen … And there were two beds, with one person huddled on a thin mattress.

"Kiddo, that's Start!" Beef Cake gushed even more enthusiastically.

The Silver Bullet made to burst forth at once, but Kiddo gripped his arm.

"Stick to the beams. I've already seen enough broken necks today."

Start's head had bobbed up as soon as he'd heard his name.

This wasn't the kind of tone he'd already come to expect from visitors up here.

"Kiddo?" Start asked as softly as he could across the distance. "Is that ... seriously you, Kid?"

Kiddo began leading the way across the wooden planks and boards between the mounds of insulation in the roof.

"It is seriously me," Kiddo told Start with a touch of warmth creeping into his voice. He was trying not to get too excited to have found one of his Razes. Not until they had taken Start out of this building.

"Careful," Start warned. "There are so many spots you could fall through. I've learned this section pretty well by touch. But they take my glasses every time I finish doing what they want."

Start reached out to Kiddo as he saw Kid's blurry shape nearing him out of the dim gloom.

His hands paused as they gripped Kid's bandaged arms, but then he stood – wobbling, and tugged Kiddo into a tight hug that muffled his half laughs-half cries of relief.

Start was a shorter, slight figure, and his face was buried into Kiddo's sternum for a good few moments before Start finally nodded against him at last, and drew back with a wan smile.

"Did you find Tiny too? He was up here with me for the first few days."

Kiddo frowned. His gaze shifted to the second bed.

"Tiny's here?"

Beef Cake shared a bemused glance with Kiddo.

There hadn't been many other possible hiding spaces for prisoners on the floor plan. Why would they move Tiny somewhere else, if he could be easily spotted?

"They beat him every time I wasn't working fast enough," Start explained with a shuddery twitch – disturbed by the memory. "They said if I didn't want him to disappear, and if I didn't want to live up here alone forever, I better stop giving them reasons to hurt him."

Start hung his head.

"According to them, I was never working hard enough. And I couldn't really see him, but Tiny tried to reassure me that he was doing alright every time they left."

"Why'd they take him away after the first few days?" Beef Cake asked with the kind of expression that suggested he didn't really want to know.

Start frowned. "He went quiet during one session on the third day. They said I'd really messed up, and when they dragged him out of here I figured it was to make me work harder to earn him back. And I've been trying, but it hasn't been enough."

Kiddo squeezed Start's shoulder.

"We'll search for him too."

There was a shout from downstairs that made them all tense to listen.

It was the first sign of any life from the household since they'd got here.

"Uh oh," Beef Cake grimaced.

There were the distant sounds of volleys of gunfire.

Kiddo checked his phone to find messages from Hato and Seethe.

Seethe: new batch of reinforcements just rocked up.

Hato: actual snatchers this time.

Seethe: good. Was getting bored.

"Start, before we go," Kiddo said briskly. "I need you to leave plenty of evidence of what they were up to for the police to find."

Start hugged his elbows. "I can't see the screens to open anything."

"It's ok," Kiddo grabbed Start's hand. "Can you talk me through what to click on?"

He guided Start cautiously over the boards to where the monitors were set up, eyeing the tech cluelessly.

"Ah, on the centre screen you want to click on the Britain files. Open the document called conversation eight."

That was achievable.

"Shit," Kiddo breathed, as the huge font Start had been using made the topic of the document jump out loud and clear.

"The Federal Commissioner was listening in on conversations between the British Treasurer and their Secret Intelligence Service?" Beef Cake gaped. "I didn't think MI6 was a real thing."

Start nodded. "And for whatever reason that my buyer was getting up to this, and a number of other things, the

Wolf was interested in all of it. It's why I was placed here; to analyse everything that an outside hacker was sending in. Now on the second monitor, open the same file, but this time document number nine. Economic conversations in China."

The Wolf had chosen himself a buyer ally who could keep tabs on legitimate branches of real world power. Had he hoped to do more than keep tabs?

Start rattled off more complicated file pathways from memory, and Kiddo opened explosive document after explosive document on each screen, before the sounds from below grew too loud to ignore.

"Let's get you out through the front while we still can," Kiddo told Start. "And don't take this the wrong way, but we'll be more efficient if I piggyback you."

Before Start could think twice about it, Kiddo had hoisted the lighter Raze member onto his back.

Beef Cake led the way across the beams this time, steadying Kiddo as needed, and then checking the ladder below.

He let out a quick whistle, and after a moment received one in turn.

"Coast's clear in the front hall," Beef Cake told them. "At the moment."

He descended first and then held the ladder.

"I can make my own way," Start reassured Kid. "Just set me on the top of the ladder."

Trusting his friend's judgment, Kiddo laid himself out flat and helped to lower Start's weight so that his feet touched down on the top rung. Kiddo dangled out as far as he could, until Start had descended enough to get his hands onto the rungs too.

Beef Cake was reaching up to catch hold of Start while Kiddo was still lowering his legs out of the roof.

Almost too quick to absorb, a group of snatchers, Bullets and Hellions burst from the main part of the house – crashing into the hallway.

There were shots ringing and fists flying.

Gangsters piled onto snatchers, holding them back and weighing them down.

The snatchers were more focused on desperately trying to give their attackers the slip than on fighting back – pinning their attention on Start and the Bullet trying to help him to escape.

"Hit that one, hit that one!"

"Careful of the smaller one!"

There were more shots fired, each crack of sound echoing down the hall.

"Woah," Kiddo cried out as the ladder swayed beneath him.

"Oh no …" Start was gaping. His hands were grabbing for Beef Cake, who had slumped against the ladder.

"Get Start and Beef Cake out of here," Kiddo called down to the other Bullets of his own team, who were all scrambling back out of their hiding places, ready to join the fray.

"Take the van," Kiddo ordered. "NOW."

The fight behind Kiddo intensified as the snatchers saw their prize, their most clever Raze, being surrounded by Silver Bullets.

Beef Cake was hauled up and he and Start were whisked away as Kiddo clattered his way down the rest of the ladder.

He ran for the desperate, messy wrestling match happening in the middle of the hallway, stomping on snatchers and pulling gangsters up as he went.

"Get out of here," he told the Hellions and Bullets. "The police won't be far off now."

The majority of the gangsters didn't wait to be told twice – extricating themselves from the fight so fast that the snatchers found themselves panting on the floor with empty arms.

But a lingering Hellion bashed open a lock and yanked Kiddo through a side door as a scrabbling snatcher lifted a gun to fire in their direction.

There were thumps and curses as the gun toting snatcher's comrades flooded their own man as if in a game of stacks on – grappling the gun away.

"Did you see who that one was?! You don't shoot that one either!"

"Idiot!"

"Don't shoot Razes!"

"But think about what's in that room guys …"

The Hellion kicked a pile of already dead security guards out of what must have been a heavily guarded doorway, and slammed the door shut. She put her weight against the door and turned to search the room for something they could use for a blockade.

Her head snapped back in surprise at what she saw inside.

"What is it?" Kiddo turned hurriedly to face whatever new threat had shocked the Hellion.

He lurched in shock.

He had to brace himself against a wall.

"That's …" Kiddo swallowed.

No way.

No *way*.

Please, no way.

"That's Tiny."

| 12 |

Twelve

They'd been in too much of a harried rush to notice the mechanical whirring sounds, or the small beeps before.

Kiddo hadn't even registered the cyclical pumping sounds of air steadily being pushed in a replication of what breaths filling lungs should be like.

A ventilator tube hung from Tiny's slack mouth. It was strapped in place, and more tubes connected him to fluids, while wires joined him to monitors surrounding the bed.

Tiny's head was bandaged. His left eye socket must have been broken. It was sunken in.

Bruising surrounded his awkwardly gaping jaw, and the purpling, green tinged corner of the left side of his mouth seemed to drag downward.

Even his fingernails were bruised. As if his hands had been stamped on.

"Shit." Kid gasped.

Shit.

Shit.

Shit.

The Hellion cried out as gun fire came from the other side of the door again, and somebody ploughed at it, making her stumble forward a step before quickly forcing her weight back against the wood.

Kiddo stepped toward Tiny as if in a trance, and took the stout man's limp hand into his own.

It was cold.

"S h i t ..." Kiddo uttered slowly in a shaky breath.

He pulled the covers up around Tiny as far as he could.

"KIDDO!" Hato's voice roared. "WHEREVER YOU ARE, GET OUT HERE NOW."

"Come on, Kid," the Hellion rasped. "The cops are coming. They'll find Tiny and take care of this."

A snatcher screamed and Seethe's laugh rang out from down the hallway.

"KIDDO!"

Shots were fired, and it sounded like the snatchers were dispersing for cover.

The Hellion left her post by the door, grabbing Kiddo's arm so that the sting of her grip brought him halfway back to his senses as she tore him away from the bed.

She threw the door open again and tugged him as fast as she could through the hallway toward where Hato and Seethe's voices had come from.

"I'll get us a car. Keep these snatchers off my tail and meet me over the back gate," the Hellion puffed at Hato and Seethe as she shoved Kiddo into them and kept running.

Seethe grinned maniacally and let off another round down the hallway to slow anyone thinking about resurfacing for pursuit, before Hato thrust both Kiddo and Seethe ahead of himself and got them running toward the back of the house.

"Did you ... get Start out ...?" Hato barrelled along behind Kid.

"Yes," Kiddo managed, gasping the word.

Numb.

"And ..." he tried to drag in a full breath.

There was that aching diaphragm again.

Constricting to snapping point.

"I ... found Tiny."

Hato nearly tripped over Seethe as he drew up short.

"Well let's get him," Seethe said. "Fast."

Kiddo slowed to turn back to them. He shook his head blankly. Swallowing nausea.

"He isn't in a state to be moved." He took in a deeper breath. "Koa ... and medical professionals ... will need to handle it."

Neither Hato or Seethe made to move again for a moment.

Seethe started cussing viciously, while Hato sagged where he stood.

Kiddo had to be the one to pull them back into action.

There were sirens approaching from outside.

Seethe kept up his furious stream of curses as they rammed their way through the back door and into the tranquil gardens, where broken security guards were scattered about like ghoulish garden gnomes.

"No, no please," a voice cried out from behind a garden shed. "Please don't!"

"Fouunnnd you," a slow, delighted answer came. "Did you

really think hiding in the bushes and getting snatcher backup would keep you safe? You should have run. What were you trying to guard?"

Kiddo's heart thudded up into his mouth as he steered toward the shed instead of the back gate.

"The snatchers are here to steal from me, not to help me! The *Wolf* sent them to take back what he sold me! Please – tell him it was an accident, I didn't mean to break what I bought – I-*I'm* the victim here!"

"Tut, tut, tut. Yorak Wolf sent me here to *deal with you*. A corrupt leader, working with snatchers in your own legitimate looking den. You are everything that's wrong with the world."

There was a strangled gurgle right as Kiddo rounded the shed, with Seethe and Hato close behind him.

"Dominic! Don't!" Hato bellowed, and the faint smile that had been on Dom's lips as he'd started to press down on the Commissioner's gullet with the sole of his boot vanished at once.

"Oh, hey guys," Dom greeted them, with eyes narrowed. "I just got back into town. Thought I might see you."

The Commissioner's puce coloured face blinked up at them.

It seemed that the man couldn't move his arms or legs.

"Don't kill the Commissioner," Hato implored, with his hands held out. "Just wait."

"Mmm. Should have known," Dom said, his electric blue eyes suddenly losing even the façade of humour as a cold glint touched them. "A crooked friend of yours?"

"We came to take him down," Seethe negated. "But it's got to be done legit. Through the law."

"*I* came to take him down, thank you," Dom cocked an eyebrow. "Worked on this whole scene all night and into the morning." He started to lean forward again, cocking his head as he gazed down at his catch. "I guess you guys are open to working with the police these days, with the very top of their hierarchy being dirty."

"The force itself is not compromised," Hato explained emphatically. "They may have had their hands tied at different times, but they're going to find enough on this guy to arrest him."

Dom eased off at last, standing straight and crossing his arms. "If you think an arrest will give you time to save this chump, you're wrong. He'll be silenced before he's had his first full night in jail."

It was true. But the arrest itself, and the attention from it, was what they needed.

The sirens were so loud now, that police vehicles had to be rolling into the driveway and around the building.

The Commissioner coughed and whimpered.

"Pleease! We ... I ... went too far, and broke one of them. But we're trying to fix it, and the genius one is still intact. I can still be of use –" the man's voice was cut off as Dom delivered a swift kick to his head.

"He makes no sense." Dom turned without a second glance.

Just minutes in Dom's presence had taken Kiddo's breath away.

He watched helplessly as Dom made to leave.

"Dominic –" Hato uttered hurriedly. Clearly wishing to try to take another Raze home from here.

And Dom paused. Peering back with a chilling smile.

"What, big man? You want round two?"

He rolled his shoulders, and turned to face them again.

"We haven't much time, but you weren't too tricky last round, and I've been practicing on all these other snatcher helpers."

"Dominic, we aren't terrorists or allies to the snatchers," Hato tried. "We haven't changed from who you remember us to be."

"Yorak believes you have, and his resources just helped me to knock off two snatcher bases," Dom shrugged. "His tip about our Commissioner's den here was correct. And I never woke up in a fog of confusion at his house, after apparently being smuggled across countries. Sooo..."

"We're Raze," Seethe cut in. "We're all Razes now."

Dom rubbed his chin. "I think you're confused. And I thought *I'd* been scattered lately." His gaze pinned Kiddo then. "Get them name badges, will you?"

Without warning, Hato suddenly charged forward.

Seethe quickly followed suit.

It was as if they were trying to catch a ghost, and it went about as well as it had the last time.

Dom ducked under Hato with a tap on the lower half of Hato's broad back, gave Seethe another jab to the ribs, and strode toward Kiddo.

"On the phone that night, Ryo seemed to think we were

an item," Dom commented thoughtfully. "I can see why he thought I'd go for you."

Kiddo held still as Dom circled him.

"Quiet. But a stand out," he mused, taking in Kiddo's features. "Did they use you to lure me out of Tokyo? They took you too? Is that where you're from?"

Hato was grasping his back as if his spine and every disc was full of arthritis. Seethe was off swearing again.

"Dom, you haven't been still long enough to look into things. Check a calendar, call Ryo again," Kiddo answered intently. "Try to fill in some blanks."

Dom finished eyeing him up and down. "I can help you if they're forcing you into anything."

"Stick around," Kiddo answered desperately. "Get to know us all again."

"Hato! Get the hell off the premises!" Koa's voice hissed from the back of the house.

Dom slipped away as if he'd been rehearsing a disappearing act instead of neck adjustments all night.

Kiddo gaped at the loss. Blinking stupidly for a moment.

Then Kiddo pivoted to where Hato was struggling.

He wrapped his arm around Hato's form, and helped Hato to hobble away to the back gate, with Seethe loping raggedly beside them, swearing all the way.

Kiddo booted the gate a few times, breaking it open rather than trying to boost Hato over.

The Hellion was parked across the street, slouching down in her seat as far as she could.

They'd got Start, the law was about to expose a major

snatcher buyer. But it still felt like this venture had been a terrible loss.

| 13 |

Thirteen

Start wiped the tears that had gathered beneath the thick lenses of his spare glasses.

"You know," he said in a quiet, quivery voice. "They kept saying that they were disappointed to have received a useless second Raze. If they couldn't have another useful one, why not a prettier one." He closed his eyes for a moment as he remembered. "They made sure Tiny knew they hadn't even wanted him, because there was no point buying brawn to keep it locked up."

Start hugged himself.

"Tiny kept encouraging *me* to hang in there. To wait for help," Start breathed the words shakily. "Even as it got harder and harder for him to talk."

Kiddo felt Dom's ring dig into his finger as he clenched his fist.

He sat shoulder to shoulder with Start; only able to offer silent support himself, as they watched the machine that was helping Tiny's chest to rise and fall.

Everyone had been gathered here earlier, as Koa had supervised Tiny's transport to the clinic. Her captain was now pulling every string that he could for her. Either in a show of support, or out of fear that if he didn't take any kind of stand, his department would lose faith in all police leadership as the corruption at the top was exposed.

Koa had been able to confirm some good news – that the evidence had been found. The media was also having a field day over this latest development in the snatcher story, with such a high ranking leader being caught possessing snatcher purchased captives.

But Frazzle had in turn given them the bad news.

The doctor had explained that Tiny had been king hit. Or coward punched, to name it more accurately. He'd had a stroke following the impact. It was unlikely that he would wake again, or still be himself if he did.

Sora had then left to begin organising yet another club funeral. This time for Beef Cake and one other Silver Bullet.

The others had gradually left the ward room, one by one, until finally, Hato had grimly offered to take the sleeping Rue to her bed. As if carrying Rue's small weight, and doing something so normal and wholesome could ground him.

Now Start shook himself beside Kiddo, and checked his new phone when he felt it vibrate.

"A message from Seethe," Start stated tiredly. "More news from Officer Koa."

"Mm?" Kiddo's voice was flat. He couldn't even muster a sense of dread over what else could have come up.

"The Commissioner had regained some movement by the time they were getting him ready to leave the property," Start read out slowly. "He was cleared by doctors. But then he died suspiciously before he got to his federal jail cell."

Start pursed his lips and pocketed his phone.

"Good," he said decidedly. "I hope it hurt."

For all his bravado, tears had begun to pool in the rims of Start's glasses again.

It was a bad sign if the Commissioner had been taken care of so speedily. Had the work been done by his own peers?

Kiddo stood abruptly, and Start blinked up at him.

"I need to get some energy out," Kiddo stated. "Do you want to head to bed?"

Start shook his head and stared down at his hands. "I'll keep Tiny company. I don't want him to be alone."

Kiddo nodded. "I get it."

"Tomorrow I'll bring my laptop down here, to focus on finding Jingle," Start added resolutely. "And on finding a way to tear down the Wolf."

Kiddo squeezed Start's shoulder.

"It's hard to feel grateful for anything right now," Kiddo admitted. "But," he said emphatically. "I'm grateful we got you back."

Then he wandered listlessly through the passage that connected the clinic to Sparks' garage, to find the whole lower level to be eerily muted.

Rows of unused patrol bikes and training equipment.

No music pounding up from the still closed Lair.

Empty firing range aisles – where Flip had once taught him. Rearranging Kiddo's fingers, and showing him how to place his feet.

Kiddo could hear the voices of a few recruits and Hellions on guard outside, talking softly about today's wins and losses.

They wouldn't be ducking across to Kid's Place after their shift. Beef Cake wouldn't be trundling in with Dolly, looking for a late night coffee.

In fact, Narkon had overseen the clearing of the rubble from the site, and no traces of shiny red booths, graduation certificates on the wall, or dainty teacups for Miss Dorris remained.

He'd been told that there had been a few nights in a row where Miss Dorris had driven to Kid's Place to find her adopted grandson, Raze. And she had been rattled to find the diner gone; her grandson missing.

Kiddo grimaced at the idea of it.

Miss Dorris felt the loss every time.

He stopped at one of Sparks' benches. Tracing its marked, polished surface as if he could be closer to her by touching an object that was so familiarly hers.

Normally covered in tools, or parts, or plans. It was too empty.

But his eye caught on something glittering faintly in a crack of the bench.

Frowning, he dug at it frantically, wiping away old dust and picking at the shining, sharp edged thing, until his fingertip dragged a piece of treasure free.

His heart lifting slightly, he hurried to the garage sink, grabbing a coarse bar of soap and rubbing at what he'd found.

The hoop was open, but not broken. The dangling, four point star gleamed as he cleaned it.

The bottommost point was elongated so sharply that it almost looked like a miniature dagger.

When had she lost this earring? Sparks had been wearing little studded stars when he'd last seen her.

Her lucky stars.

On an impulsive whim, Kiddo lifted the earring to his own lobe, and grimly forced the dagger sharp bottom tip of the star through the soft skin. The pain felt refreshingly good as he threaded the hoop through the radiating hole, clicking the clasp closed.

He would worry about the fact that he'd just performed the most unsanitary home piercing tomorrow.

Tonight, he'd needed her.

And as always, even the slightest piece of Sparks could keep him going.

"Didn't really think you were into such spontaneous violence," a voice mused.

And Kiddo froze.

His gaze darted to the grubby mirror above the garage trough.

Its reflection showed a lithe, apparently carefree figure, leaning casually against Sparks' now very shot up old Jeep.

Breathing deeply, Kiddo turned slowly and unthreateningly.

"What makes you say that?" he asked levelly.

The guards outside could still be heard talking. Necks clearly intact.

Dires roared by at incredibly frequent intervals.

How in the world had Dom got in?

Dom gave him an upraising smile.

"Just the fact that Hato and Seethe always charge at me like competitive shoppers, while you hang back," Dom explained in a friendly tone. "But here you are, randomly stabbing your own ear for the heck of it. Might be just as unstable as Seethe."

Kiddo took a few careful paces to lean against another one of Sparks' workbenches. This one had been scrubbed thoroughly. Awful things must have happened to it over raid night.

He tried to collect himself.

"I don't enjoy violence, but that doesn't mean I'm not good at living with it," he answered Dom – feeling the déjà vu of their second ever meeting. "It's a frequent reality in my life."

Dom nodded in grim understanding, less cavalier for a moment. "Was that a kind of act of self-harm, as a cry for help? Or to rebel … if they're keeping you because of your looks?"

He spoke almost gently. So naturally that he still felt exactly like Kiddo's Dom.

Did Dom think the violence Kid was speaking of living with was actually abuse from home?

The wrapped up arms and left over bruises, along with the savage scar marking the side of Kiddo's scalp probably did seem questionable.

"What brought you here?" Kiddo asked, instead of answering anything himself.

He was afraid of admitting that he was firmly with Hato and Seethe, when Dom believed they were snatcher allies.

"How did you get in?"

Dom grinned, his eyes calculating. "I can always find unexpected weak spots when I want to get in somewhere. Even though this place is surrounded like Fort Knox, I could help you to get free if you needed it. Yorak said you'd be safe with us."

Kiddo blanched.

Dom had come because he'd thought Kiddo was a victim. And the Wolf had put it in Dom's head that he should convince Kiddo to live with them.

Kid cleared his throat. "I have too many important things here. I can't just leave," he replied. He pulled himself up to sit firmly on the bench in a clear 'I'm really not budging' move.

"They're holding onto a loved one of yours?" Dom's expression darkened. He straightened. "I'll be able to get them out too."

"Ughh." Kiddo rubbed his face roughly. This was hard.

"You're battered and exhausted," Dom insisted. "Yorak has space for us both."

Oh, I bet he does … Kiddo thought dully.

"I'm just tired from late nights. Trouble sleeping," Kiddo negated. "But … how about you give me your number, and I'll let you know if I do need help?"

There were the sounds of late night movements from above. Probably Hato getting a glass of water, or Seethe peeling himself up to get a beer.

Dom rapidly crossed the space between them.

He splayed one hand on Kid's chest and the other cradled Kiddo's head as Dom tilted him backward across the workbench.

"I don't have a phone now. I avoid tech. Hate being traced," Dom said quietly, as if he wasn't holding a hand over

Kiddo's racing heart. As if he wasn't the one who had just caused it.

Kiddo stared – fixed in place.

"You're worn-out," Dom repeated. "If you're they've done something so you're not up to, or even if you're afraid of the escape, I can let you sleep through the whole thing across the back seat of one of these cars."

He made it sound so simple.

So enticing.

To be carried to the back seat of a car and driven off to sleep somewhere with Dom.

His Dom.

"I'll watch over you, until you're free and the trouble's over."

The grip supporting Kid's head tightened a little at the nape of his neck.

"No –" Kiddo gaped hurriedly, taking hold of Dom's forearm to try to prevent any movements. "I'm not afraid."

The still racing heart probably seemed to disprove that.

"You could do with the sleep," Dom smiled down at him. "While I've had plenty recently, during a number of joy flights. Let me handle this."

How could Kiddo want to be held so badly by Dom, and also be panicking quite so much?

"I have to be honest with you," Kiddo uttered in a rush.

Was he costing himself an opportunity if he stopped letting Dom think of him as someone who needed saving?

But if Dom caught him out as a liar, losing the chance for trust would be worse.

"Hato and Seethe are not bad people. They're not holding

me against my will, or making me work for them. I would go anywhere with you ... except to the Wolf."

There was silence for a moment, as Dom processed that.

The warmth faded from his countenance.

His fingers moved ever so slightly beneath Kiddo's neck, and scrunched the material over Kiddo's heart.

Kiddo didn't struggle. He held Dom's gaze.

But it seemed that Dom was hesitant, and was unsure of why.

There was a gasp.

"Please don't!" Rue's voice cried.

She stood on the stairs in her new princess slippers and matching pyjamas.

The colour had drained from her face.

"Don't hurt him!" she squealed now, and flew down the stairs toward Kiddo and Dom.

Dom frowned. "You've got a kid?"

Rue's cry had brought Seethe and Hato running too. Thundering down the stairs.

Hato caught at Rue to hold her back.

He was worried that if they rushed Dom, he would do something dramatic again. To Kiddo this time.

But Dom's hold slid away from Kiddo.

He stepped right back.

"So you really are with them," he stated.

Then he nodded coolly to himself, and turned on his heel.

Dom simply swept out the front exit this time, startling the guards as he stepped through them confidently, out of their reach before they could react.

"Um ... was that ...?"

"No way…"

"What the hell, guys!"

"You alright?" Seethe half snarled at Kiddo.

He was brittle after the day, and had clearly been woken again.

"The Wolf sent Dom to try to collect you?" Hato asked – his usually warm, russet tone now ashen.

Kiddo nodded in answer to them both and propped himself up on his elbows – shell shocked.

"It's all my fault," Rue burst out in tears. "I did that to him!"

Hato patted her head glumly, his voice tinged with regret. "We were the ones who never should have let Dominic do so many lone patrols in the first place. Knowing how fixated the Wolf was on him."

Kiddo sighed and sat up properly on the bench. "We would have lost him anyway if we'd stifled his independence back then."

Staying in one place for a prolonged time was already not Dom's style.

Rue shuffled over to grasp onto Kiddo's legs, snuffling against him. "Poor Dom. Poor, poor Dom."

"Why are you even still up?" Kiddo asked Rue wearily, reaching to dry her cheeks.

She craned to peer up at him. "I never heard you go to bed, so I was checking why *you* were still up!"

Then she cheered a little as she took him in fully.

"Hey, I like your earring," she said with interest. "It's real nice. Like, tuff nice. Did Narkon get it for you?"

Out of Habit, Kiddo glanced at Hato, as if expecting a challenge. But none came.

"It was Sparks'," Seethe answered Rue instead.

His attitude softened slightly, though he crossed his arms. "Suits you."

Hato gave a single nod.

His stern approval, and sad nostalgia, clear in that one motion.

"Real nice," Rue affirmed again, and she patted Kiddo's knee.

"You got her with you now," she went on consolingly. "So at least that's one nice thing."

| 14 |

Fourteen

Kiddo turned the thick carboard cup around in his hands, watching the buzzing movement across the road.

A few people in hard hats and high-vis vests were wandering around the cleared diner site, holding up large sheets of paper and pointing. The front carpark was even busier.

Kid's mind was only half on what he saw, and half on Narkon, who had come to join him in the rooftop garden so that he could give Kiddo an update – and a green tea.

"The food trucks are going to stay there as long as it takes for Kid's Place to be rebuilt," Narkon was explaining. "Starting from today, they'll be manned by all of your usual staff, and the community will be back to having a place that they can count on for meals."

Kiddo swilled the steaming tea in its recyclable cup. "I suppose that's if people in need want to risk being near any Razes at the moment. We're more of a liability than a protective force right now."

He felt the weight of having just attended a day's worth of funerals for Sparks' fallen apprentices, the Raze recruits they'd lost, and the slain Bullets and Hellions. Dolly had not long been released from hospital – and she had fainted in Sora's arms when they had reached Beef Cake's coffin. Jeffrey had appeared ready to follow suit.

Narkon regarded Kiddo solemnly for a moment, and Rue's voice carried up to them from the library at the pause in their conversation.

Since Narkon had passed through the library to greet her and then Kiddo, she had been reciting her ones, twos and threes multiplication tables to Miss Anushi with incredibly well projected enunciation – to make sure they, too could hear and appreciate her from the roof.

"You may not be aware," Narkon drew Kid's attention back. "But while it's not a good time to reopen the garage, Hato has been working with the surviving mechanic apprentices on the restoration of his club. And they have been joined by many willing volunteers whose faces I recognised from the diner. I also know that your clinic has been as well attended as ever, and that I have myself had no shortage of offers to help with the rebuilding of Kid's Place."

Kiddo processed that, with eyebrows raised.

He'd been spending any time when Rue was busy with her lessons wallowing down in Tiny's ward room.

Rue forced him to want to do routine, wholesome things of a morning and evening – like cooking or washing up together. Like Kiddo shaving while she brushed out her curls. Making the beds. Decorating her room. Reading. Even watching children's movies with Hato, while Seethe tried to ignore their catchy tunes.

She found each film and storybook so hilariously and beautifully innocent.

But when she was sleeping or learning, Kiddo was remembering Dom's sudden, cold withdrawal from him. He was watching Tiny's every mechanical breath. Or Frazzle and Daleeah's hopeless visits for monitoring, and Start's furious navigation through too many complicated tabs. Otherwise he was listening to Koa's depressing influx of news.

This morning she'd said a few groups of regular university students had been killed when they'd gone out searching for the snatchers they'd heard so much about – only to find them and discover exactly how dangerous snatchers could be.

He'd heard about how there were arguments in parliament house during question time, as fingers were pointed and accusations were made about why such problems existed. It seemed that tensions were high, but no solutions about poverty, homelessness, or even the snatcher issue were being offered. Instead, it was becoming a political attack point, and a feature of each opponent's election campaign ads – to belittle the opposition for having been most blind and incompetent in the past.

Teddy's quest to find Pash had so far turned up no sightings, though at least regular people were on board and being as vigilant as ever about snatchers in general now.

In the underworld itself, the under-web had been sporadically screening disturbing clips of Flip's international Raze recruits, who were apparently allowed to be terminated as creatively as possible by their buyers.

Dom had toppled a few more shocking leaders close to home; dumping them in paralysed piles outside local police stations, along with evidence of them having benefitted from snatcher capitalism. No more captive Razes had surfaced from these cases, but the fact that one dumped, unmoving superior had been the CEO of a major security company, one had been the owner of a shipping and freight empire, and another had been a respected surgeon to the stars had led to a public witch hunting frenzy. An awful lot of rich and famous people were suddenly getting quite involved in charity events, or speaking out in support of the 'catchasnatch' movement.

Yet somehow the worst news Koa had delivered, was that there were rumours of even greater global support for the Wolf amongst underworlders. The Dire boss reported that many appreciated the Wolf being able to tighten up such a colossal and lawless society, scaring influential players into line, and enforcing order through Raze – his own personal snatcher police. There was a belief that causing fear and awareness in the surface world might in fact get the Wolf more allies and a stronger hold above too.

Recently Yorak had released a temporary story on the under-web stating that 'to wield a true Raze was to have the power,' and that that was why his ultimate Raze was solidifying his own position as the Top One of all top snatchers and Hunters.

Yorak had warned, however, that you didn't just get authority by buying a Raze. You had to prove yourself as continually being deserving, by utilising and keeping hold of that Raze. With his perfectly charming demeanour, and with magnetic light and dark eyes trained on the camera, he had admitted that it was dangerous to be a buyer. Yet he'd added that he personally did not mind hearing of or causing buyer deaths, as only successfully surviving buyers were worthy.

The comments on that clip had applauded every one of the Wolf's decrees. Agreeing heartily. Praising the charismatic Wolf.

He could do no wrong.

"You're struggling to concentrate today," Narkon commented, after too much time had passed between replies and eye contact. "Have you been getting enough sleep?"

The chef peered at Kiddo closely.

Kiddo drew in a very long breath, and slowly let it out.

No, he had not.

"I just didn't expect to hear positive news," Kiddo circled the topic back. "I'm grateful for it."

Where the food trucks had not long finished being set up, he did notice that there were already some people loyally gathered there. A patient line, waiting for supper.

He took a gulp of the tea, and turned purposefully to try to hone his attention in on the chef.

"I don't know how you're finding the time to help us so much, but 'grateful' actually doesn't do it justice," Kid added honestly, and Narkon's concern eased.

"I finished at the university this week, so I am glad to entertain myself by organising rosters, orders and payrolls on your behalf." The chef gave a warm smile then. "Even moreso, to surprise my newest family member with the kinds of gifts that a child who has never been spoiled deserves."

"Your generosity gives me faith," Kiddo replied. "The top of the hierarchy isn't all about spoiled hoarders." He finished the tea. "Thought you were all a bunch of old, extravagant dragons, sitting possessively on your gold."

Narkon gave a bark of a laugh. "I have always had more money and work than time or joy," he answered in good humour. "And what a waste. Until now."

Narkon finished his own coffee then.

"One more piece of good news," the chef told Kiddo, and Kid cocked his head curiously. He'd really thought they were in such short supply of things to be thankful for.

"Mmm?" Kiddo frowned; listening.

"Now that so many of my," Narkon paused on the word, "*friends* are keen to show that they advocate for the truth as I do, I've had an abundance of partnership offers, and have begun a sponsor program," Narkon informed Kid. "Scholarship paid trainees from underprivileged backgrounds are going to be able to apply to be accepted into kitchens around the globe. I'll also eventually start a chain of restaurants in as many cities as I can, specifically for the program."

Kiddo shook his head in admiration, feeling a genuine grin tipping up the corners of his mouth. "Surely you won't use the Kid's Place business model," he teased, touching on Narkon's past, and very valid criticisms. "It's not economical."

Narkon shrugged with a smile of his own. "I was planning on calling them 'Raze Havens.' But the ideals will be almost identical to Kid's Place. No one will go hungry if I can help it."

Kiddo couldn't find words – speechlessly shaking his head in wonder. And Narkon was pleased.

The chef chuckled when Rue's hollering disrupted their warm moment then.

"Hey Kiddo!" she shouted up from the library window. "Miss Anushi is going to take me to the merry-go-round at the docks!"

Before he could open his mouth, she added: "And don't worry. I'll wear the dopey hat."

He wanted her to cover her distinctive, bright curls when she went out, and had bought her a cap with a flap of material at the back that was designed to protect the wearer's neck. Kiddo's effort at a thoughtful purchase had been received with much less enthusiasm than any of Narkon's pretty presents had.

"Bye, best uncle!" she sing-songed to the chef.

"Stay safe, favourite niece," Narkon returned.

Still buoyed just enough by Narkon's company and general goodness, Kiddo managed not to be in a dark cloud when he was once again alone in his wakefulness later.

He sat down at a table in the library to go through the activities that Rue had been completing. Miss Anushi and Rue had proudly set her best worksheets out for him to see, and she was clearly coming along well with all of the basics.

He smiled to himself as he read a simple story about The Angry Man Called Seethe. Miss Anushi's corrections helped, but Rue's punctuation was accurate and her careful letters were legible – with rounded curves and little hooked tails that suggested she cared about every single word that she made on the page.

He would have to make sure Seethe checked out the expressive crayon illustrations at some point, he snickered to himself.

He flicked through some numeracy skills sheets for a

while, loving that Rue had even put in the effort to colour the cute frog character who gave tips about each activity at the top of every page.

He could see that Miss Anushi was generous with stickers and praise, and he was even more buoyed now, with pride.

It was some time before Kiddo stretched, and registered an out of place shadow from the corner of his eye.

His heart stuttered, and he thought he was imagining it for a moment, as his head shot around to check the vision properly.

But there was Dom, seated comfortably in the large arched window's sill.

"Thought you'd be up late." Dom quirked a cool smile. His sharp featured face was half in shadow from the dimness of the library, and half illuminated by the moonlight outside.

His long legs were stretched out across the wide sill, as if it had been made to be Dom's personal rest stop.

He took Kid's breath away.

"What brought you back?" Kiddo finally asked, as evenly as possible. "And how long have you been spying?"

"Researching," Dom corrected, in as much of a response as he would give to the second question. "Trying to decide what I think about you."

Kiddo felt a spike of hope. If Dom would only begin re-searching *all* of them again, like when he'd first arrived to in-vestigate the gang, he would see what they were really about.

Kiddo set Rue's precious papers down in a neat pile. "Come to any conclusions?"

"Oh, sure." Dom straightened his spine against the thick window frame. "You're incredibly attractive."

And Dom was like a *god*.

He wore a closely fitted black trucker jacket. So similar to the leather biker jacket hanging in Kiddo's wardrobe.

"I don't think you came to contemplate my looks," Kiddo prompted, and Dom shrugged.

He swivelled to face Kiddo fully, his legs dangling down from the sill.

Kiddo was in turn on alert at once. Dom could easily launch at him like that, and reduce Kiddo to a paralysed pile of his own.

Observant as ever, Dom cocked an eyebrow and smirked, having noticed Kiddo's subtle reaction.

"Those looks do seem to keep drawing me back to initiate these intimate moments with you," Dom answered dryly, as if exasperated at himself, when he had so many other Raze things to do.

"Maybe those looks, and your reserved, mysterious ways, are why Yorak and I both want me to keep seeking you out to know more."

Kiddo grimaced.

Reserved and mysterious ways?

"I am not interested in going anywhere near the Wolf, remember?"

Dom leaned his elbows on his knees, watching Kiddo closely with eyes that glittered with guile.

"That 'Wolf' was sure you'd keep saying that," Dom mused. "He seems to think I should just carry you off so you can thank us later. It would save me being enticed to come here after you again."

Kiddo stiffened at that. "I *wouldn't* thank you for it," he said flatly.

"Not right away," Dom agreed. "Because your captors have been messing with your head, like they did to mine. Yorak said they've likely done something to you to make you want to stay."

Kiddo grunted. "What makes you so sure that Hato and Seethe were the ones who did something to your mind?"

"I woke up here," Dom answered darkly. "And I'm missing over two years of memory." Low anger seeped into his voice. "I only have a few hazy images of Yorak trying to save me each time I must have got out."

So he'd discovered the date and year, but had filled in that time incorrectly.

"Yorak helps me with the headaches I still get from whatever went on here," Dom went on grimly. "He'll be able to help you too."

Kiddo shivered at how Yorak must be 'helping'.

"It wouldn't be easy taking you from up here. The garage was much more convenient," Dom remarked. "But I'm sure I can do it. I'm very capable."

Kid puffed derisively. It was as if Dom was considering something normal and simple, like whether or not he could carry all of the groceries in one trip, rather than somebody's dead weight. And he was really quite confident that he could do it without being caught.

Then Kiddo was up out of his chair and backing right away as Dom slid down from the sill.

"Easy," Dom eyed Kiddo – contemplating his every move.

He took a step forward, and Kiddo took two more backward.

"I don't really want to do something you're not open to," Dom admitted. "But getting you out of here would be for the greater good."

Another stride forward from Dom.

"I told you … I'm totally open to doing anything with you," Kiddo took another step backward. "Except going to the Wolf."

His pulse was racing.

Dom was unconcerned.

"I've been here since I was thirteen," Kiddo added then – trying for reason and logic. "I would be aware if Hato and Seethe had any brainwashed captives laying around. You were never here against your will."

Two more steps from Dom in their little dance, and Kiddo's shoulders were against the wall.

Dom was just paces away.

"I won't forgive you if you try to take me to the Wolf against my will," Kiddo warned. "And I'll cut this conversation short to call for backup."

He wasn't stupid enough to think he'd win against Dom alone. He'd never had to contemplate it before, and had rarely been faced with a lone opponent he didn't feel at the very least equal to, but Dom was different.

"You see, while I'm wildly fascinated by you, and think you do need our help," Dom deliberated in an easy tone. "I'm not as sure of you as Yorak is. And *I* won't forgive *you* if you truly turn out to be a snatcher ally. So that makes us even."

Dom closed in, leaning an arm against the wall beside Kiddo.

Flirtatious?

Possessive?

Intimidating?

Or a distraction of seduction and sweetness. He'd already told Kiddo what he planned to do.

"Nice aftershave."

Dom reached a knuckle to trace Kiddo's cheekbone. He was much too close to the kinds of nerves that he found so easy to manipulate, but Kiddo just couldn't bring himself to make a sound that would ruin this.

Could he take a chance to try to jog Dom's memory?

Dom's gentle touch trailed along Kiddo's cheek, ready to move down to take a hold around the nape of Kiddo's neck.

Kiddo abruptly broke from the mesmeric moment.

He ducked under Dom's arm and slid along the wall until he felt the panel that stood out almost imperceptibly from the others.

With a push, the panic room door opened. And Kiddo stepped into the darkness, knowing that he was being followed closely.

Almost immediately the door swung closed, and Kiddo felt strong hands grip onto him.

"Are you panicking?" Dom whispered, and pulled Kiddo back against himself with a jolt.

But they were both surprised, and stilled at once when

they heard the door connecting the rooftop to the library suddenly opening and closing, and heavy footsteps moving through the library.

"Hey, Kid?" Jeffrey's voice whispered coarsely. "Kiddo, you in here?"

Faster than Kiddo could register, Dom had clamped a hand over Kiddo's lips – holding him tightly in place.

Kiddo's arms were mostly healed and were now uncovered, but the new skin prickled as goosebumps raced across his flesh. He could feel Dom's hard, wiry body, pressing against his. So familiar.

Jeffrey must have checked between the bookshelves, muttering in a worried voice to himself. "Not here either," he said as he passed the panic room and headed down the internal stairs. Safely oblivious to the proximity of the danger.

Dom waited for a few beats, until he was sure that Kiddo was content to be silent, before lowering his hand.

The hand settled around Kid's abdomen in a kind of hug-hold instead.

"I'm not worried," Kiddo stated, answering Dom's panic room question seriously. "I know you. I know that if you think someone has a shred of goodness, or might be innocent, you'd never hurt them. You won't betray my wishes."

"Huh," Dom's voice held an amused undertone, and his breath was warm against Kiddo's ear. "You know me so well. Tell me more."

Kiddo closed his eyes. "You're a generous ... a great ... kisser."

"Ohhh," Dom purred. "That could be a lucky guess. Should we confirm how generous?"

Kiddo felt deft fingers going for his jeans button.

"You don't seem to mind," Dom commented as the button flicked undone. "So I think I'll push your boundaries."

Oh lord.

"Fine ..." Kiddo managed. "So do it."

It was both consent, and a challenge.

The zip was open then, and a pressured hold snaked down into Kiddo's pants.

Oh lord oh lord oh lord.

Kisses were trailing down the side of Kiddo's neck.

That pressured hold was ...

Before he could get too carried away, and lose the point of this exercise, Kiddo elbowed backwards and turned quickly, giving the dark figure that was Dom a fast shove.

Moving almost as swiftly as Dom himself always could, Kid caught at Dom so that his hands made a buffer between Dom's body and the thin wall before impact. They didn't make a sound.

There was a pause.

Heavy breaths.

"You're good at throwing me against walls," Dom uttered softly, but with a trace of uncertainty touching his usually self-assured voice.

Kiddo hoped Dom could feel the sense of déjà vu this time too.

The chemistry between them was palpable. Making the air thick in the very small space.

Kiddo grabbed Dom by his jacket, dragging Dom in to steal a heated kiss that seemed to electrify every part of them that touched. Chests, hips, knees, lips.

It was better than the kiss against the wall in the snatcher exhibition. Better than the kiss they'd had pressed against Miss Lotus' hidden tunnels. Hotter than any kiss before, but just as right as all of them had been.

When Kiddo pulled back, Dom – who had been just as swept up during the kiss – seemed to freeze.

Kiddo realised that Dom was sagging against him a little.

In the silence, he heard Dom lift a hand, and he thought he could make out Dom holding his head.

"Hey," Kiddo whispered in concern. "You good?"

Keeping a hold on Dom, he reached across to feel for where he knew there was a light switch, and turned the dim light on.

Dom squinted against it, frowning.

"Are you dizzy? Is your head hurting?" Kiddo asked. "Here, I'll help you down."

For a moment Dom seemed confused, and then surprised by Kiddo's genuine care.

Then he shook himself; his defences apparently shooting right back up.

Dom pushed Kiddo away. But only lightly, to create space between them. The thrust had nothing of the ferocity Kiddo knew Dom could muster.

Dom braced himself against the wall until he was able to straighten resolutely, his blue eyes focused warily on Kiddo.

"Are you alright?" Kiddo made to get closer again, but Dom shrugged him off to avoid being touched once more.

"Back off," Dom warned. "And I'll leave you alone for tonight too."

No more threats of being carried away unconscious.

But also no admission of an onslaught of recollections.

"Did you feel anything just then?" Kiddo asked intently. "Did that spark memories of anything between us?"

Dom's face was guarded. "I felt horny. Definite spark. Don't overthink it, I've always been a flirt," he said plainly; overly non-committal. "It just means I like the look of you."

Kiddo winced. He'd been watching too many fairy tale films with Rue and Hato.

"Right," he intoned. "That's ... that's alright."

"Hey! He's in here!" Jeffrey's voice came from the panic room door then, and the panel burst inward.

Before Jeffrey could even get a proper glimpse of the situation and barge in, Dom had lashed out.

He hit Jeffrey with an upper cut to the jaw, and as Hato arrived on Jeffrey's heels, Dom brushed by him with a purposeful hand to Hato's chest – and then a violent blur of motion.

While Dom was exiting through the rooftop door, Kiddo was gaping at Hato as the big man collapsed to the floor.

| 15 |

Fifteen

"He's dead!" Jeffrey wailed, clutching with one hand at his jaw, and scrabbling to feel Hato's pulse with the other. "Oh my God. Hato's dead!"

Seethe and Koa were up the steps then, and Seethe yanked Jeffrey back by his collar as Koa hurried to Hato's side.

"Don't wake Rue," Seethe hissed, giving Jeffrey a small shake. Then his volatile gaze flicked to Koa. "Is … he dead?"

"Don't be so dramatic." Koa pummelled Hato in the sternum and then threw herself into chest compressions.

Seethe swore.

"You've got three minutes to get a defib kit back here," the cop told them, and Kiddo was off racing at once.

His feet hardly touched the stairs as he flew down to the clinic's quiet consult rooms, hauling a frazzled Frazzle up from the night shift cot, and swiping a professional electronic defibrillator pack kept ready in the office.

To his credit, Frazzle went along for the ride, sprinting up the stairs like the wind at Kiddo's heels.

The doctor hardly slowed before he crashed to his knees, working out the scene at a glance.

As efficient as he must have been as a medic in the middle of a warzone, Frazzle had cut through Hato's muscle top, slapped on the adhesive pads, read the data and told them all to back up as a charging sound whirred from his equipment.

Seethe didn't seem to notice that he was practically holding Jeffrey up by the shirt.

Kiddo held his own breath as the whirring built, and suddenly there was a fast pulse of electricity that jolted Hato's body – his broad shoulders bouncing against the floor.

Hato's eyes shot wide open, and his chest heaved as Frazzle quickly threw out a hand to keep the big man from scrambling up in an adrenaline fuelled rush.

"Calm, calm my friend," Frazzle told Hato, as Hato glanced about himself wildly.

Seethe dropped Jeffrey with a thud and sank to the floor too, while Koa scooted in closer to Hato.

"What ... the hell ... just happened?" Hato rumbled, pressing a hand to his chest.

Kiddo dropped his hands to his knees, hunching as if winded.

"Raze took you down with a strike to the chest," Koa informed Hato bluntly. Then she threaded her fingers through his in a stout grip and gave a droll smile. "But your heart was safe in my hands."

For the first time Kiddo noticed that both she and Hato were dressed for bed.

"Interesting indeed," Frazzle rocked back where he squatted. "To deliver the blow like this, at right time and pressure. Not often you can disrupt a heart like this."

The medic patted Hato's muscular arm. "You bouncing back so good probably means Raze makes a clean hit. Probably no damage," he reflected. "Aside from the blow tripping heart rhythm before – you well know that."

Koa shook her head in consternation. "Raze caused a heart concussion? I thought that was a sporting injury for kids with soft chest bones." She eyed Hato's powerful chest.

"Mmmhmmmm," Frazzle agreed. "Often yes. But Raze has extra strong muscles, bones and force. And must know what he does quite well. Might have been intentional that you cardiac arrest instead of die," he told Hato solemnly.

"You don't think Dom *meant* to kill?" Seethe asked sharply.

His face was so drawn it had become skull-like.

"Maybe we got to stop underestimating how big of an enemy we've got here."

Frazzle considered it. "Dominic's past medicals show … heart marks. He is first-hand expert in what he just does to Hato. Many many times over."

The room was silent then.

"Pharmacy experiments made *all* his body strong. Heart too. Amazing, though, that he learned from what they do. Precisely where and when they do this strike to him. Very specific."

Kiddo drew in a shaky breath and straightened, gripping the back of his head with interlocked fingers.

As a child, Dom's body had been pushed to the absolute limits in the name of experimentation.

He had clung to life every time they had tested him beyond the limits.

What greedy elites were benefitting from this research, and hoarding the benefits?

"No wonder he was able to rattle his lab buyers so much when he started to play up," Seethe scowled. "They'd created their own monster, who was probably too valuable to permanently get rid of."

"He is *not* a monster," Hato stated firmly. "Or why save that move for only when he is most cornered?" he sat up a little straighter. "Dominic has a conscience. He doesn't like doing the worst thing that was done to him, even to people he considers to be his greatest threats."

Frazzle was nodding his own belief. "He do this knowing you have a clinic right here. I am never going to let you be dead like that. I always try to save you."

Koa pursed her lips, and Seethe appeared undecided.

"Beware giving your Raze too much benefit of the doubt," the officer cautioned frankly. "I might not be so close to tide you over before help gets here next time."

Hato pulled her hand closer, as if to refute that.

"He really has no idea who we are," Jeffrey spoke up despondently then. He was cradling his jaw in a hand. "What are we meant to do? It's *Raze*."

Hato sighed cautiously. "We have to be aware that Dominic does not recognise his family right now, and won't hesitate to kill if he is sure you are on the wrong side. But ... I have to trust in who Dominic is at his core. If he wanted me dead, I'd be dead, with a seriously snapped neck or totally stopped heart." Hato peered at them all, collecting himself stoically. "So I choose to believe he's still in there, or has even the smallest suspicion that I could be good," he answered.

Seethe rubbed his eyes roughly.

Kiddo grimaced. "He did inform me that he came here tonight to 'save' me. Even if I didn't want it, he had to act for the greater good."

Seethe growled. "The Wolf has an interesting sense of the greater good." Then he raised a white blonde eyebrow at Kiddo, with a pointed look. "So fortunate Dom can still be diverted by true love."

For the first time Kiddo realised that his still unzipped pants were riding much too low on his hips after he'd flown up and down the base stairwell.

He corrected that with an eye roll.

"So I was right!" Jeffrey declared. "I knew it was a good idea to have the night duty checking up on you," he told Kiddo proudly.

Kiddo frowned.

Jeffrey coughed and quietened.

"You're lucky your hunch paid off," Seethe agreed with Jeffrey menacingly. "If you'd woken me for nothing again I'd have snapped your neck myself."

"What..?" Kiddo asked. "You guys are keeping tabs on me?"

"Damn straight," Jeffrey tried to sound more confident again. "Since the other night when Dom was ready to carry you off then, too."

Kiddo crossed his arms.

"I'm not the one Dom nearly killed tonight," Kid said

crossly. "When only I'm involved, it's not life and death. I might just be swooped off to be the Wolf's new pet. But every time someone else comes along, it becomes a confrontation. And how do you think Dom would feel if we do get him back, and he finds out he's responsible for one of us dying?"

"You prefer us just to wait and see if you show up for breakfast?" Seethe drawled slowly, with no humour in his voice. "How we gonna explain to Rue that we didn't even notice that you were *swooped?*"

That stopped Kiddo's protests.

"It's just at night," Jeffrey reassured Kid, while wincing at his sore jaw. "When you're the only one up and wandering, and no one else is around to have eyes on you."

Kiddo felt his shoulders drop. "I get it," he said, though a little testily. "I'm happy you'll all be aware if I'm snatched in the night. Rue has explained the importance of knowing where I am at all times, for her own peace of mind." He glared at each of them then. "But can you *all* stop trying to save me for the greater good? Don't get in the way, so that I don't have to watch anyone else being resuscitated on my behalf. You can rescue me later, I'm sure."

Hato, Seethe and Jeffrey all appeared ready to argue, but were diverted when Frazzle tutted thoughtfully to himself.

"What is it, doc?" Seethe asked, with an incrementally more civilised tone.

"Hmmm, hmmm, hmmm," Frazzle tapped his chin. "Just wondering how we get big Hato down to clinic safest."

Hato glowered – this time with it being his turn to feel babied and to hate putting others out.

"I will walk. Carefully."

"I've got you," Koa nodded supportively.

Seethe was already standing, even while favouring his injured side.

"Should really get elevator put in," Frazzle decided. "Is good idea."

Kiddo reached a hand out to Jeffrey. Like a peace offering for having reacted so poorly to a selfless effort on the Raze recruit's behalf.

"I'll get you an icepack," Kid told him.

And they joined a very slow, staggered procession down the stairs.

| 16 |

Sixteen

"Wakeupwakeupwakeup!"

Kiddo groaned.

He'd only got in a few hours, and Rue's excitement made for a rude awakening.

She shook his arm with hands that were like tiny vices.

"Kiddddddddooooooooo," she wailed. "Come onnnnnnn!"

He pulled the pillow over his face.

"What is it?" he asked her in a grouchy muffle.

"I can't learn today," she stated. "I just can't. You need to write me an absent note like they do in the real classrooms. Oh my God."

Kiddo lifted the corner of the pillow and squinted out at her.

"You sick?"

He added a new item to his checklist of trying to be a good guardian.

He would take her straight back to Daleeah for another check-up. This child was a robust thing, for being such a waif.

And she had now been vaccinated, vitamin-ed, listened to, tested. What could they have missed?

Maybe Dalee was free this morn –

"I'm not sick!" Rue blustered about, jumping up onto his bed to bounce over his legs.

Kiddo yawned, relaxing once more in relief. "You shouldn't try to dodge classes. You're doing so well with your activities."

She paused for a second. "Did you see I even coloured the frogs?"

"Even coloured the frogs," he agreed sleepily.

"But I'm not dodging!" she went on then. "I can't learn today because I'm too EXCITED!"

"Oh?" he closed his eyes again. "What's exciting? Something good at Narkon's food trucks?"

She snorted. "Noooooo. I'm excited because Trix is here!"

Kiddo sat up so fast that he headbutted her with the pillow, and she fell back on her haunches with an *oof.*

"What did you say?"

She recovered quickly, kicking the mattress with glee. "You know Trix is one of my favourite Razes!" she said delightedly. "And Trix brought another tough girl with her! I think it's her girlfriend!"

Kiddo gaped.

"Oh, and Flip and another guy," she added, as if that was of much lesser import. "I haven't been able to speak to them, because they went into the clinic to see Hato and Tiny, and Seethe said to give them a moment of respect." Rue pouted at that. "But it's been a whole lot of moments trying to wake you up."

"Rue," Kiddo said vehemently. "Shoo."

"Yeah, yeah," she rolled off the bed. "Privacy. I'll meet you right outside your door!"

Rue was jiggling about as if she were busting when Kiddo burst out to meet her.

"What do you know?" he asked as he hurried her to the kitchen level and grabbed her a muesli bar and an apple as a cheat breakfast.

She caught the bar as he ripped at it too hard, and it exploded free from its packet.

"Um, so I heard how surprised everyone was," Rue admitted, before urgently shoving in half the bar. "And listened in," she added around her mouthful. "Flip's accent is cool."

Reliable little spy.

Kid grabbed her before she could keep running down the stairs.

"Chew," he said firmly. "They'll still be here."

"Ahuh," she chewed on super speed. "Apparently Hato had told Trix to stay put in Miss Lotus' hidey-holes. So he was a bit grumbly that she didn't do that," Rue explained. "But, like a happy grumbly."

"Of course," Kiddo grinned.

"Then Hato was just telling them what's been happening here, so that I could get you," Rue gulped the last of the bar down. "I'll take the apple with me," she promised, tugging him back to the stairs. "By the way, why's Hato in the clinic?"

"Uh, don't worry too much," Kiddo answered. "Frazzle is

beyond impressed by how he's doing. They're just monitoring the rhythm of his heart after it got a bit off track."

Rue pushed open the door that connected the garage to the clinic walkway.

"Geeze, poor Hato," she lamented dolefully. "He's proper broken hearted over his family. Lucky Trix has come."

Rue led the way as fast as her short legs could take her, and then walked straight into Tiny and Hato's room as if the private ward was her own domain.

She barged right over to where Trix was sharing a mini sofa with Blossom, and plonked herself on the startled Trix's lap.

"I'm your biggest fan," Rue announced to Trix, making herself at home.

Blossom laughed, lifting a pierced brow. "Wanna bet, small fry?"

But Rue simply shrugged. "Play your cards right, and I could be a fan of yours too."

Ryo appeared unbothered not to have been considered, giving a small smile and a nod to Kiddo, who had stopped short in the doorway.

He had to take it all in.

Just yesterday Kiddo been telling Narkon there was so little to be thankful for.

Yet he had Hato here, looking fine. Frazzle was unworriedly updating his charts. Seethe was perched on the windowsill, his feet up on the end of Hato's bed. Start was in the chair that he'd barely left since his rescue. Trix was bemused and holding Rue. And Flip. He was sitting with Tiny's hand in his.

Kid just needed the rest of his big family. Sparks. Dom. Jingle. Velvet. Pash. And Quicklips.

"Ey Kid," Flip stood to yank Kiddo into a bear hug. "You miss me?"

Kiddo was surprised when Flip towed him over to sit on Tiny's bed, with Flip leaving his arm around Kiddo's shoulders – keeping him close.

Flip had always been a believer in personal space.

"Good, we all here," Frazzle noted. "I only have short break. Please get on."

Rue bit into her apple loudly, gazing back at Trix adoringly.

"I want to know everything," Rue agreed juicily. "Anything that's not on your Raze profile."

Hato glared dourly at Trix, but his obvious contentment made the expression lose effect. "Like why you didn't stay put," he rumbled.

"Oh, well," Start pushed up his glasses. "That's actually my fault." He shuffled his laptop and papers on his lap. "I didn't want to say anything to everyone here, in case I was wrong."

He hadn't thought they could take another blow.

"But," Start continued. "While I was in captivity, I received a message from an unknown sender. A hint of where Flip might be. When freed, I reached out to the people at Lotus to see if Trix was willing to check the tip, because it was only a twelve hour flight for her to get to Dublin."

"And *I* didn't want to tell anyone we were on our way here after, in case the wrong side caught wind of it," Trix added.

"Dublin? They took you home?" Seethe asked Flip. "Was your buyer some past enemy?"

Flip shifted uncomfortably.

"Pretty much," Blossom examined her fingernails. "I mean, when we got there, he *was* being whipped."

Kiddo gave Flip a sideways glance.

"In a kinky way," Flip assured them, trying to be as flippant and uncaring as ever.

Trix clamped her hands over Rue's ears, while Rue went on crunching happily.

"An heiress ex-lover of mine told me she'd saved me before I'd got to auction," Flip shrugged. "Didn't know she was actually the buyer. I had a great time, waiting for her to say it was clear for me to leave."

"You tried to slice your wrists with the Yorak stabber after she showed you live stream slaughters of the international Raze recruits. She told you every single Raze was dead," Trix said hotly; infuriated by what they'd found out.

"I only nicked one wrist," Flip played it down. "Few stitches."

Kiddo was shocked.

Flip had always been a fighter.

His buyer had known exactly what to say to take all of the fight out of him. Though she'd probably just thought it would keep him from bothering to try to get away.

"The woman had to clobber you over the head, call her private physician and lock away the knife so that she could keep you alive for her pleasure."

"And you clobbered her right back," Blossom reassured Trix sweetly. "She'll never touch him again."

"It was all so fast. Don't know if she was dead," Trix griped back with dissatisfaction.

But Trix released Rue's ears now, because the other Razes were so silent.

"Alright, so the early days were tough," Flip acknowledged casually, though his grip around Kiddo's shoulders was stiff. "But what a nice gesture that she paid extra to buy my knife."

"Sure. She had the complete set," Trix glowered. "You and your signature flip-switch. Lucky girl."

"Anyway, I had it easier than some," Flip countered less amiably then – his meaning clear as he held onto Tiny. "I just had to think I was locked in for my own safety, with a woman who worshipped me."

Grieving and hopeless to the point of suicide. Being used.

Kiddo slid his own arm around Flip's back.

"Who d'you think the anonymous tip came from?" Seethe jutted his chin at Start – changing the topic to less stormy waters, while his own expression was still quite stormy.

"Ah, well, I have my suspicions," Start jumped in quickly. "I am very optimistic that it might be Jingle."

Hato, whose face had become incredibly pinched and stony over yet another Raze's suffering, sat up straighter against his pillows.

"What makes you say it was Jingle?" he asked with reluctant hope. "How could it be possible?"

"Um, you see, our buyers ..." Start swallowed thickly. "Tiny and mine ... had me collaborating online with someone else on a rather frightening project," he answered. "I had to research the major markets, stock exchanges and even banks of the world, and come up with strategies on how to simultaneously hijack each unique one. I was sent many sensitive files discussing foreign economies, all coming from an unknown person. Once I'd analysed and strategized, I had to pass my plans back to this other person digitally, so that they could work out how to actually carry it out as an online terrorist. I was nowhere near done, but had sketched out a rough approach."

"So you and your buyer provided the method, and now this other person ... Jingle and her buyer, will provide the means to rob the world?" Seethe whistled. "The money is the power. Who does this reek of?"

"Jingle's buyer would of course be an ally of the Wolf," Start affirmed. "It has to be her. I don't know who else exists who would be up to the task." He took off his glasses to clean them, blinking at them all. "Anyway, I only had the capability to file share under supervision, and couldn't actually communicate with my unknown partner, or find out where in the world *I* even was. However, an odd document popped up on my screen very briefly when ... the guards were focused on Tiny. All it said was Dublin. But it had me thinking – if this was Jingle, perhaps she'd heard something. And which Raze would most likely be a hot item in Ireland?"

"Hot item alright," Flip commented under his breath, releasing Kiddo.

Frazzle had crossed to him, pulling up Flip's sleeves and exposing a bandage on the left wrist that the doctor at once began to unwind.

"I came up with a strategy for Trix to try, while I kept up my own planning and searching for Jingle," Start told them.

"Basically the strategy was the name of the city and a phone list," Trix took over dryly. "Flip has a lot of old, loyal comrades on the streets of Dublin who came out of the wood-work to join us in a search."

Frazzle peered at Flip with the most melancholic expres-sion that Kiddo had seen the pragmatic doctor wear in a long time, even after so much recent tragedy.

"You was very lucky she hit you on the head before you made it longer," Frazzle said sadly. "Deep. Stitches on the in-side and outside?"

Flip gave a curt nod. "The early days were tough. I wasn't myself," he told the doctor. "I'm myself again now."

"The woman's live-in doctor saved Flip's life twice over, and was in fact her weakest link," Ryo finished their tale. "He may have been a well-paid, private physician. However, he still enjoyed a visit to the public bar."

"Pub," Flip corrected, automatically.

Ryo accepted that with a tolerant, almost affectionate dip of his head. "One overheard whisper of the word 'Raze' at the right time, and Flip's friends were able to chase a trail."

Hato nodded gravely, his eyes travelling from Flip's wrist to Miss Lotus' protégés. "We can't thank you both enough for staying with Trix, and helping to recover Flip. We know how much Lotus Bar, and the Tokyo underworld count on you both."

Blossom and Ryo's work for Miss Lotus, and with Dom, was one reason that the underworld in Japan had become so clean, as far as underworlds went. True evil couldn't get a foothold there.

"Trix is as much Lotus as she is Raze now," Blossom answered a little possessively. "We've got her covered. But our mistress has also let us come to you with other motives." She brushed her long, glossy ponytail off her shoulder and Rue stared at it admiringly as she chomped through the apple.

"We want to see if Ryo and I can be bait to lure out *our* Raze, so you can catch and treat him," Blossom went on. "And if you can't cure him, we'll take him back so Miss Lotus can attempt to."

Kiddo leaned his elbows on his knees, twisting his ring. "Dom knows that it's been over two years since he was based in Japan now. He might not feel too kindly about it if he thinks you waited so long to get him."

Blossom waved that concern away. "That's no matter. Apart from him being our Raze, Dom is the Wolf's key to success at the moment. The whole underworld – and I mean the whole underworld – is buzzing with what the Wolf's weapon has been getting up to in a matter of weeks." She tapped black fingernails on the arm of the couch. "I mean, the Wolf just needs an official crowning ceremony, because he's pretty much the king down there, with Raze boosting him up. And, with Start's revelation about the surface economy, and legitimate leaders allying with him, who knows if Yorak has plans to be king of *both* worlds down the track."

"We can target Raze while Start continues his work, as you at least know where Raze is based," Ryo also reasoned smoothly. "And Raze would likely blame himself, more than us, for us apparently not knowing his whereabouts for so long, or if we seemed confused about who he had been with."

"Why?" Seethe stretched his legs out further on Hato's bed. "Doesn't he remember you three as being reeeaaal close?" he drew the word out, and both Trix and Kiddo winced – knowing exactly how close both Blossom and Ryo had enjoyed being to Dom in the past.

"Oh, the Hot Shots and sex were great. Dom's a master," Blossom smirked, as Trix grabbed for Rue's ears again – too late.

Ryo closed his eyes, as if to gather his inner peace.

"While Raze could seem uninhibited," Ryo smoothed his hair absently. "In reality he was so intent on his goals, that –"

"He rarely initiated things," Blossom cut in tragically. "Others always followed or sought him out, even while knowing that to get involved with him could lead to the other person's heartbreak."

Ryo's expression suggested that he knew this with painful experience. He sighed and tried again. "In reality, he was so intent on his goals that we were only included in his ventures if we were lucky. Mostly, we did not know where he was."

"We certainly were *reeeaaal close*, and would fall over ourselves to do anything for Raze," Blossom echoed Seethe meaningfully. "But there was always something you couldn't quite get a grip on, or hold onto about him. He had his flings and joined in if he liked what was on offer, but he didn't pursue or commit to anyone. Before you," she directed this at Kiddo.

Ryo cleared his throat, and sent an apologetic glance

Kiddo's way. "Raze became our great friend. He was willing to put everything on the line for us, and for the vulnerable people of Tokyo. We were honoured that we could count on him … when we had him," he explained, somewhat regretfully.

"I do you remember when I first came to ask Miss Lotus about him," Flip nodded, recalling what had happened. "Even Miss Lotus couldn't contact him once he'd left."

"He always had our numbers, but his changed often," Blossom confirmed primly. "We only had his details if he remembered to let us know. But it was part of his appeal. It was a pleasant surprise when he was in, and he would apologise from the heart … and on his knees … after being too long out."

Ryo cradled his brow, embarrassed.

Kiddo shot Blossom a glare. Was she trying to provoke him, and Trix?

Though Trix had apparently grown more accustomed to how much Blossom relished her sordid memories.

Blossom seemed to think honesty was the best policy, and that it was a delightful story to share with a room full of people – current partners included. She didn't see why oversharing might be less enjoyable for others.

Ryo was still grimacing as he tried to smooth things over; his gaze often returning to Kiddo to check that he was alright.

"Raze didn't even have a traceable bank card. He was able to thrive on his unpaid life's mission, because many people that he saved or who understood what he was about wanted to pay him back. It meant he had no shortage of new phones, as well as meals, clothing, even his beloved leather jacket.

They were all gifts. He did, however, become less paranoid and unsettled after joining your gang. Finding himself a true family," Ryo concluded, and Kiddo appreciated Ryo trying so gallantly to change the tone.

"Bottom line," Blossom announced. "Raze won't think it's our fault if we seemed out of the loop. He'll apologise to *us*, for leaving us no trails because of his hard to reach ways."

Trix gave Blossom a 'you done?' expression, before releasing Rue's ears this time.

"Oh, well, you see, the problem is," Start answered with a frown of consternation. "Dom's gone back to those impossible to reach ways. He only has time for one person in our gang at the moment, and apart from him seeking Kiddo out, we have no way to set this up by letting him know you've come."

"As you said, he'll see me," Kiddo suggested heavily then. "I could go to him this time."

"Go to Yorak's mansion?" Hato appeared ready to revisit his cardiac arrest. "Just take yourself into his lair?"

Rue scoffed. "You've got to be joking, mister. It's a no."

She'd been aiming her apple core for the bin, but the core hit the trash can so hard that the whole thing tipped over with a metallic clatter.

"You'd all still know where I am," Kiddo replied weakly.

"Sure, sure," Seethe crossed his arms. "And you plan on just knocking on the door for a visit? The Wolf should love to hear that Dom's friends from Japan would like a chat."

"He's not into selling Lotus people. He likes a more limited edition type of collectable, so he wouldn't snatch us if he found out," Blossom contemplated it.

"He might decide to *kill* you," Trix derided, just as ardently against the idea as Rue was from in front of her.

"I said no," Rue repeated decidedly. "End of story."

"I don't fancy mourning your death again," Flip also muttered to Kid.

"No, no, Kiddo is the last person Yorak wants dead," Start assured Flip. "But I don't see why he'd let you go once you get there," he told Kiddo with a frown.

"Hear me out," Kiddo held Hato's gaze, and then Rue's in particular.

Neither one made it easy.

"Dom thought I was from Japan. I could say that I want to go back there, rather than stay with the Wolf *or* with Hato. The Wolf would show his true colours if he still forced me to stay. His whole argument has been that he just wants to get me away from Hato and Seethe so that I'm safe – not so that he can have me instead. And I could find a way to let just Dom know that his own Lotus friends have offered to help Dom and I to get back to Tokyo safely, to entice him out."

"I'll make you a covert origami note to slip to Dom with meet up details for tomorrow evening," Blossom was nodding. "A menko envelope. Which is thick, but barely the size of a business card. Try not to let the Wolf see that little exchange."

"Yes, Raze will recognise the characters for his name on the front, and our names at the sign off," Ryo considered it.

"He'll know my handwriting. I'll tell him we're here to get you both out, or at the very least to see him."

"Then he'll definitely come," Blossom stated confidently. "He knows we don't leave Miss Lotus lightly. And even if the Wolf has brainwashed Raze into thinking he loves him, I'm positive he'll keep the note private, as any of us would with a Lotus letter."

"It won't take me long to get ready," Kiddo added quietly. "I could drop it off today."

Rue was gaping around at Kiddo, Blossom and Ryo in disbelief.

"This is stupid," Rue insisted. "Shut up about it. You're wrecking my exciting day."

Kiddo slipped off Tiny's bed to cross to her. He knelt in front of her as she sat, sulking now, on her idol's knee.

"Rue, what if I can get the Wolf to talk to me, and I find out something important? I might find out more about his plans, or what he's done to Dom, so we can fix it," Kiddo told her softly. "What if Blossom and Ryo can help us to catch Dom, if I just set it up?"

She wouldn't meet his eyes.

Instead, she pushed off Trix, and wrapped her arms around Kiddo's neck, plonking her light weight onto his lap as hard as she could. It was as if she thought she could anchor him to the ward room floor.

"Yeah, well what if I lose you as well as Dom, and it's all because I didn't stop something stupid from happening again?" she retorted into his shoulder. "This isn't like when you went searching for Start at some smarmy buyer's house.

This is the *Wolf.* The guy who caused the problems of every single person in this room."

Kiddo held her as he lowered them both all the way to the floor, crossing his legs.

She refused to pull back, hiding her face against him, and he peered around at the solemn room.

Hato was silent.

Seethe shrugged, palms up.

Even Blossom held her tongue.

They all knew that both Rue and Kiddo made good points.

"The difference between my situation and Dom's, before he was taken," Kiddo said slowly, as calmly as he could. "Is that the Wolf is more careful with my health. He's not going to suddenly pull something too serious on me. Dom's in there, and I don't think he'd let anything overly awful happen to me either. I've also had a chance to know all the facts, and know what I'm going into."

He hugged her close, trying to find a way to make a terrible situation alright.

"I want to do this because I've thought it through," he went on. "And I'm sure I'll be able to get through it to come back to you."

She was breathing heavily against him. But he could tell her silence meant she was listening.

"I know it is a risk, and I hate to make you worry. Just like how I hated letting you take a risk by going off alone the other night," Kiddo admitted. "However, I had to trust that you knew what you were doing, and that you felt certain you could come back to me too."

She fidgeted against him. Her fingers were knotting in his t-shirt.

He felt her sniff.

But it was Ryo who cleared his throat to speak again after a moment.

"If I can also suggest something that might help," Ryo began politely, and Kiddo peered up at him curiously.

"I wanted to remind you that Raze is very protective of those he cares for. And he can also be somewhat ... jealous, too." The conservative young man blushed slightly. "As Blossom said, the Wolf may have planted ideas of love in Raze's mind. That is why he has stayed with Yorak for an extended period. But with Kiddo, the love is real. He stayed and he loved by choice. Raze's subconscious has not forgotten that, and he still seeks Kiddo out." Ryo dipped his head subtly. "Kiddo, you may be able to use Raze's jealousy. It might make Raze actually want to get you out of the Wolf's mansion and reach. Or it might make him lose his temper if you need him to exit the situation."

Kiddo's eyebrows lifted.

It was a strong tip. One he could very well have need of, if he had to count on Dom to behave in a certain way to save him from anything nasty.

"Thank you," he replied with gratitude. "I'll make sure to keep that in mind."

As always, no matter his own feelings toward Dom, Ryo proved himself to be nothing but gracious and generous.

"Rue ..." Kiddo tried again tentatively. "Do you think you can trust me to take this on? Do you trust me to decide what risks I can handle?"

There was a heaved sigh.

And a churlish nod.

"But if you don't get out … I'm going there to kill everyone myself," she swore with a passion. "I'll kill them until I'm dead."

It was the best he was going to get, and Kiddo's heart tightened for the poor little mite.

He really would do anything to get back to her.

"You can do some knife throwing lessons with me when he goes," Flip offered Rue. "It always cheered your Kiddo up."

"And I can show you how to ride a patrol bike to put all those Dires floating around outside to shame," Trix made a stiff effort to be accepting of the plan too.

Kiddo felt another sullen nod against his shoulder.

These weren't the types of lessons she would get from Miss Anushi.

"But first, you can help me get this all important Lotus note ready," Blossom told her. She stood, taking Rue's hand from Kiddo's shirt to pull the child up and into action. "We need to get this right."

Rue was too surprised to protest for a moment, but then gave a purposeful nod.

"Ok."

| 17 |

Seventeen

"You are repulsive," Kiddo muttered drunkenly.

One eye icy blue, the other near black.

Dark hair, swept back in tousled waves.

An elegant tuxedo, and air of magnetic confidence.

Striking.

The Wolf's lip curled. He was leaning over Kiddo, one hand on Kiddo's chest, the other with fingers pressed into the groove of Kid's neck – feeling his pulse.

"Your body's reactions say otherwise."

Kiddo tried to shove the Wolf backward, but there was not enough force behind the blow.

"Rest easy," the Wolf murmured soothingly. "You look tired. You really haven't been sleeping enough."

He tipped Kiddo's chin so that Kid's head tilted back to lean against the velvety, high backed armchair that he'd just been so tenderly lowered into.

Mere minutes earlier, the Hunters had all been happy enough to let him in, and the Wolf had personally greeted

Kiddo in the front foyer. Before Kiddo had suddenly been crawling in snatchers.

Even worse, after smothering him in every way possible … they had quietly deposited him in a monster sized master bedroom.

"I knew keeping a trial sedative on hand would be a good idea," the Wolf told him, smoothing Kiddo's hair. "To calm you right down, without knocking you out if you paid a visit."

"You think this is the movies?" Kid slurred, unable to help closing his eyes. "There was chloroform on that cloth?"

The Wolf chuckled. "Chloroform is too slow acting, or indeed fatal as an inhalant to be anything like they show in the movies. But, I have useful friends in pharmaceutical experimentation, remember?"

He was patient and charming, as if explaining something to a curious youth.

"This is a similar kind of anaesthetic. It is not a risk with your … addictive nature … and getting a minute of it into you has been safe enough, with your conditions and heart history." The Wolf seated himself on the arm of the chair and touched Kiddo's pulse again, pressing his wrist this time.

"You don't feel like you are having any unreasonable conflicts with your other medications? Or a seizure coming on?" the Wolf enquired.

"I feel like … I've been drugged," Kiddo snarled. "By a psychopath."

Kiddo managed to open his eyes long enough to catch the Wolf's speculative expression.

"I'd thought I had more sociopath in me," he mused.

"You promised Dom that the other Razes would go to the

best buyers ... and would be safe," Kiddo accused. "You feel nothing for other people."

The Wolf tilted his head in amusement. "Ohhhh, I don't know," he contemplated it. "I feel certain things toward *you*. Right now."

There was a sound from an adjoining room. A shower starting?

"And my Raze does not remember me promising that," the Wolf traced Kiddo's lower lip now, making it tingle. "But if he ever does, he'll realise that I saved him from the regret of killing Hato and Seethe, and I let him punish any especially disappointing buyers."

Kiddo frowned, and the weight of his brows was enough to force his eyes closed again.

"In fact," the Wolf crooned slowly. "Raze could use your help to continue with his high workload. You would be joining him in doing exactly what you hoped for anyway – taking down snatcher bases, and *terribly* rotten people."

Kiddo muttered sourly against the Wolf's fingertip. "Just the ones conveniently selected by you."

"You can only protect him from me, and from danger on his missions, if you're with him. With us. I already have him convinced that the right thing is to make you stay."

Kiddo sneered. "I'll convince him otherwise."

"Hmmm. I do not think so," Yorak tutted. "I'm the only one he trusts. When he looks at me, he sees the one person who is trying to get the corrupt underworld system under control."

"Only so that you can lead it," Kiddo bunched his fists,

feeling incrementally less vulnerable and weak with the passing of time, along with the building of his temper.

Yorak leaned further in so that his body pressed against Kiddo's. He'd noticed the angry gesture, and peered into Kid's face.

"Deep breaths," Yorak's voice purred.

Then Kiddo tensed at the unexpectedness of a purposeful hand pressing a cloth firmly over his mouth and nose again.

The chemical smell rolled down Kiddo's airways at once, making him choke and cough as he tried to clutch at Yorak's wrist to tear it away.

But after a few moments, it was an effort just to hold that wrist.

"There," Yorak pulled the cloth back. "Just enough to keep you placid."

He stroked long fingers across Kiddo's brow

"*Anyhow.*" He elongated the word so that it sounded somehow extravagant as it rolled off his tongue. "If Raze learns anything too detrimental about me, I can always play a little, and muddle his short term memory." The Wolf resumed their conversation once more, as if Kiddo had been fretting on the Wolf's behalf about Dom catching him out.

"I *had* hoped I would have longer before Raze checked a calendar," the Wolf added with low amusement, and with a long caress from the top of Kiddo's crown, down between his brows, along his nose and to his lower lip again.

"I had truly feared that he would wrack his brain for memories and slip backward, forcing me to use harsher conditioning," Yorak told him indolently, drawing down on that bottom lip ever so slightly.

"But it was in fact quite useful. You should have seen the rage he had toward Hato and Seethe that day," the Wolf reminisced with pleasure. "I was sure I'd convinced Raze to lure you out of their clutches, and to be willing to force you to remain under my protection after that."

Yorak took no offense when Kiddo didn't bother mustering a response.

He enjoyed a captive audience, even if it was a disapproving one.

"I'm not a barbarian, you know," Yorak sighed tragically. As if he had been grievously misunderstood. "I don't want my Raze to lose who he is. Making him a follower would defeat the whole purpose and allure of having him in the first place. So I don't go too hard on him anymore."

Kiddo did snort sarcastically at that. Contempt written all over him.

"Come, come," the Wolf scolded, incredibly sedately. "Even during the worst of it, I took my time. Leaving Raze's personality intact, and carefully filing away his memories so that I could have room to implant my own suggestions."

"You tortured him," Kiddo growled drowsily.

Though Kid hadn't missed the Wolf's phrasing. Perhaps Dom's memories were simply locked away, rather than deleted.

There was the sound of running water being shut off from the bathroom.

"Mmmmm. Shocks and hypnotism are a snatcher conversion therapy specialty," the Wolf assured him. "We are good at what we do. Even if it was slightly different in Raze's case."

Kiddo flinched when he felt Yorak move against him again, but it was just so the Wolf could bend to examine the sharp piercing at Kid's ear. Touching the dagger-like point.

"Raze's torment then, throughout the corrective therapy, means that now I don't have to be so severe when I want to make him listen to suggestion. Just a few trigger words coming from my voice, and he is calm and grounded in his loyalty."

Kiddo mustered up a glower. "False love. False loyalty." He took a steadying breath. "You must be so proud."

The Wolf smiled down at him. He twisted in the chair so that he could stoop closer.

"One thing I'm proud of," the Wolf mused. "Is that I have some new ideas on how I can do something similar to you."

Yorak brushed two featherlight kisses across Kiddo's eyelids, forcing them closed again.

"How convenient that you are here for us to try some of them."

Kiddo felt like he was on the very edge of slipping into a deep sleep. If he wasn't careful, he would lose his grip on everything.

"Thought you … didn't want to take any risks," Kiddo gritted out. "With the issues I already have in play."

"True," light fingers brushed the scar along the side of Kiddo's scalp. "I didn't want to push that fitful, hyperactive brain too far with our typical methods, and do anything I couldn't fix." He spoke with a tone of light affection. "But my new shock therapy solution for you has been inspired by

Raze's own skill set, and by helpful developments in the medical field. Have you heard of vagus nerve treatments?"

Kiddo felt his stomach clench.

"You will have surgery to fit you out with your own device. A perfectly safe implant, that will give me a fun controller, and you the intermittent electrical stimulation that you need."

"*Need?*" Kiddo growled. "No thanks."

"The shocks work simultaneously with my hypnotism. And this current anaesthetic seems to make you nicely compliant and easy to work with," the Wolf answered with satisfaction. "Each of these things together will help you, too, to become as loyal as I need you to be."

Kiddo puffed a brash laugh, which came out more like a husk of breath. "Don't. Think. So."

"Yorak..." Dom's voice called from the bathroom.

Kid froze at the familiar sound. With yearning. Then despair.

Dom was calling for the Wolf, with casual, comfortable ease.

"Yes, dear one?"

Yorak in turn sounded pleased.

Had he registered the pain on Kiddo's face?

"I can't self-tie this bloody self-tie. Open bow tie is a thing, isn't it?"

"Come to me. You know I am always here to help you," the Wolf called back contentedly.

Then he spoke more quietly again to Kiddo.

"I am quite confident that I will succeed with you too," the

Wolf said softly. "It worked when I used Rue to inspire Raze, and he'd only just started to care for the child. Imagine how quickly you'll let me in if Raze is the one at stake?"

Yorak spoke in an even lower voice then, and Kiddo shivered.

"How many more years will I need to strip from him, before you give in?" he asked plaintively. "Do you want me to take him right back to his suffering in the lab?"

Kiddo's breaths were coming faster.

To make Dom forget everything but the experiments they'd put him through. Their chemicals, their bone snapping, their nerve work, their heart stopping.

Dom had already been rebellious and fierce enough back then to still be of use to the Wolf in that state.

But he would lose years of progress, growth and … all of the consolation of razing such underworld corporations to hell in retribution for what they had done.

There was the sound of a door opening.

A pause.

There was the crisp scent of fresh cologne, paired with the softer aroma of soaps and shampoo.

Humid air.

"Yorak …" there were swift, purposeful steps. "Did you drug him?"

Yorak's lithe weight slipped away from Kiddo's side, to be replaced with the pressure of two hands leaning on the armrests on either side of Kiddo.

The breeze of air that came with Dom's haste touched Kiddo's cheeks and softened the frown he hadn't realised had been once again weighing down his face.

"I did," Yorak answered without shame or concern. "It is a simple relaxant. He is quite well."

"You drugged and forced him here?" Dom's voice sounded annoyed, though just the night before, Dom had been willing to haul Kiddo off himself.

"He came of his own volition," Yorak answered genially. "But I don't have your skills. I had to use what methods I could to keep him here." So reasonable. He sounded as if he was trying to coax a put-out lover to see things his way

"He'll think coming to us was worse than staying with Hato," Dom countered in concern. "Why didn't you just come in and tell me?"

The Wolf's voice was like satin. "You have a busy night ahead. I didn't want to disrupt your shower."

"It's never stopped you before."

Kiddo bunched his fists again now, and forced his eyes open.

Instead of directing a toxic look at the Wolf, his eyes clapped on a narrow waist, tapered in by a wide satin sash, and form-fitting pants that hugged Dom's hips.

Every piece of Dom's tuxedo was black, and a breathtaking mix of classically dapper, and rough grunge.

An edgy, blazer style jacket – fitted and unbuttoned. A sharply cut lapel, covered in dark punk studs. Studded buttons were at his cuffs and ran down his shirt front, with the top few still undone, and the loose, butterfly wing ends of his tie hanging open under his shirt collar.

The only addition of colour was a deep burgundy pocket square. Like mulled wine. Or spilled blood.

"Hey …" Dom stooped a little lower to peer into Kiddo's face. "You good?"

His hair was still wet, with sharply defined flicks.

"I feel," Kiddo swallowed thickly. "Under dressed."

The Wolf was leaning nearby, a figure of poise against the wall to ceiling window.

"I would love to see you even more under dressed," Yorak commented laconically, his eyes on Dom and Kiddo.

When Dom raised an eyebrow in an '*you're not helping*' expression at the Wolf, Yorak simply smiled lazily.

"I meant, I haven't had the chance to check him for weapons or devices," the Wolf elaborated. "To ensure our safety."

Dom sighed, and began to pat Kiddo down – his hands running over Kiddo's arms and down his sides with a firm pressure.

There was only one important thing, waiting to be found. Kid hadn't even brought a phone.

"We have a charity dinner with a very important banker," Yorak went on to explain to Kiddo aloofly. "I'd invite you to join us, but it is an extremely exclusive, intimate event. And Raze has to focus carefully on some things he needs to do there."

Sounded like some unfortunate banker's friend was scheduled for a neck snapping.

Dom's hands were kneading along Kiddo's calves now.

His lotus tattooed finger, and the start of the Japanese dragon scene beginning to coil down from behind an ear, were the only parts of Dom's ink on show tonight.

But they were still there. Tangible connections to Dom's remembered history. Parts of him.

"Though we won't be out late," the Wolf promised breezily. "And I shall make sure you can wait for us comfortably here, in my own private bedroom."

This time Kiddo did get to deliver his most toxic expression Yorak's way, over Dom's shoulder.

"Why did you –" Dom's voice paused for a moment as he gripped Kiddo's hips and felt the slight, but firm shape of the Lotus letter in Kiddo's front jeans pocket. "Why did you come to us this time?" he went on, as if he had felt nothing.

With a deft move, the letter had been thrust up, and out of Kiddo's pocket. Dom had registered what it was, and the small note had disappeared before Kiddo's eyes.

Kiddo took a deep breath.

"Wanted to ask you … to leave for Japan with me," he told Dom.

Dom's electric blue eyes burned with interest. He knew exactly who the letter was from. And Ryo and Blossom had been right – he was not going to reveal it to the Wolf, no matter how 'close' to Yorak he had been made to feel. Simply because he did not see any reason that the Wolf or anyone else needed to know Lotus business.

"Some friends can help us," Kiddo went on. "And then I don't need to stay here," he threw a fierce glance at Yorak again. "Or with Hato."

Dom's eyebrows rose. He sat back on his heels.

Yorak's handsome face had darkened. Kiddo had just given Dom the perfect reason not to believe that they should hold Kid 'for his safety'.

"If I leave Yorak now, all the things he's helped me to do to the snatchers could get him in trouble," Dom answered slowly. "I can't do that."

Kiddo grimaced.

If Dom could only see that he was in a mansion full of unmasked snatchers, playing a part for their Raze warrior, and protecting the Wolf themselves.

"Think about it," Kid groaned, sitting up slightly with an effort. "And let me leave. Because I have … no such attachments to this man."

"I must apologise," the Wolf drawled unapologetically. "Profusely. But I simply cannot let you leave in this state tonight. It's all my fault."

Dom pushed up from the arms of the chair.

"If he's escaped Hato and has somewhere else to go to that's secure," Dom sighed. "We don't need to make him take shelter here."

The Wolf shook his head in false disappointment. "I wish I could believe that Hato hasn't done anything that would force our friend back to him. But with Kiddo so vulnerable right now, imagine him leaving us to travel the streets? We have no time to deliver him elsewhere safely, or with adequate research into that place."

Kiddo scowled. "Whose fault is it … that I'm half asleep?"

The Wolf straightened and approached Kiddo. "You really must see, I have no other choice. You need to stay until I've thought this over, and I have to make sure that you do until we can be back here. Raze and myself are the only two people I trust to help victims of Hato and Seethe, such as yourself."

Kiddo gripped the armchair as he saw that Yorak was back to holding his drugged cloth again.

"Yorak," Dom said uncomfortably, raking his wet hair back. "It doesn't feel right."

With every bit of energy that he could muster, Kiddo pushed himself up from the chair and tried to dodge Yorak's advance.

Dom caught him before he could fall, and hoisted Kid up to stand against himself.

"Trust me," Yorak told Dom soothingly, as he came to clamp the cloth back over Kiddo's mouth and nose.

The energy began to loosen in Kiddo's body, and he sagged in Dom's arms.

Yorak leaned over Kiddo to whisper into Dom's ear.

And as Yorak whispered his words, Dom's expression became less concerned.

"Thank you," Dom nodded, pulling back.

His gaze had become blank, flitting back and forth between Yorak's icy blue and dark eyes.

"Of course I trust you. We need to keep him here until we can come back and take care of this."

Yorak helped Dom to support Kiddo to the king sized bed.

"I knew you'd see things my way," the Wolf wheedled Dom, reaching to pull back the covers.

Kid's t-shirt and shoes were removed, and the two of them laid him out under the bedding. Arranging him into a relaxed position with care.

Kiddo was dimly aware that two Hunters had filed into the room. The Huntress grinned as she licked a sharp tipped tooth and eyed his prone form.

A helpless Raze member was a Hunter's favourite type of Raze.

"Check his breathing and heart every now and then. Make sure he doesn't choke," Yorak was saying. "And too much movement means another dose can be administered. Apply the cloth for just a minute. There are to be no new marks on him when we return."

There were nods. "Yes Yorak."

"We'll take good care Yorak."

Dom was silent, seated on Kiddo's other side. Not interfering. Detached and beautiful.

The Wolf held Kiddo's gaze as he wetted his cloth again, and lowered it to Kid's face. Forcing Kiddo to breathe in its heady fumes.

"You need the sleep," the Wolf told him. "We are helping you."

This time the Wolf was in no hurry to remove the cloth.

He kept his hand splayed over Kiddo's panicked heart.

Holding and waiting until its thudding beats slowed.

| 18 |

Eighteen

He stirred in the dark, rousing at the feel of a cool touch running up the smooth ridges of his stomach and over his bare torso.

The city lights decorating the night beyond the wall length window dimly illuminated the room. The stretching shadows seemed to warp and extend in Kiddo's still barely lucid vision.

His first lethargic thoughts were for Rue.

She would be freaking out.

This was bad.

"For an unfeeling psycho," the Wolf's voice mused with a touch of amusement. "I sure enjoy *this* type of feeling."

The covers had been pulled back to expose Kiddo's body, and Yorak now reclined on the mattress beside him. He was lounging comfortably against the plush headboard.

Kiddo didn't move.

His head pounded, and his limbs felt like they were cemented to the bed, but he was sure they would work. If he could just avoid giving the Wolf another excuse to dose him.

"Raze feels just as mouth-wateringly good as this," the Wolf smiled a wolfish smile. It curled coldly at the sides of his mouth. "I unwrapped that gift the first moment I ever got him home," he went on. "And the Japanese ink truly is marvellous ... It made me less regretful that I couldn't send him out against Miss Lotus, and any other power player allies that he remembers having."

Kiddo's face was like stone.

"Dom was completely confused that night," he whispered accusingly, winded by the idea of it.

"But not unwilling," the Wolf's smile widened. "Not at all."

Keep calm. He had to keep calm.

The Wolf's fingertips were making light trails over his heart.

If its pace gave away his sluggishly returning adrenaline, and anger, Kid could kiss goodbye any chance to get up and out.

"Where ... is Dom?" Kiddo asked slowly, wishing that the Wolf had not once again sought for the two of them to be alone.

"He'll be along. He likes to check the property. Make sure I'm safe."

Keep calm.

Keep calm.

Dom was keeping his greatest enemy safe.

"But isn't it nice to be able to talk so openly together? Just the two of us first?"

Kiddo shivered as the Wolf's fingers wandered over his collarbones.

Not the pulse, not the pulse ...

"You talk too much," Kiddo responded flatly. "Monologuing villain."

The Wolf angled himself closer to Kiddo. "You are the perfect listening type. And I can't exactly say it all to Raze, now, can I?"

Kiddo tried not to flinch away as that roaming hand tickled along his ribs.

"And you won't remember much of this soon anyway," the Wolf assured him. "During the car ride home I booked your surgery. You'll get your implant in a few weeks, and then we can get to work on breaking you in."

Oh lord.

Oh lord.

Keep calm.

"You plan to …"

Deep breaths.

Deep breaths.

"… convince Dom to keep me incapacitated here – for *weeks?*"

The Wolf shook his head with a glimmer of that smile again. "I've had time to think on that. I will simply give you the date and time to return here. And because of Raze – along with the fact that I *could* reclaim your other rescued Razes if I really put my mind to it, you will."

Yorak's touch roamed over Kiddo's biceps, over his forearm and to his wrist.

Not the pulse!

But Yorak instead went further, to stroke Dom's ring on Kiddo's thumb so that the chain rotated slowly.

"I can gauge that right now I don't have either you or Raze in the right condition to make it work smoothly if I tried to keep you," the Wolf went on. "So it's best you're not around to trigger him too much, or to raise contention, until I have the chance to get you into line."

In and out. Just breathe.

"Why am I still here then ... listening to this?" Kiddo growled in a low voice.

His head was throbbing.

All he wanted to do was throw the Wolf off himself.

He hated how appalling, and how pleasurable each caress was feeling.

He hated this man.

The Wolf gave an almost inaudible laugh. "Two reasons."

He slid further down on the bed to lean an elbow on Kid's pillow.

"You pointed out that I like to speak," the Wolf teased. Quite enjoying his games.

"Perhaps it stems back to my childhood," he continued; lightly mocking. "As a product of the Top Two of a major city. I was forced to be seen and not heard, and now it seems I crave to be heard by anyone who most hates to listen to me."

Child of the Top Two?

"Great," Kiddo answered flatly. "I thought most snatchers were sterilised to prevent family networks. Shame your parents weren't."

The Wolf was pleased by his reaction. By his repulsion.

"Oh, it was a sterile environment in any case. It helped to make me the obsessive, ambitious man before you."

More like half on top of him.

"But it was you, and the Raze gang coming to save you at that exhibition, that truly gave me the room to step up," Yorak said thoughtfully.

He took Kiddo's chin so that Kid had to face the Wolf, and the Wolf's burning eyes lingered on Kiddo's lips. As if he might kiss him.

"You were the turning point."

"Great," Kiddo intoned again. "I thought all high ranking snatchers were at that event. Shame you were left at home that day."

"I am truly grateful that you culled every other leader of the snatcher world, so that I could become the new power." The Wolf spoke with relish – unbothered that it had meant that his own parents had been wiped out too.

"As the only strong, well known deputy left in the whole snatcher system, all of the new, inexperienced Top Twos who were floundering in their roles turned to me. The Raze gang continued to scare snatchers and buyers to me from then on. And because of it, I am now creating something better out of our system," Yorak dipped his head close to Kiddo's chest, breathing each word across Kid's skin.

"More change is coming. Everywhere. Surely you don't want to let Raze work through a revolution alone?"

Yorak brushed his lips against Kiddo's goosebumped nipple.

Kiddo clenched his jaw.

Then he gasped as he felt the teasing bite of Yorak's teeth.

"And … the other reason …" Kiddo husked hurriedly. "That I'm still in your bed?"

Dread had settled in the pit of his stomach.

"Ohhh," Yorak sighed against him. "The second reason is my favourite," the Wolf stated in silken tones.

Kiddo chewed his lip with the effort not to react as another bite was followed by the flick of a tongue.

The Wolf enjoyed drawing things out, and taking breaks between answers.

"The time might not seem right to have you here, but I can still *try*," Yorak replied at last. "See if I can show you what we three could have. Test how well you both take it."

Kiddo's head was reeling. There was no hiding the fast pulse now.

Yorak had to know that his blood was back to pumping as strong as ever.

"I'm not convinced that you're unwilling." The Wolf placed a firm hand over the bulge straining against Kiddo's jeans. "I'm not convinced you'll hate it."

Yorak's lips pressed again to Kiddo's skin, higher up, and Kiddo cried out at the roughness of the next bite, which had to have got close to piercing the flesh.

"Hmm," Yorak paused a moment. "That might bruise."

He smirked. Before kissing and sucking as if no pectoral muscle had ever impassioned him quite so much before tonight.

Kiddo hated his body right now. It was betraying him. Showing every sign of lust.

He was dizzy, and would lurch around like a drunkard. But could he strike the Wolf hard enough at this point to somehow get out of this?

There was the matter of the two Hunters lurking somewhere nearby. And the mansion full of snatchers.

If he waited to get out, he might have some steep regrets. But he also might sober up enough to have a better chance of a successful exit later.

If he didn't wait to get out, he might have a fight that he wasn't up to scratch enough to win.

He needed help.

Desperately.

"You getting arousal out of me won't make me yours," Kiddo managed. "I survived on the streets giving parts of myself away for a long time. Never fell in love from it."

The Wolf was undeterred. "You did become addicted to the highs you got, though," he reasoned. "And I can give you a life of highs."

Kiddo scoffed, and then took in a sharp intake of breath as the movement jostled the Wolf's undulating grip on him.

The Wolf smirked, and angled himself up so that he could position a knee between Kid's legs, leaning over him with a hand beside Kiddo's head.

"I won't suddenly become addicted to *you*," Kiddo groaned. "Of all the things I could get hooked on."

"Let's see."

Kiddo grunted as the Wolf lowered himself fully, covering Kid's lips in a luxurious kiss that was exultant and tantalising rather than forceful or cruel.

Kiddo moaned a protest – just as much at his own dreamlike enjoyment, as much as at it being Yorak who was doing this to him.

He tried to push at Yorak's weight, wedging his forearm between their chests and struggling to lever a gap between them so that he could turn his head, or roll away from that attentive grip.

He made a despairing noise, heaving uselessly for another moment.

Before suddenly he felt Yorak being hauled off the bed by someone else.

"He's mine," Dom's voice said shakily. As if he hadn't registered that those two words were coming before they could pass his lips.

Kiddo lay panting, his arms still raised in defence.

Kid hadn't heard the door, but Dom was now holding Yorak back, as if to keep him from losing control and falling all over Kiddo again.

"Couldn't he be ours?" Yorak asked fairly. "You're mine, and he's mine?"

A furiously jealous expression crossed Dom's face for a split second, reminding Kiddo of Ryo's observations.

This could be his ticket.

Kiddo fought to sit up, pulling himself away from the two of them so abruptly that his stomach nearly heaved.

"He's not into it, Yorak," Dom reprimanded heatedly, letting Yorak go and massaging his temples. "He won't be ours if you truly do seem worse than Hato."

Kiddo staggered off the other side of the bed, holding onto the mattress for support. "Right now I'm nobody's but my own," he said vehemently. "You can both leave me alone."

Dom took a step toward him, hands held out placatingly.

"I think he wants us," Yorak commented with a stirrer's

wicked smirk. "He practically threw himself at me, and can't keep his eyes off you."

"Leave it," Dom hissed back.

Kiddo whipped around wildly and sped as fast as he could toward the door.

He misjudged, his vision whirling, and hit his shoulder against the doorway; accidentally falling into a surprised Hunter's arms outside.

"You best escort him to wherever he thought he would feel safest then," Yorak sighed with feigned sadness, as if he felt deeply misunderstood.

However his expression was completely unbothered and unsurprised.

Yorak and Dom watched Kiddo ram a heavy elbow into the Hunter's ribs and then the jaw as the man hunched over. Then Kid pushed off and skidded down the hallway, picking up momentum.

Three more snatchers came running. The first copped a fist to the kidneys as Kiddo ducked around her. And the second got booted in the guts as Kid rose again; grabbing onto a grotesque fixture of modern hallway art – made up of criss-crossing black poles taller than Kiddo was, to swing himself from the frame like it was some monkey bars.

The third snatcher backed off as Kiddo dropped down, while Dom's yell not to touch Kiddo echoed around the level.

Kid felt too sloppy for stairs.

When Dom shouted again it was at Kiddo himself, as he watched Kiddo hazily leap up onto the level's railing to half fall against, half wrap himself around a glossy pillar, which he slid down at much too high a speed.

His skin felt chafed and his knees gave out as he landed, but when a Huntress at the front entrance came at him, he grabbed her by the shoulder and hauled himself up at the same time as clunking her forward into his pillar.

The only reason he wasn't being crushed in a tidal wave of Yorak's people was because Dom was hurtling down the stairs and bellowing at them.

Kiddo shoved past uncaring bodies that were between him and the door, and wasn't halted by anyone as he lurched out into the night.

He was proud of himself for managing a jog to the front gate, which he shouldered his way through obliviously before it had finished buzzing all the way open.

He only stopped when the circling feeling in his head caught up to him, making him stoop over to hold his breath and try to hold the contents of his stomach in.

It was then; gaping and blinking down at his bare feet to collect himself, that he noticed the Hellion lying in the bushes outside Yorak's mansion.

"Hey ..." he gasped. "Are you ...?"

In the dim streetlight and through his light-headedness he couldn't make out her face, until he dropped to the grass to shift her long hair in search of a pulse. That was when he saw clearly that her throat had been slit, and that she was the same Hellion who had found Tiny with him.

Kid swore and reeled backward, this time unable to keep from unloading his stomach into another patch of bushes until he felt near ready to pass out.

He hoped beyond all hope that anyone else who had come

out to see if they could check up on him had just been chased away.

It was only the low murmur of an approaching, quiet cruiser, coming from Yorak's long driveway, that got him limping on unsteadily again.

The bike pulled up close to him, and its rider – still all tuxxed up, stepped off to catch him by the wrist.

Kiddo threw Dom's hold off instinctively, and tried to ignore that the move nearly made him collapse now.

He may miss Dom with his entire being.

But he was done with the men of that mansion touching him tonight.

"Stop," Dom said quickly, stepping around Kiddo to cut him off. "Tell me where you're going, and I'll get you there."

Kiddo rolled his eyes, but that sent his vision into a revolving whirlwind and he nearly dropped on the spot again.

"Please?" Dom asked nicely. "You're half naked, and that biker woman's body over there says there are dangerous people out tonight."

Kiddo steadied himself, and made to go around Dom. But Dom shot out an arm to block him.

"I don't want to fight," Dom appeased him – as if Kiddo could do much right now. "I liked your style by the way. Kind of parkour. Even missing half your senses."

Kiddo fixed Dom in his sights, and said as distinctly as possible: "coming to the 'safety' offered by the Wolf ... was the most dangerous thing I'll face tonight. I'd prefer to take my chances."

Dom took hold of both Kiddo's shoulders and Kiddo

tensed, glaring into Dom's face. But he didn't throw him off again.

"I'm sorry it went down like that," Dom shook his head. His gaze flickered to Kiddo's bare chest, and then darkened as he caught sight of something.

"It must have seemed full on," Dom took a deep breath, as if trying to reassure himself. "But Yorak would do anything to protect a victim of snatchers and their allies. Even if he gets caught up in extremes."

"Yup," Kiddo said angrily. "No amount of drugging or molestation is too much in his quest to save me."

His skin crawled at the memory and he shuddered. Realising how cold he was.

"And you," Kiddo carried on. "You were happy to drag me off against my will before this. Would you really say that holding me there felt right tonight?"

Dom ducked and angled his head to catch Kiddo's gaze again. "Yorak shouldn't have let his desire spiral out of control like that."

The most disturbing thing had been that the Wolf had seemed *completely* in control the whole time.

"It all felt wrong," Dom confessed. "Too wrong for it to be the greater good. So let me take you where you need to go so that you don't get into any other wrong situations."

Kiddo knocked Dom's grip away with his forearms and took a halting step backward.

"I'll let you get me close to where I want to go. But that's it. I don't trust you with my friend's location."

"Alright," Dom agreed easily. "Even if they are my friends too?"

Kiddo grimaced as he realised Dom had read the note, and that Kiddo himself was in the midst of setting Dom up for an experience close to what Kiddo had just had.

Having been entrusted with a token from Ryo and Blossom was likely what had made Dom less reserved and more believing and protective of Kiddo now.

"Those friends are tomorrow night," Kid uttered in response. "It's just my own friend tonight."

Dom cocked an eyebrow. "Who?"

A tiny flicker of jealousy touched his face again.

Kiddo clicked his tongue in annoyance and turned – too fast.

"Sorry, sorry," Dom steadied him and shepherded him towards the bike. "None of my business, as long as this person isn't a snatcher ally."

"He speaks out against snatchers publicly," Kiddo replied dryly. "And he lives just close enough to here that I can hold off from passing out."

Dom hesitated. "If you're not up for a ride, I promise I can protect you from anything if you want to stay here with me. Yorak can win your trust back, but I can watch over you until that happens."

Kiddo managed to mount the bike. "If you ever see me anywhere near this mansion again, assume that I'm having the worst day of my life. And if you really do care about helping good people, help me get out of there."

Dom sighed, and started to take his tuxedo jacket off.

"Don't," Kiddo stopped him. "I don't want one thing of the Wolf's. Not one thing."

Kiddo reached up for Dom's graceful neck tie and tugged it open, ripping it free.

Dom grinned. "What if he says *I'm* his?"

Kiddo grunted as Dom stepped over to take a seat in front of him. "You are your own."

Dom reached back and pulled Kiddo's legs closer so that Kid's knees closed in tightly around him. When Kiddo looped his arms snugly around Dom's middle, Dom took a hold of Kiddo's wrists in case he swooned again and fell off.

"I need you to get me to the traveller's hotel strip near the train station," Kiddo decided. "I'll do the rest."

Surely he'd be able to make the walk down a few streets to the classier hotels alone.

Kiddo had to close his eyes and put his head against Dom's back as they kicked off and the road began to blur by.

His brain was surging with aching waves, and his stomach apparently hadn't got done with being emptied yet.

He squinted queasily when the bike pulled up to park again, and Dom turned to eye him with doubt.

It was hard to let go.

This felt so very much like *his* Dom.

But Kiddo clambered off the bike and hugged his arms for warmth.

"I'm not budging until you go," he told Dom bluntly. "I don't have far to get on my own. But I don't want you following."

Dom's face was anguished. "This whole situation is

messed up. We both can't accept each other's groups. The other night, I needed space. Now you want space, and for some reason, I really don't want to give it to you. And Yorak … well for some reason he took it from you without any restraint at all."

Kiddo rubbed his eyes. "It's messed up. But today, I just had to get you your note. If I see you tomorrow, even just to talk to our two friends, that's my job done."

He felt Dom's supportive hand at his elbow and realised he must have teetered.

"It's not far?" Dom asked uneasily. "And this guy's a good guy?"

"He's never drugged, threatened or got undesirably physical with me," Kid answered dryly. "So he's winning. I'll be safe crashing with him."

That touch of envy clouded Dom's features before he could hide it.

If only Kiddo really could get him to run away to Japan, where they could hunker down in Miss Lotus' empire and escape every damn thing.

"Look, if you want me to actually get to where I'm going, it needs to happen soon," Kiddo warned then. "Or I'll crash sooner than I'd like."

Dom slowly withdrew his hold from Kiddo's elbow.

"I'll see you tomorrow."

Kiddo managed a smile – that guilt hitting him again like a battering ram.

"I'll be there," he answered.

And he watched as Dom kicked off from the curb to disappear into the night.

| 19 |

Nineteen

"Oh my God, what happened to you?"

A white light flickered on and Kiddo became aware of the feel of the cold bathroom tiles against his cheek.

"I thought you didn't drink!"

Kiddo felt Narkon's hands turn him over so that the chill of the tiles touched skin that wasn't ready for that kind of sting. He flinched.

"I don't," he answered groggily.

"What are you sleeping off, then?" Narkon felt Kid's forehead. "Curled up so close to the toilet bowl?"

By the time he'd convinced the night reception of The Vire that he wasn't a random, half naked vagabond, and that his name was on Narkon's list, the effects of the day had truly caught up.

The upward motion of the elevator had turned his stomach into a churlish swamp, and his head into a spinning top.

"Wolf's ... drugs," Kiddo admitted. "Asshole anesthetised me."

He'd barely made it to Narkon's bathroom before he had

become well and truly acquainted with the porcelain − putting his head and absolutely everything he had to give into that toilet, and more.

The heaving had made the headache intensify to bursting levels, and his limbs had refused to keep holding such a heavy body up. So he had slithered down and stayed there, where it was safest.

He'd woken twice more to offer up whatever foam was left at the pit of his stomach, before sliding back down to shiver on the floor.

Kiddo frowned as he heard the shower turn on. He curled up carefully, holding his stomach.

"Alright, up you get, come on." Narkon's strong grip was on his arms. "You need some heat."

Kiddo moaned sickly at the jostling, and clutched his middle.

His head sagged backward as Narkon levered him upright.

"No, no, no," Kiddo pleaded. "Don't. Don't move me."

Even words coming out of his mouth made him feel like he had to wretch up more burning fluids to follow.

How had he survived the come down, getting off hard drugs as a kid?

"Your lips are purple, everywhere else is blue," Narkon told him. "And the water will wake you up."

"Ohhhhh mannnnn," Kiddo complained in horror as the movements Narkon made sent shock waves of nausea through Kid's core, and up his oesophagus, to dance at the back of his tongue.

He had to focus every ounce of his being on not throwing up all over his world renowned mentor.

As if he wasn't taking such a great risk, and as careful as a father with a baby, Narkon rested Kiddo's forehead against his shoulder, wrapping his arms under Kiddo's so that they could stand together.

Then he shuffled them both into the shower – uncaring of his own lovely dress clothes being saturated by the warm jets.

Narkon held Kiddo in a solid grip, until Kiddo had stopped unconsciously shuddering with the cold. Then the chef got them both out, and wrapped Kiddo in a fluffy hotel towel.

"Are you alright to stand alone for a few moments?" Narkon asked, and Kiddo nodded dully.

Too much touching and helplessness in one night. He was ready to be left alone.

He was spacing out blankly, holding the towel protectively around himself, when Narkon returned and put a hand on his back.

Kiddo nearly jumped out of his skin as he broke from his reverie, backing right up against the mirror, and then clutching at his head as his brain floated around, bobbing in sickly loops around his skull.

"Sorry," Narkon gasped with concern and wide-eyed shock. "Didn't mean to startle you."

He retracted the hand that had been reaching out for Kiddo.

The chef had changed, and had brought in the same comfortable clothes that Kiddo had borrowed last time – now dry cleaned and neatly folded.

Narkon cleared his throat uncomfortably. "Do you think you can deal with wet denim by yourself?"

Kiddo backed up again, retreating toward the sink with a hand up to stop Narkon from coming closer.

"M'fine, it'll be right," he promised.

Though he couldn't face the idea of stooping down to scoop up the towel that he'd dropped in his momentary panic a minute ago.

As if reading Kiddo's mind, Narkon bent to pick it up for him, and tucked it over the rack.

"Did ... did something happen, that you might want to talk about?" Narkon asked sombrely – appearing slightly unwell himself.

Kiddo followed the chef's gaze, peering down at where a very prominent, bruised love bite blossomed on one pectoral muscle.

Kid winced in revulsion, and turned to grip the basin, worried that he would be sick again.

"No," he puffed through some heavy, slow breaths. "Dom stopped the Wolf before ... he got too far."

Steady. Breathing in and out.

"It's just brought up some old trauma. And ... general discomfort in my own skin. After having had the wrong hands on me."

Kiddo caught Narkon's reflection – the chef's temples were pulsing as he clenched and unclenched his jaw.

Kiddo used the basin as a support as he turned back around.

"It's fine," he said with an effort. "Thought I'd buried the old demons."

He shuddered, and held his middle, sick to his stomach over the whole lot of it.

"But right now, no matter how long it takes, I can do my own pants."

Narkon appeared ready to swoop in to hold Kiddo like a child in need of comfort and support again. But he nodded, as understanding as he could be, and maintained the distance between them.

"Is there anything I can do, while you are changing?" Narkon asked, using as much of his usual composure as he could gather.

"Could … you contact the clinic? Hato should start a group call with whoever's up," Kiddo exhaled. "Rue is going to be mad at me. And I should fill everyone in on the progress I managed to make."

"Of course," Narkon granted, though he seemed dubious that any kind of positive could have come from the night. "I'll meet you in the living area. You can call if you need me."

Just as he had when Rue had been frantic about Kiddo's safety, Narkon left the bathroom door open by the tiniest sliver.

After the mammoth effort of dragging off heavy jeans, and having one more shoulder shaking, intestine heaving encounter with the toilet, Kiddo found a mug of ginger tea waiting for him on the coffee table in the lounge.

Kiddo groaned to himself as he saw that, beneath the mug, there was a newspaper with the headline: SNATCHERS DE-CLARE WAR.

There were humungous photos of wall posters made my Pash and Teddy's social movement followers, which had been defaced by snatcher graffiti. Comments like 'catchasnatch? …

We dare you,' 'watch your back,' and *'The Hunt are coming for you'* were spraypainted over the posters in stark red.

The messiness of the dribbling paint rolling down from each threat just added to the menace.

Taking up the mug with a sense of nihilism, Kid eased himself back onto the same sofa that he and Rue had passed out on after the fire. He made sure Narkon's loose comfort wear covered the marked, tainted patch of skin left from Yorak's violent bite and attentive kisses.

Narkon could be heard from the kitchen, trying to turn on the camera of his phone, with Hato's voice giving unhelpful suggestions.

Thankfully, Trix apparently joined the conversation at that point, and guided both men to a solution.

"Where *i-is* h-he?" Rue's tearful gulps came from the kitchen then, and Narkon entered the living area with the phone.

"He's here with me, Rue," Narkon assured her, bringing the phone to where Kiddo was staring with the warm tea clutched in both hands.

The ginger smell was tolerable, and even comforting.

Narkon sat beside him so that they could both be seen, though not so close that he was infringing on Kiddo's space.

This man really *was* the best fake uncle.

Trix and Start were both already in the call, but Kiddo felt his eyes burn as he took in Rue, who had found herself the most secure, sheltered spot in the whole warehouse.

She was burrowed down deeply between Seethe and Hato,

backed right into the sofa cushions and huddled under Hato's huge arm, hugging herself tightly.

"I'm alright, Rue," Kiddo gave a wan smile. "Didn't you sleep at all?"

Seethe made a disbelieving sound; arms crossed. "We're lucky she didn't burn the whole world down as she took turns at rage, fear and hysteria."

He was offhand, but he was sitting just as protectively close to her as Hato was, forming a comforting barrier at her side.

"Even Duncan Jr. was alarmed by all the antics going on," Flip commented from the dining table behind them. He was holding a carton of orange juice. No glass. "But it's not like any of us were going to sleep a wink waiting to hear from you anyway."

Trix's moving screen made Kiddo hold his middle again. She was carrying her phone up the stairs. In a blur, she had switched on the light in her old bedroom to wake Blossom – who clearly *had* been sleeping away many winks without trouble.

Ryo had already been awake in the corner, reading by phone light on his unrolled sleeping bag. He obviously hadn't felt right, taking any of the beds left empty by still missing or hospitalised Razes.

"You l-l-look gr-ey," Rue snuffled as she eyed Kiddo, wiping her nose against Hato's arm. "And you were ... were just m-meant to take a note!"

Frazzle and Daleeah both signed on from the clinic computer together, and the fact that they were holding hands seemed like the greatest thing Kiddo had seen in an age.

"You do have a grey colour," Daleeah commented with apprehension. "What did they do?"

Kiddo's eyes flicked to where he and Narkon's small tile showed on the phone screen. He had a definitely seedy appearance.

He cleared his throat. "I had a bit of a reaction to the sort of ... anaesthetic Yorak chose for me," he answered carefully.

"MOTHER FU –" Rue's outrage was cut off by Hato's quick hand.

"– ucker." Seethe had been saying the exact same thing.

"But ... I really am alright," Kiddo added queasily. "The last big dose was maybe four or five hours ago now. So the effects are clearing up."

"He inject you with anaesthetic?" Frazzle asked. "Keep you still or knock you out?"

Kiddo swallowed down the threatening taste of bile just from thinking about it.

"Not an injection," he answered. "More like Hollywood smothering cloth. And ... both. At different times, with different doses. But I could still feel. Everything."

Narkon's temples and jaw were working again.

Daleeah's upset face moved closer to the screen. "It made you quite ill. You are dehydrated. Did it trigger a fit? Any trouble breathing or thinking clearly?"

"We get an anti-nausea. Electrolyte. Your medication. You need pain killer? Yes, we add headache killer." Frazzle was already typing up a script to email to The Vire's front desk.

The poor night stewards would really begin to resent Narkon having Kiddo as a guest. They likely thought he was a troublesome thug, the way he kept arriving.

"I'm fine," Kiddo watched Hato, now on mute, cradling and swaying Rue as she hyperventilated. "All is well." He gritted his teeth. "It was just a slightly more dramatic version of the old snatcher injector-rings. But I need to get out everything I heard before I sleep the rest of this stuff off."

"Alright. What went on, Kid?" Flip asked, signing in on his own phone so that he could see everything himself.

Kiddo paused. Preparing. He had no choice but to warn them.

"First," he began stiffly. "I learned that the Wolf has come up with a treatment plan so that he can condition me, like he did Dom," Kid grimaced as he said it, expecting the onslaught of chaotic sounds coming from all of the different people reacting to that.

He closed his eyes to let it wash over him until they settled.

"He's scheduled a surgery," Kiddo added resignedly. "Where he plans to implant me with a shocker device that can work with epileptic treatments, and anaesthetic style drugs, so that I can be hypnotised too. And likely be used against you."

"Like hell he will," Trix cut in.

"Also," Kiddo ploughed on with a big breath. "Some of the other things he was saying in regard to that were significant."

He took in the settling ginger scented steam. Pacing his sentences so that nothing unpleasant came up with them.

"When Yorak was telling me how confident he was that

he'd be able to do all this to me, he described how carefully he'd worked on Dom. Locking away Dom's memories of us, and implanting his own ideas and words of control," Kiddo stated. "I don't think the memory part of Dom's brain is permanently effected. They're still in there."

Start cocked his head thoughtfully, his glasses reflecting his screen. "So we're dealing more with the brainwashing side of things, rather than amnesia. If we can break the mind control that's causing a blocker, we're dealing with the main problem that's keeping Dom trapped."

Kiddo nodded faintly, feeling fragile in every way.

"This more a strategist, researcher area, than a doctor's," Frazzle shared a glance with Daleeah. "Need our clever Raze to work out the lock words."

"I'll go through the Wolf's torture footage of Dom again," Start agreed with distaste. "See if I can pick up on any of the secret words by lip reading or on the audio."

"I wasn't very with it," Kiddo admitted. "But I may have overheard enough sounds that if you do brainstorm some possible phrases, I might recognise them."

He remembered vaguely that Yorak's whispers had seemed short and broken up. More like a list.

"Great, I'll run anything I find by you," Start avowed, rubbing his hands together as if ready to tackle this new problem at once. "Hopefully I've got some ideas before your meet up happens tomorrow."

According to the flickering of the changing screen reflected on his glasses, he was already starting on something.

"Yeah, did Raze recognise the note?" Blossom yawned over Trix's shoulder. "Did he take the bait?"

"Mm," Kiddo affirmed glumly, after a very tentative sip of the now tepid tea. "He said he'll be there."

"I'm not looking forward to breaking his trust," Ryo confessed uneasily. "Even if it is hopefully just for the short term."

Kid had to take one awful night at a time.

"Two more things," Kiddo forced himself to add. "Important things."

The effort to lean forward and set the mug on the coffee table made him suck in his breath again, while the others waited for him to work himself up to going on.

"There was … a dead Hellion by the Wolf's gates," Kid informed them with an effort.

The image of her sliced throat flashed in his mind, and his stomach protested over the vision all over again.

"Madam Hellion knows," Hato's voice answered grimly, the sound coming from Flip's microphone.

On the tile that Seethe and Hato shared, Rue was still trying to settle herself down. Kiddo gazed at that little square sadly. He couldn't see much of her, because she was wedged so far under Hato's arm now, that she had almost disappeared.

"A few recruits and gang members decided it was worth checking out the area, when you were gone so long," Hato went on. "Nobody else was able to get as close as she got, to see what was going on."

Kiddo shifted in frustration, and also saw in real time as he paled on the screen from that exertion. "She paid the price," he uttered.

"They organised that little effort on their own," Seethe countered. "Take it as a compliment that they knew there was next to no chance of safely catching a glimpse of you, and then went anyway."

"I'm still in shock over how ... friendly ... the Dires, Hellions and Bullets have become with each other," Trix shook her head in amazement.

"And they're listening to Jeffrey," Flip interjected with a chuckle. "Always knew he had it in 'im. Promising little brat is really stepping up."

The Wolf had actually helped to unite factions who had seemed impossible to unite when he'd attacked their bases. But it had been his first step in sending a message to every other small gang or underworlder in the area – that he could take on the biggest of them. That he was the biggest now.

"What was the other thing, Kiddo?" Dalee prompted sympathetically. "Tell us, and then you can get some rest."

Kiddo's brow furrowed as he thought it out. It was something that had been floating around in the back of his mind.

"It's fuzzy," Kiddo told them. "But I remember telling Yorak off for talking so much and making me listen."

Blossom snorted. "He really does do that," she reminisced. "I had been *shot*, and I still remember vividly how happy he was to chat to you by the pool."

"Your restaurant lunch date," Trix also added in disgust. "He had time to order a dessert. And to make you pay for it."

"Right," Kiddo sighed. "But he's not just an over sharer. He ... always has a motive."

"First encounter was to sus you out," Blossom decided. "Second time?"

"Was to get all the home Razes to drop everything and

go out on a wild goose chase while The Hunt set up the gang attacks," Start ventured. "Even oversharing with Dom's torture film was to hold our attention and get a reaction while The Hunt prepared for all of us to be," Start swallowed. "Snatched." He shifted in agitation. "The problem is that he gets you in by saying things you want, or need, to know more about."

"Then what do you think the Wolf was doing with his spiel for you tonight?" Flip asked Kiddo.

Kiddo considered it tiredly. "He hoped to make me want to join him and Dom. To make me choose to keep Dom from facing danger alone. He was trying to get into my head. Planting a seed, and … opening me up to the possibility before he starts forcing the intention into me himself."

Trix scowled. "Ew."

"Well first step is to take Dom out of the Wolf's equation," Blossom stated flatly. "Take the Wolf's weapon."

"Mm," Kiddo took the phone from Narkon as the chef rose to answer the door for Frazzle's delivery.

"But when he was describing the danger Dom's facing," Kiddo recalled the conversation dimly. "Yorak asked if I really want Dom fighting a revolution by himself …" Kiddo repeated. "And a key word there, is revolution."

There was relative silence for a moment. Ryo put down the book he'd been ignoring, and Flip paused in swigging from the juice carton.

"I do have a theory, after contemplating some of Yorak's choices," Start spoke up after thinking on it. "I've wondered at why he might have sought to find out what different country's leaders are talking about. Why eavesdrop on their problems and conversations?" he rubbed his stubbled chin. "Unless you want to know how to stir up dissent within current governments, or hold something over them."

Start glanced over his shoulder – toward where Tiny's bed was in the ward.

"Why search for a way to sabotage and take over the economy?" he questioned. "Unless you want to have power over legitimate businesses and the market. Making top capitalists afraid, and both private and government security appear inept."

Narkon shared a nervous glance with Kiddo as he passed Kiddo the paper pharmacy bag. He didn't like what he was hearing.

"Why snatch a popular, well-known figure like Pash – Raze or not, when it's so risky?" Start went on, his brow furrowed with unease. "Why let the original Raze take down bases in such obvious ways, with such short intervals in between? And then why let Dom and *us* put a spotlight on once respected or prominent buyers as we take back each Raze?"

"Unless, maybe the Wolf *wanted* all this to be noticeable – to go public?" Trix asked suspiciously.

Start bobbed his head in acknowledgment. That was precisely his theory. And a frightening one.

"The Wolf could have predicted that the media and a vast majority of regular people would fire up about these social, and very class oriented issues surfacing. He also could have foreseen that leaders would be slow to know how to respond. Or covert in their responses, to try to keep their distance from the mess. They would lose popularity and confidence from the people in the process."

"He wants to tighten up the underworld," Flip surmised. "And cause instability and discord in the surface world."

He pushed his juice away completely now; totally put off.

"So our guesses about Yorak's long term plans earlier may be something quite tangible to fear," Start concluded. "Especially when he throws around the word 'revolution'."

"Why start *here*, though?" Blossom asked. "Apart from this being where the Razes are based? Geographically, things are much easier to reach if you start off somewhere in Europe."

Start would usually pull out his maps and launch into an enthusiastic lesson at a question like that, but he reined himself in when he saw Kiddo pass the phone back to Narkon to lean his head wearily in his hand.

"In short, anywhere bordering the Pacific is the right place to be at the moment," Start was counting on his fingers. "We have space and resources. We have to ship all the time, and imports and exports are right up a snatcher's alley. We have extremes of wealth and luxury, as well as poverty and homelessness. We have an exhausted and dissatisfied middle class. And leaders who are caught in a vicious cycle of gathering allies, building attacks on the opposition, and securing votes, rather than being able to develop unified approaches to betterment." Start raised his brows at them all with a shake of his head. "After all, our city was able to develop the largest snatcher hub in the world for a reason, before we blew it up."

"So we're ripe for the picking, and appealing to boot," Seethe's voice asserted moodily. "Perfect bedtime thoughts."

Every single tough as nails Raze, Lotus apprentice, doctor, chef, and ex-baby snatcher stayed quiet at that.

There was a strong sense of dread creeping over all of them.

Start, in particular, seemed particularly strained. He was trying desperately to concoct a plan of their own that might confound anything the Wolf was lining up, while searching for Jingle to help him to execute it, and while looking into ways to take Yorak's live weapon away from him.

"Ayyye, oh well," Flip at last managed in his usual resilient manner. "Things aren't all so bad." He unconsciously pulled at the sleeve covering his bandaged wrist and grinned. "For one thing, Rue introduced Trix and I to a famous chef today. And we got a free lunch out of it. That was one real nice thing to happen at least!"

Kiddo realised that Hato had coaxed Rue to turn around in his arms, but she made for a miserable picture. He could finally make out her patchy, puffy face, and he made an effort to sit up straighter.

"Rue," Kiddo said in a shaky, but cheerful sounding voice. "Do you have any nice things of your own to tell me, so I'll be able to sleep?"

Her lower lip wobbled dolefully and she shrugged.

Hato put a giant, comforting hand on her head, almost encompassing all of her hair like a bonnet.

"A second nice thing," Dalee supplied in a warm, smiling way, "is that, aside from some Koa sized handprints on his chest, Hato has received a clean bill of health. And both officer Koa and Rue were there to help him move back up to the base."

"Fascinating case," Frazzle could be heard muttering in Daleeah's ear. "Miraculous."

"Oh, a third very nice thing," Flip kept the game rolling. "Was that Rue threw the Yorak stabber so that it hit the target nearly every time." He leaned back in his chair with satisfaction. "Her timing was much better than Jeffrey's, and many of the recruits. Barely hitting the board hilt first at all."

Hato's hand moved up and down as Rue gave a faint little nod at that.

"Rue, that's amazing," Kiddo congratulated her, putting some energy behind his words, even as he felt himself blanche with the projection. "Flip isn't easily impressed. I remember."

"And another nice thing," Trix announced, not to be outdone. "Is that we raced some Dires and Bullets, and the Raze bikes won for speed. Of course."

Kiddo's brow furrowed in disapproval. "Also … very … amazing." Did 'we' mean Rue had been riding too?

"Well I know what Rue's *favourite* nice thing was," Blossom teased with a cajoling tone. "I was sooo jealous. But I'm not going to say it unless she does."

Kiddo pulled a face. "Not fair," he husked. "I'm so tired. I won't sleep."

Blossom just tossed her hair and sank back into her pillows contentedly. "I will."

"Rue … what was your favourite nice thing?" Kiddo wheedled her softly. "What could make Blossom jealous? I really want to know."

Rue cuddled against Hato, her lip still wobbly and weak against the emotions of a very upsetting day.

"I … liked," she said in a small voice. "Miss Anushi's present."

"She got you a gift?" Kiddo asked with a smile. "That's so generous of her."

That housekeeper turned tutor was another priceless nice thing in her own right.

"It's b-because I've," sniffle, "been reading so good."

"I'm so proud of you," Kiddo managed. Feeling half ready to bawl. "What was the gift?"

Rue leaned an elbow into Hato's stomach as she rubbed her eyes. "She s-said it's a sari," Rue answered. "And it's," a shuddery breath. "Pink and green. Which looks nice on m-me."

"I bet it does," Kiddo answered.

"That is going to be a hard present to beat," Narkon cut in as he saw Kiddo fading with emotion himself. "Perhaps someday Rue and I will go shopping so I can be back as the winner of best gift giver," he joked with a kindly tone.

"Yep. Tomorrow evening," Seethe suddenly announced.

"Oh?" the chef was taken aback. "Tomorrow evening?" he repeated in surprise.

Then he realised what was meant to be happening with Dom back at the base tomorrow evening.

"Tomorrow evening will be perfect," Narkon affirmed then, covering his surprise with enthusiasm. "If the shops start closing … we could see your first ever movie at the cinema," he thought it through on the fly. "We could go to a restaurant. And we could ask Miss Anushi to join us, as a thank you for her hard work too."

How could Rue refuse a growing adventure like that?

"Maybe someone like Jeffrey should also tag along," Flip speculated. "I'm getting more faith in that guy's skills to protect you from atta–"

"Jeffrey probably loves movies and shopping," Hato agreed.

"And a free meal," Seethe smirked.

"Alright. That all sounds fine to me," Narkon answered, taking the abruptly evolving plans in his stride. He didn't mind that he suddenly had a whole entourage to take out for a child's vision of a great evening ahead.

"Do you agree Rue?" he asked encouragingly.

She nodded again, a little happier. "We can get i-ice-cream? And m-maybe popcorn?"

"I'm sure we can eat low quality food, just this once," Narkon assured her. "And I'll bring a less dopey hat for you to wear out."

Rue gave a smile to the camera then, that made Kiddo swallow down a lump instead of anything nastier.

"I th-think we should brush our teeth. I want to go to b-bed," Rue told Hato then. "So it's tomorrow quicker."

"Yes, Kiddo needs take his remedies," Frazzle said then. "And also go to sleep."

Kiddo could see that he gave off the image of the undead, staring at them all with glassy eyes.

"Kiddo …" Rue asked. "You'll … come home? And see me, before my special treat tomorrow?"

"Sure will," he promised with what energy he had left. "I'll head over when I wake up."

"We'll sign off now," Hato agreed hesitantly, waiting to see if there would be any sudden backtracking or outcry from Rue. But she just held onto him and watched Kiddo's face.

"Thanks for telling me about your nicest thing, Rue," Kiddo told her with a smile. "I'll have sweet dreams now."

When she waved her little hand at him, and her picture froze as the call came to an end, Kiddo sagged back against the couch. Depleted.

He thanked Narkon as the chef handed him his pills, followed by the horrible, salty mixture of electrolytes.

Then he rolled his head to the side to eye the older man, too delicate to even slide down to sleep horizontally on the couch.

"You should get to bed yourself. I take it you were working the food trucks for most of the day and night … and that's why you were home so late."

The chef cleared his throat. Not budging.

"If it's alright by you," Narkon answered cautiously, seeing how Kiddo would react. "I'd prefer to stay out here, in case you have a fit or your reaction continues."

Kiddo gave a lazy smile, shutting his eyes. "Why wouldn't it be fine by me? Except that you've earned your own comfortable bed in the other room. And I think I'm all good. Nearly."

He realised he was still holding his stomach, as if he could settle it down by comforting it. However, he would be back camping on those bathroom tiles if he really thought he couldn't keep his fluids in now.

"I realise that you might not…" Narkon paused, and Kiddo heard the tinge of sorrow in his voice. "Feel comfortable having people around you at the moment."

Kiddo was certainly glad he hadn't had to physically face a whole room of people for the conferencing session just now. He wasn't up for much. But he realised Narkon was thinking back to what had distressed them both after the shower earlier.

Kiddo opened his eyes, and was dismayed to find the usually imperturbable chef to be sitting on the edge of the couch, elbows on his knees as he held his arms – as if he was the one who had felt personally invaded tonight.

Narkon's eyes had reddened.

"I'm alright," Kiddo said more seriously. "It didn't happen."

Narkon cast his eyes to the ceiling, speaking with difficulty. "But it did happen, at another point in your life."

Kiddo swallowed the taste of gingery, salty bile now.

"I made very poor choices, and got myself into very hard situations on the streets, when I was very young and foolish," Kiddo stated slowly. "But then I made other, better choices. To work with the help I was offered. To be educated. To be strong. To not feel like a victim, and to keep others from being victims."

Kiddo disliked talking about any of this immensely. He had shut down therapist after therapist until Hato had conceded that he was not ready to address that particular part of his past, and might never be.

Sparks had waited years for him to be capable of romance rather than the sheer survival he'd used his body for before.

But he'd come a long way, and he tried not to shut down on Narkon now.

He gingerly tilted his body ever so slightly toward the chef.

"I'm even starting to think ..." Kiddo swallowed. "That Yorak wouldn't have actually forced me all the way tonight anyway."

Narkon was back to looking like the sick one. "This man. This awful person. I wouldn't put it past him to have wanted to do something as an act of dominance. As a method to claim you or undermine your mental state."

Kiddo rolled his head slightly from side to side. "Everything he does has a premeditated rationale behind it. Or a game. But a crime of passion ... sexual assault ... just doesn't seem his style."

Kid tried not to think too closely about what had gone on in that bed.

"If he brainwashes you into wanting him, it's still against your true will," Narkon grunted, his face hard but his eyes still burning and red.

"But it's not a violent, unplanned thing," Kiddo put a hand to his own eyes. "He seems to relish the fact that Dom has been swayed to a point of accepting and enjoying what they have. Like successful seduction."

He took a few good moments before going on with such vile thoughts. He did not wish to feel the burn of hydrating fluids coming back to haunt him.

And, with me, tonight, he *knew* Dom was coming any minute. He even drew out the conversation while he waited

… talking about his childhood of all things, and only pushed me too far at the end."

Kiddo inhaled and exhaled deeply.

"It's nothing like any of my past experiences. Where everything felt out of control, needy or messy. I think he wanted to see how Dom would respond, and if he could get me on board even without conditioning. He … did and said certain things that would make me react, and that would push Dom's buttons."

"Then," Narkon considered what Kiddo was saying unhappily. "What purpose do you think he got out of that particular endeavour?"

Kiddo scowled. "He saw that that kind of thing still freaks me out, and he saw Dom still wanting to run after me – but ultimately going home to the Wolf. He just wanted to try us out."

Kiddo made an effort to shrug it off. To bury it all again.

"Anyway," he shuddered inwardly. "I shouldn't have let it bother me so much. I didn't … realise it was still a pressure point of mine."

"You don't think anything ever," Narkon's voice dropped almost to a whisper. "To Rue…"

"No," Kiddo was firm to reassure the chef.

This poor man had only had to worry about what country he might travel to next, or which high end event he might deign to be part of before he'd met Kiddo.

"Dalee didn't have any concerns after spending time with her. And, though I know Rue's seen too much, I do not have any reason to believe anything like that ever happened to her," he comforted Narkon.

It was one thing Kiddo could thank his lucky stars for, just as Sparks would.

"She has so quickly become kind, trusting and joyful. She's also told me that none of the other snatchers could ever be bothered with her. The majority of them even shunned her in case knowing about a baby snatcher could get them in trouble."

"Oh, thank goodness," Narkon uttered. His shoulders sagging. "Thank *goodness*. In this case, lonely was safer."

The chef leaned his face in his hands for a few moments, shaking his head slightly.

Kiddo reached out to pat the man's shoulder.

"You ok?" he asked sympathetically.

Narkon chuckled into his hands, but when he lifted his face, Kiddo could see that the stubborn tears that had been threatening before, had spilled now.

Narkon brushed at them with the back of his hand.

"Am *I* ok?" he repeated with another sad chuckle. "Every time I see you, or any of the members of your Raze gang, I see you all burning up or burning out. You all throw every bit of yourselves into your cause, until you have nothing left."

The chef quivered then, as if someone had walked over his grave.

"On the night of the fire, I saw Hato bolt in one direction to tear masked fiends away from the clinic doors. He was unarmed, but unstoppable. I saw Seethe cutting his way through snatchers– trying to get *into* the hellish warehouse scene. I saw you dive inside a burning building when they said Rue was in there," Narkon described. "All while the rest of us stared in shock."

"Actually, you ran into the tunnels to smuggle us out of there," Kiddo corrected softly. "After taking over my shift for me. Thanks for that, by the way."

Narkon refused to be diverted.

"You live such extremes, and suffer for it so terribly," the chef went on, aghast. "I am horrified that you have all had to take on such lives, and so very grateful that you have. The idea of there being nobody who is doing what you are doing is just as awful as knowing that you are the ones who have to."

"We're all normal people," Kiddo assured the chef faintly. "We just don't always get to do ordinary things." He yawned. "But when you have to fight for your place in the world, it bands you together with others like you, in a way that is deeper than family. The people around me ... make each hurdle bearable."

He shied away from thoughts of Tiny. Beef Cake. The Hellion with the cut throat. The burns on Teddy's face. The things that had happened to Flip. Dom, in Yorak's bed right now. Miss Dorris, finding out that Raze was missing, every night.

"We bicker." Pash and Velvet. "We're messy." Quicklips and Flip. "We can seem tough, vicious, or downright scary." Seethe, and Velvet again. "But we tell sweet stories about favourite nice things, and have our little girl wipe her nose on us. We overfeed fish. And we always pick each other up and dust each other off," Kiddo said with lethargic gratification.

Narkon had pressed a fist to his mouth. Absorbing.

"I'm glad to know you," the chef gave a muffled murmur. "You are all terrifying, good people."

Kiddo cracked a half smile. "Good's pushing it," he answered. "But I'm very glad to know you too."

He closed his eyes once more, half drowsing as he spoke now.

"I always avoided getting to know 'normal people' … and I guess famous people too," he jested quietly. "Because it's easier to be with your own kind, who understand. Without explaining it all, or having to deal with anyone else's pity or shock."

Narkon didn't say anything. Just listening.

"You're one of the first outsiders I really bothered to let in," Kiddo sighed.

He was only half aware that he was still even talking.

"Because you kept trying. You persisted."

The volume of his voice was petering out.

"No matter how dark it got, and how much sweeter it must have been to be ignorant, the truth was important to you. Supporting a cause that didn't have to be yours was important to you. And it was important for me … to discover a person like that."

"I am deeply sorry that I first misjudged you as a 'ruffian who was wasting his talent.' I shudder to think what you had been doing in between training in my kitchens," Narkon confessed with great sincerity.

But Kiddo gave a tiny shrug. "S'alright, I would have judged me too. And now … you're one of my kinds of people." His voice was trailing off. "I felt safe enough to come to you. On a night when I was at my lowest."

When he fell silent for a while, he dimly felt Narkon edge off the couch.

But he barely stirred at all when a blanket was draped lightly over him, and as the chef settled on the other couch to stay close for the night.

| 20 |

Twenty

Narkon had woken him with his dried jeans, a bottle of water and some slices of plain toast.

Kiddo now gripped that bottle of water like a best friend as they took The Vire's dreaded elevator down to the carpark basement level. Thankfully the ride down was much less nausea inducing than the ride up had been, and they'd just beaten the morning rush of business people who would soon be cramming the elevators for work.

"I'd forgotten what a hangover felt like," Kiddo told Narkon as the doors parted. "Being so *fragile*."

But the chef spluttered in surprise as they stepped out, and Kiddo thrust the bottle into Narkon's hands.

"What –"

The chef watched in disbelief as Kiddo leaned over a giant pot containing a synthetic tree, to haul a struggling man out by his collar.

Kiddo had the man in a sleeper choke at once, though he didn't press so tightly as to completely cut off the man's blood flow yet.

"Media?" Narkon gaped. "Why would they –?"

"Snatcher," Kiddo growled. "Rare older one. Check the pockets."

"Piss off!" the man squirmed; swinging his arms around crazily to try to reach Kid, and then realising that the squirming was cutting off his air supply.

Kiddo added just enough pressure to make the purpling man wheeze like an asthmatic, forcing him to instinctively scrabble to get a hold on Kiddo's forearm – which was tucked so snugly around the man's gullet.

While the snatcher's hands were busy, Narkon warily rifled in the man's hoodie – pulling out a utility knife, and a mask with fangs printed on it.

"You can't be stupid, to have lived past thirty," Kiddo spoke in a low voice. "So you know I won't hesitate to kill you to protect my friend's location."

Narkon gaped at them both.

The snatcher stopped tugging so much at Kiddo's grip. He did know.

"There are cameras down here," the snatcher hissed in a squashed, barely projected voice. "You're not stupid either."

"They're facing the cars, not this glorified plant box," Kiddo dismissed that. "Anyone else know I have such a close ally in this building?"

The snatcher coughed and gasped, acting like he couldn't answer.

"Come on," Kiddo demanded. "You're hardly seeing stars."

"Yorak'll wanna know you got sick. He'll wanna know

who helped you. And I've told everyone *exactly* who!" the man sneered in a rasp. "So better run!"

Kid kicked a foot into the back of the man's knees so that he overbalanced, and Kiddo quickly tugged him all the way backward by his hood.

With a winded yelp, the snatcher's skull hit the ground, before he curled up and inward under the weight of Kiddo's knee sinking into his stomach.

Before the man could suck in one gulp of air, Kiddo thumped his free knee down on one of his prisoner's elbows, while yanking the other arm so far across the man's pinned body, that he was now near strangling himself.

"Why's it just you behind the decorative plant then?" Kiddo puffed, peering down. "You hoarded the info, didn't you?"

The aggrieved, bulging-eyed expression that he got in return made Kiddo laugh.

"You fluked seeing me last night, right? Thought you'd wait around and work out who I was with?"

The snatcher managed some very faint expletives, with Kiddo's mass still forcing his stomach into his spine, and his pretzelled arm nearly popping from its socket.

"Wolf … would make … me … a Hunter … for something like this," the man finally choked out.

Kiddo nodded sagely. "Probably would have. And it's about time, considering your years of service. Too bad for you."

"Kiddo," Narkon said nervously. "Are you really going to …?" he couldn't say it.

"I don't have to," Kiddo smiled down at the snatcher grimly. "Put his mask on for him."

"Wha –" the man wriggled and gurgled. "Why?" he wheezed.

"The catchasnatch movement just saved your life," Kiddo explained, as Narkon falteringly pulled the balaclava over the man's head. "They'll get you a nice cosy stay in jail, where they will be very curious to know more about a live snatcher in captivity."

The snatcher struggled more furiously then. "Will … be … put … down!"

"If your friends can't trust you not to talk, you will," Kiddo mused.

"The elevator numbers are moving downward," Narkon warned. "We'll have company in a moment."

"Perfect," Kiddo decided. He gave the suffocating man another thump against the ground so that the snatcher's eyes rolled back.

Kiddo released the man's slack limbs, grabbing the Stanley knife and thrusting the blade up. He pressed the hilt into the snatcher's hand, and was stepping back to Narkon's side as the elevator dinged.

"Attack! Help!" Kiddo yelled desperately while the doors were opening. "A snatcher! Snatcher attack on the hotel!"

There were gasps and jostling motions as the elevator full of business people swarmed out.

"Oh my God!"

"It's a real one!"

"They're real!"

A security guard from the boom gate box came hurrying across the basement carpark to see what the fuss was about.

"He's armed!"

"Get the blade away from him!"

Phones were being whipped out.

A circle was forming as everyone crowded in.

"Police!" Kiddo exclaimed again. "Call the police!"

He had grabbed Narkon's elbow so that they could back away, escaping unnoticed.

"Don't worry," Kiddo reassured Narkon as the chef stumbled against him. "He won't get a chance to pass on who I was with. The Hunt he wanted to join will make sure he never gets another chance to speak."

"That was horrifying," Narkon uttered, leading the way to the car. "Absolutely horrifying."

"And a fluke. He just happened to be out at the right moment that I was stumbling by last night," Kiddo scowled with distaste. "I nearly cost you your stay at The Vire."

Narkon collapsed heavily into the driver's seat of the car, handing Kiddo his water bottle.

"I made my peace with the fact that it was a risk to speak out publicly and to continue working with you," Narkon conceded. "They would already know I'm an ally."

He gripped the wheel tightly as he pulled out of his car spot. There was no queue at the boom gate, where he had to swipe his card to exit. Everyone else was still clustering around the unconscious, real-life snatcher that had appeared in their midst.

"I prefer they don't know we're quite so close that I have

sleepovers," Kiddo remarked dryly. "You don't want any kind of misguided jealousy or focus from the Wolf. Or Raze."

Narkon shuddered.

He turned on the radio to search for an upbeat song or some kind of talk show banter, but it offered no escape.

"The drug lords were deposited outside a police station last night, exactly as the corrupt leaders before this have been found. Temporarily paralysed from the neck down, and with incriminating files on their persons.

"We do know that the king pin and queen were taken from a black tie event – with his tuxedo embellishments and her earrings alone being worth millions. And it begs the question; how do such people get invited to exclusive functions ... unless they have friends in high places who support what they do?

"Another thing we know is that our vigilante seems hell bent on exposure of the truth over all else, because nothing is ever taken from those who are dumped. Nothing other than the crooks' mobility and their secret, sordid lifestyle that is!

"It remains to be seen if these particular crooks will find themselves silenced on the inside, following in the pattern of the others."

Narkon switched the channel.

"So another kind of snatcher exists, you say?"

"Yes. The head of the #pashwatch herself announced it. Darling Teddy, who has never steered us wrong. She has issued warnings that you must look out for overly sharpened canine teeth. Like wolf fangs."

"Oh, see we have to be careful there! Some people just have pointy teeth. I'm no trafficker, but I'm no dentist's dream either ..."

Then the chef simply switched off the radio altogether.

He cleared his throat. "Do you feel alright after moving around quite so energetically?"

Kiddo fidgeted with his air vent. "I could be blown down by a breeze," he deadpanned. "But not by a lone snatcher. I'll be right for a quiet day with Rue. And I'll be up for tonight."

Narkon darted a glance at Kid. "I take it you'd rather not face tonight's ordeal, even if you have to."

Kiddo shifted in his seat. Not wanting to face this ordeal, or any of them, was an understatement.

"There are plenty of things I don't want to face," he confessed. "Like what might be happening to Sparks. Jingle, Velvet. Like, how badly Quicklips and Pash were hurt in that crash. Like Frazzle, telling us we need to think about how long we're going to force Tiny's body to stay alive, and who we're really helping by keeping the life support going." The plastic bottle made crackling sounds as he squeezed it in his hand. "But in the short term, I am most definitely not looking forward to this encounter with Dom."

Narkon's eyes were sad as he nodded, repeating his concern from last night. "You all live in such extremes." He shook his head to himself with a pained expression.

"I'd much rather hear about your non-extreme things." Kiddo swapped to twisting his thumb ring, to save the bottle. "I mean ... apart from walking in to find half-dressed young men on your floor, what other things does a high profile, but otherwise normal person get to face?"

With a reluctant quirk of his mouth, Narkon considered it. "Well in my case," he pondered. "I pick the tardiest, roughest, least ambitious, most ungrateful student I've ever met, and organise their diner to be rebuilt."

"Of course a student like that would have been careless enough to lose the first one," Kiddo sighed.

"That, at least, will soon be remedied. The slab for the new Kid's Place is being poured tomorrow," the chef informed him. "And a frame will shortly follow."

Kiddo's eyebrows rose. "That's *great*," he breathed with surprise, genuinely diverted from his fidgeting.

"The Lair is reopening too," Narkon went on, diligently settling back into his role as good news giver.

"And aside from that, I will be very busy taking my fake niece, her security guard and her teacher out for a wonderful evening. For which I must ensure that I have purchased a stylish hat to please that niece first."

Kiddo's eyebrows lowered. "Odd. Her guardian already bought her a pretty nice one, I thought."

"Dopey," Narkon corrected.

And Kid grinned. Wishing he was going to be joining Rue and Narkon for movies and treats instead of living in those extremes again.

When he ducked under the roller door to Spark's garage, Rue squealed immediately, and Flip quickly plucked the Yorak stabber from her fingers as she wheeled away from the target area in a blur of pinks and greens.

"Do ladies in small saris usually throw knives?" Kiddo asked while she at once assumed her position as his belt.

It all looked adorably awkward, tied in bunched knots over a pair of overalls, with any trailing bits pulled up under the overall shoulders to keep them out of the way. Miss Anushi had clearly not overseen Rue's second adornment in this garment.

"Why not?" she asked as he shifted her hold from his hips so that he could swing her up.

Even without adrenaline, he felt almost back to usual strength. If a little shaky in the arms, and delicate in the centre.

"Huh," he considered it. "You're right. Why not?"

Flip gave him the nod as Kiddo carried Rue off toward the stairs.

"Start said when you get home he'll come and speak to you about some words and plans he's got," Rue snuggled into him.

"He's going to leave the ward?" Kiddo asked. "That will be good for him."

"He already had Blossom, Ryo and everyone else come to him in Tiny's room this morning," Rue explained; kicking her legs, and crinkling Narkon's light, stylish sweater. "He said you might be more comfortable and feel better away from sick people after a sick night."

She scrabbled up straighter to holler up the stairs then – close to his ear.

"HATO! SEETHE! KID'S HOME!"

"Oh ... wow," he winced as she slid down for him to plant her feet on the kitchen floor. "Much more comfortable. Much better."

"Since when do you dress so fancy?" Seethe turned from rifling in the pantry as Kid straightened beside him.

Seethe had been about to flick the decorative buttons on Narkon's V-shaped collar when he froze.

"Ouch. What's that?" Rue asked, reaching to prod the top of Kiddo's chest.

The material had dragged as he'd put her down.

"Nothing," he told her, pulling the fabric back up. "Nothing," he said more firmly to Seethe. "Trust me."

Seethe slammed the pantry door shut and turned on his heel to go through the fridge instead.

"Don't," Kiddo warned Seethe as Hato's heavy steps began to descend from the bedroom level. "It's fine."

Seethe banged a glass bottle down on the table and 'hrmf-phed' into a seat.

"Bit early for a beer, isn't it?" Koa commented as she followed Hato into the kitchen.

"Don't," Seethe said acidly, crossing his arms. "It's *fine*. I wasn't the one anaesthetised by a predator last night."

"Good to see you all in one piece Kiddo," Start smiled as he hurried up to join them.

"Even with a few extra colours," Seethe sniped under his breath.

Kiddo was now much more aware of how Seethe displayed concern. But this kind of response to a sensitive topic would have killed him when he was younger.

"I heard Rue's shout when I was in Frazzle's office," Start explained to Kid. "Thought I best fill you in." He held up a vial. "The doc gave me something to spike Dom's drink tonight."

Kiddo groaned.

He sank into a chair across from Seethe, slumping deject-edly.

"This is exactly the situation Dom just helped me get out of."

"Not *exactly*," Seethe quipped. "We're not a bunch of *animals* like the Wolf."

"Dom doesn't know that," Kiddo replied discontentedly, and Rue patted his arm.

"I can always stay and help," she comforted him. "A sweet kid like me being around would make it seem less scary."

"Oh, no, I couldn't ask that," Kiddo grimaced. "Narkon's already out buying the hat, and is very excited to hear of your progress from Miss Anushi directly."

Rue nodded apologetically; shrugging in a self-sacrificing 'it's out of my hands − I'm needed' kind of motion. "Jeffrey's already looked up all the movie options, too."

Start set the vial on the table. "Blossom said she'd do it, when she orders her different ingredients for some, ah, Hot Shots, was it? And we've booked you an outdoor table at the bar, so we'll all be able to surround the area and move in swiftly."

"I'll be driving the van," Hato rumbled.

Kiddo cringed.

Honestly, this was exactly like a snatcher grab.

"There's not much else you can do," Koa shrugged uncom-fortably. "Think of it more as an intervention rather than an abduction. Like I have to."

"If it helps, once we get him here, we'll be doing the complete opposite to the kind of conditioning snatchers do.

Giving awareness and self-possession, rather than taking it away," Start told Kiddo sympathetically. "Because I did have a light bulb moment last night, when I was going through Dom's torture clip. I'm hoping that I've found the right words. Or at least some of them."

Kiddo sat up straighter. "What did you come up with? How'd you work it out?" he asked – impressed, and more hopeful now.

"I got some indirect help from Jingle's past hard work," Start answered proudly. "You remember how she got into the top snatcher base's first system, when Dom was down there with you, using their computers?"

Kiddo could hardly forget. "She was able to access the buyer files at that time. But they changed their system after that."

"Jingle never lost her copy of the old stuff when the snatchers scrambled to get a new system up," Start informed him. "And I got to thinking ... exactly how far back did those old snatcher records go? Because it was very likely that the kinds of words that could have such a strong, triggering impact on Dom now, would have to be words he'd heard during the most traumatic stage of his life – when he was a snatcher product."

"I'm not following," Kiddo admitted. "Why would the snatchers have used repetitive words on him when he was a kid, if they were selling him on instead of conditioning him?"

"No, no," Start halted him there. "I only needed the snatcher records to find which *buyers* had purchased a specific blue-eyed, eight year old boy. To narrow it down, he needed to have a snapped wrist, but high spirits and strong health, and to have been sold to a pharmaceutical company. From there, I followed the trail to find out which company it had been, and what experiment records they had. It wasn't the words of the snatchers I was interested in, but the words of the doctors in the labs."

"That would have been like finding a needle in a haystack," Kiddo gaped in disbelief.

But Start shook his head. "Actually, Dom wasn't lying when he once told us he would have been a winning candidate if there'd been a snatcher exhibition related to the sciences. His case stuck out, as one they'd pinned great hopes on. They couldn't bear to put him down, no matter the trouble he began to cause, because he was the only successful body and immune system enhancement case they ever completed."

Seethe was staring moodily at his beer bottle. He'd heard all this earlier, and it was turning into quite the trying day in terms of unpalatable details.

"They could never quite figure out how to replicate it, or how far they could take it with him," Start went on. "They'd done all they could in terms of injecting him with illnesses, bone breaks, frying his nerves, manipulating his body and heart, and he always came back from it all – while leaving them none the wiser as to why. So, sending him to mines, sweatshops, terrorist organisations – it was all actually more testing to see if the worst of conditions for prolonged amounts of time could finally bring out more answers, or an end to it. When they thought it was the latter, that lab was actually closed down."

Kiddo swallowed the tingling feeling at the back of his

tongue. He felt worse now, after hearing that, than he had the night before.

"The good news is," Start tried to bolster Kiddo's spirits. "Frazzle believes Dom's brain will come back from all of this with time, if we can keep him away from the Wolf doing any maintenance work. And I believe that, if I've got the words right from his lab file, I can start the process of snapping him onto the right path tonight. The length and flow of the words does possibly match up to the whispered phrases the Wolf used in the clips."

Kiddo cleared his throat. "What were the words?"

"A few phrases he would have heard quite often, when his suffering would have been at its greatest, were the words 'break, clear, hold, enough, relax'. It was a process outlined on his file, where the verbal cues were a signal for the professional, and also indirectly to Dom, of what was coming. To hear those words and associate them with pain again years later would have an adverse effect, especially when coupled with hypnotism and brain shocking."

No wonder Dom had often thanked Yorak, and relaxed, on the final word and with Yorak's assurances that he was there to help and to love Dom.

"The word 'break' was obviously for when they were performing their bone work," Start pushed on. "And 'clear' was for heart work, 'hold' was for nerve work, 'enough' was for when they had to stop before going too far. 'Relax' was to tell him to stop panicking and that it was over for the day."

Koa pulled Hato closer to herself as the big man passed the back of his hand over his eyes. Exhaling heavily.

Dom had once told them that he had called for Hato as

a child in that lab. That memories of Seethe and Hato had been the only things that had kept him going. And that he had never come home when he'd got free, because he'd heard they'd been snatched and possibly turned to snatchers themselves. He hadn't been able to bear the thought of his heroes being ruined. Then he'd woken up with the Wolf telling him that his fears were all true.

"The words won't do anything to him when they aren't said in the voice of his mind controller," Start told Kiddo. "But without Yorak's voice adding new power to them, Dom will definitely recognise the phrases, and it'll all get him thinking."

"Or turn him even more homicidal," Seethe hissed after a sizable gulp from his beer.

"Making Dom aware of the words and how they are being used can help him to break free," Start countered. "I hope."

He have a jittery smile that wasn't too reassuring.

"The length and rhythm of the words in that order," Kiddo nodded glumly. "It could be close to the kinds of things Yorak whispered last night."

"Yeah, well, fingers crossed guys," Rue said with a resigned face. "Otherwise … we're all screwed."

| 21 |

Twenty One

"Stop fidgeting," Blossom scolded Kid, leaning back on her bench seat like a Japanese goddess – cool and untouchable.

Her elbows were up on the wooden tabletop beside Kid, and she was facing outward, observing the busy street life around them.

Despite her two companions, more than a few party goers hanging out in their own neighbouring beer gardens had let their gazes wander toward Blossom. Roving up her long legs as she lounged confidently – an image of chunky platform boots, black leather pants, plunging top and lace choker.

Exactly the kind of memory Dom would have of her. Exactly what he would be expecting to see.

"Thought Kiddo was meant to be the show stopper," Flip murmured over his shoulder from the table behind Ryo. He was hyper aware of the fascinated stares Blossom was drawing as well, but the tone of the crowd's gaze was more of awe than that of capitalist-snatchers.

"I don't carry that kind of compelling attitude," Kiddo muttered to Flip's back.

"You get used to it," Ryo commented blandly. "The attitude, and the show stopping. Means when I'm with her I can get things done quietly while she distracts the crowd."

"Should see when it's Blossom and *I* together," Trix's comment carried back to them breezily. "Couple of killers."

She was seated next to Flip, where they could both turn around fast to seize the person who would soon be sitting in the empty spot at Ryo's side.

"Ryo and I will blend our roles this time," Blossom informed them. "I'll put on the usual show to make everything seem fun and natural. But Raze will be more diverted by any subtle comments Ryo can come up with while I'm the busy one."

Ryo reached across the table to pat Kiddo's arm as Kid twirled the metal table number holder. Kiddo gave the other young man a bashful look and released the number, not wanting to seem obviously out of sorts or nervous.

Ryo had kindly volunteered to take the seat that would be shared with Dom so that Kiddo wouldn't have to do any grappling if it was necessary.

"Chatting amongst tables is not advisable," Start warned, as if speaking into his phone. He was perched nearby on a barstool at a beer-keg-turned-table. "Our van has been doing the rounds. They haven't spotted him yet."

"He's probably been watching this whole area for the last hour," Blossom yawned. "He's no fool."

"Except to trust us," Kiddo deadpanned.

They were counting on the fact that Dom would have no

memory of the other Razes, and wouldn't recognise them or be concerned enough to be deterred in meeting up.

"We're helping him," Blossom batted her eyelashes Kiddo's way. "It's for the greater good."

There was that greater good again.

"Your drinks order, and glasses," a dazzled cocktail waitress smiled at Blossom breathlessly; almost starry-eyed. "We've never had someone insist on mixing things themselves."

She carried a tray of five assorted liquor bottles with pour spouts attached, and three shot glasses. Not the usual kind of order.

Blossom reached forward to run a hand over the bottles in inspection.

Easy laughter came from a small group passing by on the pavement then. They brushed by Kiddo's elbow, which was now leaned up on the beer garden's picket fence.

"Set it all down," Blossom instructed the waitress after a moment. "I hope it's better quality than that saké was before. You ought to know you shouldn't chill such low grade stock."

Kiddo blinked as a lithe figure broke from the passing crowd, leaning over Kid at the low fence, and placing a kiss on Blossom's cheek.

Then a tattooed arm was wrapping around Ryo's neck in a warm embrace, before Dom stepped over the fence and slipped onto the bench seat beside him.

"You shouldn't flirt with the wait staff," Dom told Blossom affectionately. "It scares them."

The waitress hurried to set down her delivery, glancing

around their table as if she'd stumbled upon her favourite band, all posing for an album cover.

Kiddo noticed that now there were six liquor bottles in front of them. One of them having been carried here by Blossom herself.

Blossom flapped a hand at the young woman, finally swivelling all the way on her bench to face forward. "Come back for the tray later. I think I best take care of this."

"Y-yes, of course," the woman even opted to bob slightly before she retreated.

"So I missed the saké stage?" Dom asked with a grin; more natural and genuinely at ease than Kiddo had seen him in a very long time.

Kiddo noticed Dom's eyes on him, though he'd directed the question at his two friends. His electric blue gaze was almost doing a scan to evaluate how Kiddo had pulled up – lingering on Kiddo's drawn face, and moving to where the Wolf's hidden mark stood out like a brand on Kiddo's chest beneath his shirt.

"Well that's your fault," Blossom shrugged, pouring just a sparing dash of honey coloured liquid from one of the bottles into the three glasses. "You're late."

"You chose a busy place," Dom countered. "I had to get a good feel for it."

"Near the docks, nice sea breeze, vibrant community, trendy clientele," Blossom huffed. "Perfect location."

"And all seemed well?" Ryo asked Dom. "You saw nothing questionable?"

Dom at last shifted his gaze to Ryo, and Kiddo noticed

Blossom taking her chance to add some drops of her special tonic to one shot glass only.

"There's an Irishman drinking with a First Nations woman behind you," Dom answered. "Spicy mix. Could be fake. But it's more likely a first date with zero chemistry. Their hair is doing way too well to be in and out of balaclavas."

"You're right, great hair. Look at her afro," Blossom continued with a new bottle now. "She's pretty hot. I bet if he doesn't do it for her, I could."

"That one over there had my attention for a while," Dom went on easily, jutting his chin at Start. "At first I thought he gave off creepy loner vibes. He's flicked through about twenty different apps on his phone. Closed them all, opened and closed them again a bunch of times. Even faked a phone call not long ago. But I think maybe he's just been stood up and can't admit."

He leaned his chin on his hand, eyes back on Kiddo.

"Aside from that," Dom mused. "You three are the most dangerous and fascinating people I could see here. And, while it's busy, your table is close to the road for a quick getaway if we need it. So I decided it was time to come on over."

"Good choice," Blossom congratulated him – filling the last parts of each small glass. "We've missed you."

Dom straightened, becoming earnest, and sad.

"I truly am sorry that I went off your radar for a couple of years this time. Please believe me when I say it was not my intention to leave you with no idea of where I was."

Ryo cleared his throat. "Your friend here," he gestured to Kiddo. "Has given us some insight into what you think went on. Please forgive us for our ... confusing response when you first called us a couple of months ago."

"I'm a bit murky on how you knew of Kiddo at all," Dom frowned. "Did I contact you in the past and tell you I was happy? Kiddo doesn't think I was being held prisoner, but Hato and Seethe have a clinic that likely messed with both our heads."

Blossom pushed Dom's specific glass across the table and into his hands. Then slid one to Ryo. "Miss Lotus could assist you to work all this out."

"We did find Kiddo in the hopes he could help us to trace you," Ryo said calmly. "And we had thought he was your partner. There is definitely a lot of confusion to sort through."

"Yup," Dom agreed. "But right now I've got someone I'm working with to move forward. I can't head to Miss Lotus' underground now and get stuck on trying to look back."

"What if I just want to bundle you up and drag you home with me anyway?" Blossom asked flirtatiously. Only half joking. "Reliving what came before could heal you right up."

Ryo clinked his small glass against theirs, and lifted it to his lips.

"You're not having one?" Dom asked Kiddo, instead of lifting his own.

Kiddo shook his head, struggling to make eye contact. "I don't drink."

"But he's fine with his friends drinking," Blossom announced, and threw back her shot. "Empty your glass so I can refill it."

Ryo tipped back his glass, and watched as Dom emptied his.

"You want a water or something?" Dom questioned Kiddo, before pulling a sour face. "The recipe tastes different, Bloss."

Blossom raised a pierced brow in disapproval. "Mhmmm. Foreign imitations. Not the same as what I've got to work with in Lotus Bar." She set the empty glasses in order again. "Still, it's good enough for more rounds to come."

Dom shook his head. "Not too many, I've had a busy day, and another busy one tomorrow. Tonight's not going to go how a night of Hot Shots in Tokyo would go."

Blossom pouted as she poured.

"Kiddo *could* use that water, Raze," Ryo suggested softly then. "He said your new associate gave him something that sickened and dehydrated him last night."

A pained expression crossed Dom's face. He stood quickly, but didn't notice when he overbalanced a touch, and gripped Ryo's shoulder. "I'll get it," he promised Kid. "Extra ice. Little umbrella. The works."

When he headed inside to the bar, Blossom used the opportunity to add a larger dash of Frazzle's serum to her mix in Dom's glass.

"No chemistry?" Flip could be heard guffawing to Trix. "Can you believe that? We're sexy as hell."

They'd been straining their hardest to eavesdrop, while also acting like there actually wasn't anything dodgy behind their 'spicy mix'.

The shots were lined up as Dom returned, a little unsteadily, with a tall, icy water – a colourful paper umbrella leaning on the rim as promised.

Of course he could sweet talk, or swipe, anything from the bartenders.

"Would you consider leaving your new associate, if we said that we do not like the sound of him?" Ryo asked Dom carefully.

The three of them tipped back their glasses, and Kiddo twirled his tropical umbrella.

"Look," Dom set his glass down, grimacing at the taste again. "Yorak's *a lot*. And Kiddo didn't have a great meeting with him yesterday. At all."

His words were slightly less distinct than usual, though Dom himself hadn't noticed it yet.

"But he's the only person who has been able to take on or subdue the snatchers so effectively." He tapped a lotus tattooed finger on the table. "As a team, we're tearing down bases and exposing buyers like it's nothing."

"The team's one sided," Blossom growled under her breath to Kid. She was working on more refills and waiting for Ryo to take Dom's attention again. "And the asshole knows where the bases are."

"What if we were to say that we've done our research into Hato and Seethe," Ryo asked thoughtfully. "And that we don't think they are who Yorak says they are?"

Ryo definitely had Dom's attention now, and Blossom was done with the third round. She'd finished the vial completely.

Dom passed a hand over his eyes, squinting and blinking. "Then where the hell have I been?" Dom questioned less patiently. "Why do I have short glimpses of memory of Yorak trying to help me get away when I was unwell?" he shook his head, as if to clear it. "And I found out Hato and Seethe call themselves Raze, after *me*," he said with disgust. "It's wrong. As if Raze would refuse to work with the only person who has any power against the snatchers."

"What if your Yorak is the wolf in sheep's clothing?" Blossom asked sweetly. "Rather than Hato and Seethe?"

Dom tsked in frustration. "Stop it. I won't hear of it. That 'wolf' was able to get me into Mumbai. You know how long I slaved to make things better there, just clearing out small-time dens. Then the two of us tore its capital base down in a *day*."

Ryo nodded in understanding.

What he really understood was that they had no choice but to carry out their plan.

"We hear you, Raze," Ryo assured him gently. "We don't mean to upset you. Let's just enjoy each other's company, and celebrate that we have found you well enough, and as righteous as ever."

The placid, sweet natured young man passed Dom his final drink.

Dom's shoulders lost their wary tension, he tilted somewhat drunkenly toward Ryo.

"Thank you," he told Ryo in relief. "Above all, I need the support of my greatest friends."

The only ones he would let his guard down with. The only ones who could do this to him.

Ryo and Blossom raised their glasses to him, watching as Dom downed his last dose.

"You can take Kiddo back to Miss Lotus, and I'll find you all there, when I need a break," Dom swallowed heavily.

"It sounds nice. If you were assured to survive the crazy pace you're keeping," Blossom sighed, mournful rather than triumphant in her success.

"You know I can take more than most," Dom reassured her in a slur – showing consternation over how frequent and languid his blinking had started to be, as if his eyelids had become unbearably heavy.

He tried to concentrate on the three of them.

"I can usually take much more liquor than this, too," he at last mumbled. "You don't even seem …"

He took in the fact that Ryo and Blossom barely even had flushed cheeks, while three shots had nearly knocked him out.

The colour drained from Dom's face.

A moment of heartbreaking realisation made Dom's breath suck in as he fought to focus his gaze on the bottles. One unusually small, empty one. Suspiciously unmarked by any branding.

Blossom pressed a hand over her heart as a pang of distress and grief seemed to physically wound Dom before her eyes.

"It's alright Raze," Ryo breathed, taking a hold of Dom's shirtfront to try to keep him from bursting out of his seat, as well as to keep him upright. "We are your loyal supporters still, and we've got you."

Intoxicated or not, Dom was still fast in grabbing Ryo's thumb and twisting it so that he winced and had to let go of Dom's shirt.

"Lured me out," Dom whispered in disbelief, gutted by the hurt. "No friends of mine."

But he couldn't bring himself to do anything more to the three he had trusted.

Dom crashed up from the table, nearly toppling the bench seat with Ryo on it, and stumbled backwards. He was about to stagger over the garden's picket fence beside their table, when Flip swivelled and rose to throw a strong hold around his teetering form.

Dom instinctively kicked backward into Flip's shin, and threw the back of his head against Flip's forehead. But it was the last he could manage.

The Irishman grunted and let Ryo catch Dom safely as his body sank down between them.

Blossom sniffed and dashed at her cheek before taking a resolute breath.

She stood up noisily, making sure to jostle the table and all of its bottles so that anyone around them who'd begun to stare, switched their attention from what was going on with the men to her.

"Oh nooooooo!" she cried out. "Please, can you help me to get him out of here?" she asked Flip and Ryo dramatically – like a flustered damsel. "He's had too much!"

Kiddo discreetly rose and stepped over the picket fence.

Start was already hurrying away across the road.

"Don't panic, we'll help!" Trix stood to comfort Blossom loudly. "Your friend just needs to sleep it off."

With Ryo under one arm and Flip under the other, Dom was swiftly swept away from the bright lights of the beer garden.

"I just don't want to get in trouble," Blossom gushed while Trix escorted her out. "My father's picking us up!"

Hato's van was pulling up across the road even as Ryo and Flip crossed, with Kiddo close behind them.

"Shhh, shh, it'll be alright," Trix held Blossom as they stepped onto the road too.

The sounds of chatter filtered from the beer garden again as the crowd gradually returned to their own gossip and brews. Luckily, and disturbingly, catchasnatch movement or not, there didn't appear to be any suspicions raised.

Kiddo opened the front door of the van for Flip and Ryo to pass Dom up to where Seethe was waiting.

Seethe tucked Dom under his arm, buckling him in.

"Let's hope we've got some time before he wakes up," Seethe uttered before Kiddo closed the door. "Or my ribs are gonna hate this."

| 22 |

Twenty Two

"Elevator is good idea, I tell you," Frazzle commentated as he and Kid followed Hato up the stairs.

Hato was carrying Dom in like a ragdoll.

"Also, you watch out, he wake soon. Breathing changing."

Dom's head rested against Hato's immense chest, and he seemed so powerless and helpless right then. But at the doctor's warning, Hato eyed him like a grenade that could go off at any moment.

It would do them no good to underestimate the original Raze while it seemed like all of the fight had gone out of him.

"You got any more zip ties?" Seethe was asking Flip.

They stood over a steel interrogation chair that Seethe had somehow procured from somewhere. They'd cleared out space in the kitchen, and had pushed aside the loungeroom couches for what Koa had described as their 'intervention.'

"I've got one for each wrist and ankle," Flip stated. "That's plenty."

"Add more," Seethe disagreed, adamant after their recent experiences.

"They're metal clasp, industrial zip ties," Flip argued.

"Ahh, make haste please," Frazzle interjected, his eyes on Dom.

"I'm not messing around," Seethe insisted, when Flip frowned disbelievingly.

While Hato set Dom in the chair, Dom's brow was already furrowing. His head hung forward as he groaned.

"Do hurry up," Blossom added cattily – still visibly upset despite her best efforts. "But don't cut off blood flow. Watch the ink."

Flip begrudgingly set about fastening Dom's ankles, then his calves, wrists and the crooks of his elbows to the arms and legs of the chair.

Dom was taking deep breaths, trying to lift his head by the time Flip was done. He managed to drag his head up, to tilt it against the high backed chair, but was struggling to open his eyes.

"Get in a circle," Hato instructed them all grimly.

Kiddo watched nauseously from where he leaned against the bench. Duncan Jr. made lazy circles of his own, in no way interested as everyone else fanned around the chair.

"Remember the first time Dom ever came here for dinner?" Trix asked the gang. She was holding Blossom's hand rigidly. "Some of this feels similar."

Hato had thrown Dom up against the pantry door before he'd finished climbing the stairs. None of them had realised exactly how much self-restraint Dom had practised back then, and the kinds of tricks he had up his sleeve.

In fact he'd apparently never felt the need, or felt so cold or trapped, into using his worst tricks in the entire time that he'd been part of their family. He'd been efficient, he'd been brutal when it suited, but he'd never resorted to the cruellest tortures that had been used against himself.

Dom inhaled deeply, as if he was working himself up to something big.

But then he simply opened his eyes. Taking in his binds, and then glaring flatly down his nose at them.

Ryo was the more stoic one as those electric blue eyes fixed on him for a moment. When it was Blossom's turn, she looked ready to shrivel on the spot.

For someone who had just woken, and who was slumped in exhaustion, there was an awful lot of malice behind that narrowed gaze.

"Well played," Dom complimented them, with a voice of deadly calm. "The unexpected friendship trap. The ties. Can't just snap a wrist out of these."

"We didn't make you sick, like Yorak did to Kiddo," Blossom couldn't help but point out to him.

Kiddo wondered if the chain might twist right off the ring on his thumb, but he couldn't seem to stop his repetitive turning of it.

"Your drinks didn't," Dom agreed with Blossom civilly. "But you do."

Blossom flinched.

"I find betrayal hard to stomach."

"Raze, the fact that we went to such lengths to aid these people, should tell you something about the extent of our convictions," Ryo tried to protect Blossom from the acid of Dom's attacks. "You know that Blossom and I want to do right by you."

Dom nodded slowly. "I'd thought that, yes. But I'll learn from this."

His fists were bunched, and he tried to roll them from side to side, as if craving to launch those fists at all of them.

"Dominic," Hato began then, drawing Dom's now murderous gaze to himself. "Seethe and I never forgave ourselves for letting you go to that newsagent's alone. You were our kid brother, and our carelessness let you down. You didn't trust us when you finally found us again, but you did your research –"

"Oh, don't worry," Dom said pleasantly. "I'm doing my research right now. Confirming a whole host of doubts I'd had about you."

Hato regarded him wretchedly. "You told us you didn't come back for so long because you were worried that we weren't the same people you had wished for when you were stuck in that lab. You were worried the snatchers turned us."

Dom had stiffened. But he managed a faint flicker of a half-smile.

"*True*," he uttered darkly, drawing the word out. "I'd wanted to die in that lab. So many others got to. But they just wouldn't let me. My own will wouldn't let me. And the memory of you. What a joke."

Frazzle made a choked sound in the back of his throat then. "Stop that, not do that."

Kiddo only noticed then that Dom had still been almost imperceptibly straining and manoeuvring his wrist against one of the ties. Disguising it as angry fist bunching.

The rubbing had sliced into the inked skin, and blood had

just started to roll down the metal arm of the chair. It was the first drops of blood that had drawn Frazzle's eye.

With Dom's concerted efforts, a tiny fraction of space had opened up between the tie and the arm of the chair.

"I'd prefer to make at least some sort of effort here," Dom gave a slight shrug. "Or to gradually rip off both my own hands, rather than be conditioned into someone else's tool," Dom explained rationally. "One thing those scientists could never toughen me up against, was blood loss."

"The Wolf is doing exactly what you think Hato and Seethe were doing," Blossom said pleadingly. "He's using you."

"You dislocate your shoulder, elbow and wrist before chop off hand," Frazzle stated urgently.

"Hmmmmmm," Dom contemplated it. "Let's see."

Dom's lips formed a grim line. He tensed, ready to make a wrenching movement powerful enough to peel the skin of his hand off like a glove, when Start yelled.

"Enough! Relax!"

Dom stopped short, his hand still bunched in a tight fist and small drizzles of blood still rolling down the top of his wrist.

"Break. Clear. Hold. Enough. Relax," Start gulped in a rush.

Dom's eyes flashed dangerously in Start's direction as his shoulders heaved with long, harsh breaths. Every muscle in his body seemed to have become taut.

"So *that* was your game ..." he hissed. "Clever, clever. The trauma would crash through my brain like a pickaxe to the head." He gave a humourless laugh then. "You really did your research. I've never mentioned that process to anyone, let alone let myself dwell on those words."

Start held his hands up in innocence. "Raze, it's not my voice using those commands that affects you. If you think about it, whose voice did you last hear saying them?"

Dom visibly calmed himself. Sitting back in the chair.

"Alright," he conceded unhurriedly, as guarded as ever. "I'm thinking."

He rolled his head to either side, frowning, with his simmering anger only apparent in the way his jaw clenched and unclenched.

Start gulped as Dom's sharp gaze followed him when he backed up to the TV in the lounge.

"This is something that Yorak sent to us, on the night that he took you for himself," Start explained nervously, picking up the remote to turn on the screen. "I found it left over from the clean-up, after Yorak attacked all of us who had joined your Raze gang's cause."

When Start pressed play on the footage of the Wolf's ongoing torture of Dom, the others were uncomfortable, or as perturbed as the first time they'd seen it. But Kid couldn't help but watch Dom himself.

The rise and fall of his chest was becoming more rapid. His face was stony as he tried to comprehend what he was seeing. As he recalled how many times Yorak had held him and whispered just like that in recent weeks.

Kiddo could see Dom battling with his perception of Yorak. With excuses. Could the film be doctored?

But Yorak's appearance and his mannerisms were so very

unique and striking. What actor could have impersonated him so closely? And there Dom was. It *was* very clearly himself, being subjected to things he had no memory of.

Start wasn't done with just that clip. He went on to play the clip of Yorak's speech at Seethe's auction day in Japan. Where the gang's hidden camera had captured Yorak openly outlining his role as the head of the snatchers, and indeed of The Hunt itself. The Hunt for all Razes.

"We wanted to make you conscious of the trigger words Yorak has been using against you," Start explained timorously. He turned the volume down and stepped in front of the footage of the battle that had broken out in the auction room.

Dom managed to tear his haunted gaze away, squinting at Start again as if his head was aching.

"If you know what's happening to you, and you see the signs, you can actively try to avoid being drawn in or perhaps even break free in future," Start said hopefully. "I believe that you can overcome what the Wolf might try to do to you from now on, by maintaining deliberate focus on your own will, and perhaps remembering what you used to do to mentally escape or survive the experience when those words were used around you as a child."

Dom's expression stiffened as he involuntarily flicked his eyes toward Hato and Seethe.

"Frazzle and I believe that, with your new mental empowerment, even if you are sometimes re-hypnotised or subdued, your mind will stay somewhat open and become stronger against it every time," Start went on promisingly, while the doctor nodded just as winsomely beside him. "Your memory should eventually become something you can access again."

"Brain is muscle. We exercise! We keep you in ward to recover –" Frazzle began enthusiastically, joining his hands together in readiness.

"No." Dom ground out through gritted teeth. "You will not be keeping me. And I don't do hospitals and doctors."

He was straining both arms again now.

"You *need* rest and doctor," Frazzle answered with a disconcerted step forward. "That's me. Or my Dalee – who love you. You be with your Razes."

"Or Miss Lotus could…" Blossom began imploringly.

"No," Dom repeated. Both forceful and quiet. "If you are all the kinds of people you say you are, you'll let me go now that you've said your piece."

"Dominic…" Hato beseeched, with heartfelt intensity.

"Stop it," Dom cut in. "I listened. I want out. I promise not to touch anyone, if no one touches me. Just cut these off, and no harm done."

He turned to Kiddo at last.

And beneath the fierce, buzzing energy radiating from him, Kiddo could see the shattered awareness of the night's truths in Dom's gaze.

"I won't forgive you if you keep me against my will," Dom said emphatically, throwing Kiddo's own words back at him. "If you truly care about doing what's right, you'll get me out of here."

Kiddo straightened.

"You let him go, you'll lose him," Seethe pushed Kiddo back toward the bench.

But Kiddo just patted Seethe's grip on his shoulder, and then slid it off.

"If we don't do what he's asking now, we'll all lose him forever," Kiddo answered gravely.

Flip shot a look of disagreement at Hato as Kid approached to take the Yorak stabber from Flip's hands.

"He's heard what we had to say," Hato gave in heavily. "If he won't stay by choice, we'll be doing more damage to his trust in us than helping his brain's health if we force it."

Seethe crossed his arms, icy with discontent.

Trix was holding Blossom in support. She and Ryo had become grim, silent observers.

Reluctantly, Flip gave the knife up.

Kiddo was cautious in approaching the chair and flicking the blade open. He slid the knife under the bloody chair arm first, and sliced through the underside of the tie. He was gentle as he peeled it from Dom's bleeding skin.

As promised, Dom did not move while Kiddo carefully cut through each bind. Holding perfectly still until he was free.

Then Kiddo sat back on his heel as Dom thrust himself upright.

"Don't trouble me, and all will be fine," he reiterated. "Don't follow me."

"How 'bout you just don't go?" Flip suggested, taking a few steps forward to help Kiddo up. "Reconsider it, mate?"

Flip was a dauntless and highly skilled Raze in his own right. Though also a touch cocky.

He was about to clap a sociable hand on Dom's chest.

"Get to know us again –" the Irishman made to continue.

And he found himself blinking up from the floor as Dom was stepping over him.

The others cleared a path while Dom headed for the stairs, and didn't reach out for him as he passed.

| 23 |

Twenty Three

"You not hearing from Raze doesn't mean he won't come round."

Narkon and Kiddo stood on a concrete slab, surrounded in the open framework that had sprung up to make the new skeleton of Kid's Place.

Kiddo rubbed his jaw.

He felt like he could hardly talk. But Narkon seemed to sense that he needed to, and was trying for the right prompt to help.

"It's hard to accept that Raze simply returned to the Wolf," Narkon admitted. "When he saw what Yorak had been doing. But he must be in shock, and snatcher conditioning must be extremely hard to break out of."

A nod from Kiddo this time.

"The Dires taking breaks at the food trucks have been quite vocal about Raze's continuing exploits," Narkon commented conversationally. "He has certainly continued to be a success when it comes to terrifying the underworld."

A grunt of acknowledgement.

The Dires were definitely not wrong. Dom was still the Wolf's most chilling weapon.

"But at least you know Dom's as strong as ever. Perhaps if the Wolf has made him forget again, it gives your team a chance to have another try at bringing him in."

Silence.

That wasn't the right prompt either.

"It's great that your friends from Japan have been able to stay on, to help in the face of everything …"

Narkon's voice trailed off as Kiddo wrapped his arms around himself, gripping his elbows and turning away from the base. He squinted up at the sunset through the roof beams, without seeing any of it.

Narkon sighed empathetically. "I'm sorry. Earlier this week, Rue told me about another loss that you suffered, which I am sure is upsetting you deeply. I'm so very, very sorry."

Kiddo took a shuddery breath. Trying to be stoic.

This prompt had to be addressed.

"For the best," he uttered flatly. "Brain dead. Machine and feeding tubes were keeping him going. Wasn't peaceful." He swallowed around the lump in his throat. "Was in adult diapers for God's sake. Would've … would've hated that."

Tiny had developed ventilator-associated pneumonia. The sound of the struggle, the wet, suffocating mess going on inside Tiny's body, the suffering they were putting him through every time that machine ded forced his lungs to breathe, had become too cruel.

His body had stopped working, and he had slipped away mere minutes after everything had been switched off.

Kiddo scuffed his shoe roughly. "Had only half his family there with him. But what can you do? Others might be in the same shape when we find them."

Narkon couldn't help but reach out to wrap an arm around Kiddo then.

And though he kept stiffly holding himself in a self-hug too, Kiddo allowed the man to pull him in. Needing the comfort.

He clunked his forehead down on Narkon's shoulder, hiding his face in the shadows between them.

"Was wondering if…" Kiddo grimaced to himself – finally forcing out the tough thing he most needed to say to the chef.

It was weighing on him so very heavily right now, with everything as it was.

"Wondering if, when we work out identity papers … You'd agree to be Rue's next guardian. If anything happens to us … If we ever can't keep her safe enough."

A pause stretched between the two of them, and Kiddo squeezed his eyes shut.

Narkon's grip had tightened about Kiddo's shoulders, but Kiddo couldn't bring himself to lift his head and face meeting Narkon's gaze.

"Kiddo?" Narkon asked hesitantly, suddenly searching for words too.

The shark sounded hollow now himself.

"You once said to me that you might not show up to work because you'd be organising someone's funeral, or because somebody might be organising yours."

Morbid words.

They definitely rung true.

Gangster funerals. Recruit funerals. Apprentice funerals. Now Tiny's too.

Tiny.

Gone …

Kiddo realised he was shaking his head against Narkon's shoulder.

"Mm."

"You said that snatcher at The Vire was lucky to have made it to his thirties," the chef went on tentatively.

Building up to his real concern, and kneading his firm grip against Kiddo's arm as if to keep Kid grounded. As if to make sure he stayed tangible.

"You don't think you'll make it to thirty either? That it's the same for Razes?"

Kiddo finally straightened a little, but the chef kept Kiddo by his side; his arm around Kid's shoulders in a comforting weight, rather than as an added burden.

"There are no international Raze recruits left," Kiddo replied slowly. "Only half the local recruits. Marco and Tiny never made it to thirty," he listed, sighing. "Don't know how Pash and Quicklips are. Hato was in cardiac arrest just the other night. But Frazzle's somewhere in his thirties, and Hato's nearly made it." He shrugged, moving Narkon's arm up and down. "I don't know. I just want Rue to have options. She can't end up on the streets again."

The idea of Rue having found her own family, having made her own room, flourishing so beautifully with care and support, and then losing all of that, was enough to drive him mad.

"I cannot articulate how much I want to take you home to France with me," the chef announced in return. "You already do feel as much like a nephew of mine as she feels like a niece. And, frightening, clever or lovable, I wish I could let your whole gang hide away to live safely from here on out."

Since his attention had been drawn to the unfairness all around him, and since it had started to effect people in his own personal life, Narkon had been unable to come to terms with the reality of the way things were.

It troubled him. Disillusioned him. And brought out the best in him.

"But rest assured," Narkon went on. "Rue has already told me she is planning her first overseas trip to visit me when I decide to head home. She will *always* have a refuge with me."

Kiddo gave a faint smile. He'd desperately needed to hear that.

"The moment we became an open presence here, and Yorak created those underweb Raze profiles, we knew we'd be known and hunted no matter where we settled in the world. But while the rest of us would never go unnoticed for long, Rue would have a chance of going under the radar without us."

"Think on that no more," the chef assured him. "From now on, she will have every chance and every opportunity. If it comes to the point where she needs to take shelter elsewhere, she will find it with me."

"Thank you," Kiddo said emphatically, exhaling heavily and sagging a little with a sense of relief.

He felt like a retrospective, tired old man who'd just set out his will and testimony – just in case.

"And Narkon …" he added in a serious tone; wanting to make sure everyone here could rest easy.

"You should try not to dwell on how things are with us, either. We chose this path," Kid conceded. "And, anyway, Razes are smarter than snatchers. Most of us haven't had any mental manipulation into distorting our reason."

Narkon snorted. But then drew up short.

"Razes are more cognizant, but they're also more self-sacrificial."

"Mm," Kiddo agreed. "That must be where we're going wrong."

Narkon gave Kiddo's shoulders a squeeze before he released him. "In many ways, it makes you the most right of all."

Kiddo gave him a smile, turning back toward the direction of the food trucks as a dazzling blur of pinks and greens skipped toward them from the nearest van.

They both felt the gloom lift slightly at Rue's approach, seeing that Miss Anushi's sari had acquired some fresh souvlaki sauce stains in the last fifteen minutes.

But for once Kiddo didn't mind. Stains like that could be fixed.

He was in fact getting so good at not minding, that he used his own sleeve to wipe Rue's greasy face as she pranced closer.

"So, that wasn't on Frazzle's diet plan," Rue grinned. "But it sure felt good for me. And Miss Dorris had one too. She wasn't certain about what she was sad to have lost tonight," Rue confided. "So I said a souvlaki might have been it."

"Dom and souvlakis are both hard to go without," Kiddo

affirmed. "I'm sure Frazzle wouldn't mind, when you're being kind to someone else."

"Yeah, thought so," Rue threw a long bit of loose sari over her shoulder, as if it was completely natural for the garment to be an everchanging, shifting mass. "And it's Teddy's first time back, so I was kind of being there for her too. Letting her load me up with the lot."

"You didn't have the onions and garlic sauce, did you?" Narkon asked, accepting her sticky hand as she threaded hers into his. "It'll keep you awake," he admonished.

"Who in their right mind skips the juicy bits?" Rue gaped; aghast. "And an onion and a garlic are plant foods. So healthy."

She slapped her other little hand into Kiddo's and tugged them to follow her out of the construction site.

"Crafty thing," Kiddo remarked dryly. "An answer for everything."

Rue cackled and kicked up her legs so that Narkon and Kiddo had to quickly swing her between them, making her squeal with glee all the way through the food trucks.

"Don't worry, anyway," Rue giggled at a high pitch as she swung. "Miss Anushi had me counting in patterns and practicing reading animal facts all the way to our field trip today." She beamed as her feet finally touched back down to cross the road. "Jeffrey said I'll sleep like a baby."

"Jeffrey will be the one to sleep like the baby," Kiddo countered with amusement. "He got sunburnt at the zoo."

"I was fine because I had my hat," Rue told Narkon sagely. "And Miss Anushi used so much sunscreen on me, there wasn't a whole lot left for Jeffrey. She felt bad."

Narkon couldn't help but chuckle. "She only planned to take care of one child on the outing, I suppose?"

"Jeffrey likes her," Rue stated knowingly. "Which means he really likes being my bodyguard. And I can get him to tell me great Raze stories when I'm too tired to do number patterns on bus trips home."

"Oh?" Kid asked suspiciously. What kinds of stories could a Raze recruit possibly have to share with a child? Especially the child they were all trying to get away from a life of blood and gore?

"He tells me different adventures of the original Razes that he's heard about," Rue explained happily. "The things that The Hunt never knew about to put in those profiles. Like, cool things, and nice things, or exciting things."

Kiddo was wincing as they drew to a stop outside the warehouse roller doors.

"He better stick to the nice things from now on," Kiddo decided. "But he's so recent, he wouldn't know most of the nice things."

Kid couldn't bring himself to remember how very unaffected this girl was with less nice things. Like at his own first meeting with Rue, when she hadn't batted an eye as Kiddo had carved his way out of a snatcher attack with a butcher knife. At another point, he'd witnessed Rue herself, casually pushing a Huntress off a roof.

Rue bounced on the spot, tugging on their arms. "Yesssssss. *You* can tell it better. How 'bout my bedtime story tonight can be your personal favourite memories of Sparks!"

she shook Narkon's hand in hers. "You want to hear them too, don't you?"

Kiddo cocked his head and shrugged at the chef. "Come up and see the room you almost single-handedly fitted out for your adopted niece."

Narkon was dragged forward before he'd had a chance to respond.

"Sparks' is a good story for me to hear," Rue filled Narkon in. "She's no dummy. And I'm going to be like her."

Kiddo nodded wistfully, leading the way up the stairs. "Hers is a great story."

Narkon tried not to overbalance as Rue towed him up after her eagerly.

"Oh?" he managed. "I will be glad to hear it."

"Sparks is a year older than Kiddo," Rue added for Narkon's benefit, before turning back to Kid. "What was she like when you met her?"

Kiddo smiled nostalgically. "Hmmmm."

Grease patches on coveralls, tank tops and short spunky hair. Straight forward, and straight into Kiddo's otherwise hard to catch line of attention.

On her first day Seethe had picked her up from the Bullet base, like a smug middle finger to Sora. When she'd stepped off the back of Seethe's bike, she'd tossed Kid her bag and had asked where Hato was. Then she'd told Seethe the gang was going to need to invest in equipment, and had pointed out where it should go.

Kiddo had simply stared, and Hato had just listened and nodded when she'd introduced herself. She'd immediately gone on to outline her short and long term plans for a garage, and exactly what she could bring to the gang.

"Well …" Kiddo mused warmly. "Sparks has always been the capable kind of person who just says how things are going to be, and then that's how they are."

She had such an air of self-assurance and competence about her. She thought things through, and got them right. It sure made others listen.

"Sparks told her big boss Sora that she wouldn't keep stealing or racing cars when she first joined the Bullets. She said she was going to run his workshop at the same time as studying. And instead of being a full time recruit, that's what Sora let her do."

Narkon's brows were raised. "Sora is quite the intimidating leader. I'm not sure many people would feel confident making demands of him."

"Keep in mind, she was barely a teen at that point. A runaway, with only a moderate reputation to advertise her skills, going into an auto gang as if she was weighing up if they were the right fit for *her*," Kiddo added with affectionate admiration.

Even being a runaway and joining a gang had been part of Spark's overall plan. She'd only stayed in a bad family situation long enough to learn everything her parents knew about mechanics. They'd been opportunistic thieves, turning cars over for a living.

"Legendary," Rue crowed, hardly watching where she stepped as Kiddo led her into the bathroom and put her toothbrush into her hands. "What a girl boss."

Narkon leaned in the door frame while Kiddo sat on the edge of the bath.

"She also told Sora that she was going to get so good that she wouldn't stay on a junior apprentice wage for long." Kiddo spread the multicoloured toothpaste over Rue's toothbrush for her. "And then Seethe noticed her. So that quickly made her premonition about earnings come true too. Sora never forgave Seethe for tempting Sparks away from the Silver Bullets."

Rue gave a drippy grin. "Jeffrey said that Seethe stole the Bullets' cars for ages when this was just an empty warehouse and he and Hato were strapped for cash. Then he stole their prized mechanic later on," she chuckled.

"Couldn't Sora have offered to increase Sparks' wage?" Narkon asked curiously, getting drawn into the details himself. "If he saw such potential, and was so loath to lose her?"

"Too risky," Kiddo reached to wipe at where Rue's chuckle had projected some bubbly droplets onto the mirror. "The Silver Bullets are a huge gang," he explained. "There's a certain order to things. A hierarchy. If you don't want to ruffle too many feathers, you can't just promote the youngest, most recent mechanic apprentice. Especially when she's only there half the time, and still working on her qualifications."

"Even if she was pretty much running the show while she was there anyway?" Rue asked through an alarmingly growing mouthful of foam. "Bunch of Bullets said that. She was a pro."

Kiddo tugged at one of Rue's red curls, and then leaned forward to grab her magic panda hairbrush for phase two of winding down for the night.

"You've got to be more careful in a massive gang. It's more political," Kiddo answered, over the sound of Rue now gargling loudly. "Their whole focus is on their members earning their place, dominating in their specialty area, and holding the gang's turf."

"It sounds almost as cutthroat as the elite kitchen arena," Narkon remarked blandly then, and Kiddo nodded – only half in jest.

"The sharks aren't quite as frightening, though."

"But Hato and Seethe ... you guys were just another gang to join," Rue commented in puzzlement. "A smaller one. So why'd she choose here?"

Kid pulled Rue to come and lean back against his legs, and she obediently gave Kiddo her head of wispy hair to work on. He was getting better and better at making soft, wavy clouds, instead of pulling out raging red knots.

"Working for Hato was different," Kiddo told her. "Being a small gang meant there was no need to quibble over positions. We were only focused on creating a safer place around The Lair for ourselves and for others like us. All Hato wanted was to make a better life for the people under his wing. Sparks liked how Hato made the base feel like a home, and she had a vision for the ground level that made sense."

"Alright ... I get that Hato was happy for the ground level to become all about training, cars and weapons. It would've suited Flip, Sparks, and all of you lot really. But the library?" Rue snickered. "I've never seen him up there reading with Seethe."

Kiddo paused, and raised his eyebrows. "Huh. You're right."

Not long after Kid had arrived, Hato had built the shelves for the library. He'd carted in the books, desks and chairs. But he'd never cracked open even one of those books.

"Perhaps Hato made the library because he wanted Sparks and yourself to keep up your studies," Narkon commented with respect. "The library is an escape. A completely different pathway, away from the more violent or grownup things going on below," the chef went on. "He was wise beyond his years."

"I did do Hato's books and slog through many assignments up there while the others patrolled," Kiddo lamented the hours of drained restlessness and hardship.

Maybe Hato had given him such steep responsibilities on top of his homework to keep him at his desk instead of out in the action so much.

"And Sparks got all of her licensing finished up there. Jingle did her online courses and started her empire up in that library too. Then who knows half the things Start planned from those tables."

"Guess it's like playing music to a baby to make it smart," Rue tapped her small palms on Kid's knees. "Put books around your kids and they'll start to learn. I like doing my learning there," she admitted. "So, why'd Sparks drop out of school?"

That was a painful memory. She'd been one of the only things that had kept him in school in his own early and middle years.

"Hato used money from the club to pay for all of us to study anything any of us wanted. But no other gang I've heard of would just pay for every kid they take on to go to school," he began thoughtfully.

Kiddo put the brush aside, leaning around Rue to turn the tap on, and holding a face washer under the slowly heating water.

"They want their members to be committed to the gang alone," Kiddo reasoned. "So even before she left the Bullets, Sparks had put *herself* through the start of high school, with scholarships for hard work. But later when she stopped getting what she wanted out of general schooling, she moved on."

"This is quite the interesting tale," Narkon admitted appreciatively. "I feel I should be reading this as part of a biography on standout people, working their way to success."

Kiddo gave the chef a smile. Narkon's admiration of Hato and Sparks made Kiddo himself glad for some reason.

"I showered already," Rue protested when Kiddo held out the warm face washer. "Miss Anushi said I had to get all that zoo and sunscreen off."

He plonked it on her face. "You've added souvlaki and toothpaste to your look since then, and grubbied up your hands," he told her teasingly.

She'd never been so consistently clean in all her life. But she sighed through her facecloth-drape and started rubbing it over her chin and cheeks so that Kiddo would be satisfied enough to keep talking.

"So Sparks came here, because she could study better?" Rue grumbled around her wiping.

"Sparks could be her own boss here, make her own way,

while also helping bring money in to meet Hato's goals for the area," Kiddo asserted. Taking the face washer to dab at her hands and clean the stubborn creases of her fingers next.

"Fairy nightie?" he asked her when her hands and face were scrubbed pink.

"Warrior princess nightie tonight," she corrected as he stood. "Suits this kind of story. But don't say anything more while I'm changing," she warned – as if Narkon would be pushing Kid for the best details without her.

So Narkon and Kiddo dutifully waited for her to call them into her bedroom, where Narkon was suitably enthused by what she'd done with the space.

He gave the right amount of compliments to how her three dolls were arranged to be drinking tea with her three action figures. And he was happy to see how her cars were on show beside her doctor's set.

"You know, Rue," the chef ruminated as Kiddo pulled back the plush covers for her to bounce on in. "By the sounds of it, you already have similar qualities to Sparks. You are both very strong and intelligent young women."

"But Sparks is like a genius," Rue despaired. "She wound up making herself into the kind of mechanic, and weapons master, that everyone respects. Absolutely bad-ass."

Kiddo tucked her in. "Sparks would tell you it was all hard work, not automatic brilliance. She does naturally see how things fit together, but I can attest to how much her sheer determination and motivation got her the rest of the way."

Rue squirmed around – messing her nicely combed hair against the pillow. "Miss Anushi says I've got good motivation. I'd bet I have a heap of determination too."

"An abundance of it," Narkon agreed.

Kiddo sat on the side of her bed and smoothed Rue's curls again.

"Hato *was* crushed when Sparks dropped out in her final year," he remembered with a smile. "Until he realised how seriously she was going to focus – solely on her passions. She went the way of Jingle, and slogged, then excelled her way through course after course. An absolute star."

The luckiest, most hard-working of stars.

"You're so proud of her," Rue said dreamily.

"And you," Kid confirmed, tapping her nose lightly.

Rue reached up to touch the sharply pointed star hanging from his ear.

"When did you realise you loved her?" she asked curiously.

"Oh …" Kiddo took Rue's hand, and tucked it in under the covers. Pausing over the pang in his chest.

He took a breath.

"The minute I saw her," he managed as smoothly as possible. "She was like … everything in one. And she made me feel normal, instead of like … I was everything too much."

Rue gave him a sympathetic look. "You miss Sparks and Raze a lot, huh."

Narkon's gaze was just as sympathetic, knowing exactly the kinds of things bottling up inside Kid right now.

Kiddo ran his fingers lightly over Rue's forehead, and tried to stay in the moment with her, instead of with those things he was bottling.

"I miss the loves of my life," he answered very seriously.

"But it's *very* lucky I've got you, and good people like our chef here too."

Rue bit her lip. Mulling over something.

He waited patiently.

She wouldn't switch off if she had even just one more thing in mind.

She was currently close to being at 'placid level', but he needed her at 'sleepy'.

"I've thought on it," she said softly at last.

"Oh?" he asked, tracing over her brow and down her nose.

Last time she'd said something so solemnly, she'd announced she was going off alone to get information from the snatchers.

Thankfully, that didn't seem to be the case this time.

"I think you ought to know," she said quietly, in an almost vulnerable voice.

She shifted a little under the covers.

"You should know that I've decided I love you."

And just like that, she'd stolen Kiddo's breath away again.

His tracing faltered, and he stared at her.

The warmth of her words spread from his heart to the pit of his stomach, replacing the slightly off feeling it so often contained these days.

"Thank you for telling me," he replied gently.

As if the moment was a fragile one and he was afraid of breaking it.

Narkon seemed to have become completely still with the same sense of delicacy.

"I love you too," Kid told her – meaning it with every bit of his heart.

She nodded.

Of course.

She'd been sure he did.

"That's my favourite nice thing for today," she resolved with a satisfied smile.

Even though today she'd gone to the zoo for the very first time, and had eaten a loaded souvlaki from Teddy.

Kiddo smiled a true, grateful smile back.

"It is most definitely my favourite nice thing too."

| 24 |

Twenty Four

Kiddo laid his dark shirt and trousers over the back of his reading chair for the next morning.

He rubbed the creeping stars of exhaustion from his eyes.

He'd noticed the pinpricks of light gathering in his vision when he'd walked Narkon out a while earlier, and knew he should try for an earlier night.

A seizure hitting at Tiny's funeral was the last thing any of them needed. But it was just so hard to lay there and wallow sleeplessly every night. So he always put it off. And now …

He swallowed a metallic taste in his mouth, and frowned down at his hand on the black clothing.

Did that really have to be his hand, on a set of his now much used funeral clothes, ready to say goodbye to his friend? It didn't feel like it was his hand. His clothes. His friend.

He wished it wasn't.

An aura of light was beginning to surround that hand. The pinpricks were joining together to form a sadistically euphoric glow.

Kiddo pulled back with a grimace, feeling claustrophobic.

Hemmed in.

He pulled his shirt over his head.

Too quickly.

He put that hand of his out again to steady himself against the bed.

"I'm fine," he told himself. Straightening again. "Need sleep."

And then he went down.

He became aware of someone holding him.

Hands on his arms. His forehead.

Next he felt the comfort of a mattress beneath him.

Fingers on the side of his neck.

The relief of the slow, moving pressure.

The tension easing from his muscles.

Lips pressing to his lips?

Kiddo sat up in a rush. Then clutched his head.

Had he felt what he'd felt?

"Easy there."

Dom was on the reading chair. Out of reach. Surely too far for a stolen kiss.

Was that even what had woken him? Or had time passed?

Dom's eyes flickered over Kiddo's bare torso, the sheets now puddled at his waist.

Dom was slowly turning something in his hands, watching Kiddo closely.

"That wasn't ..." Kiddo gathered himself, trying to surface from the haze. "Wasn't Hato, Seethe or our doctors' fault. They didn't do anything ..."

"I know," Dom reassured him. "I didn't know that I knew," he added wryly. "That you have epilepsy. But somehow I found my hands working on your neck in a way that seemed to help."

He shrugged.

"My hands don't usually benefit necks. Unless you want me to help you get more sleep."

Kiddo squinted everything into focus.

"Is that your jacket?" Kid asked fuzzily. A new item of black clothing had been added to the back of the reading chair Dom sat in.

Dom had found his leather jacket.

Dom had been in here with him long enough to explore the room.

"It'll look good on you tomorrow," Dom told him. "You can carry the original Raze you knew to the funeral."

"It's yours," Kiddo shook his head. "You should wear it there yourself."

Dom set the item that he'd been turning over in his hands aside. It was Miss Dorris' gaudy peacock brooch. Her gift to her adopted grandson, Raze.

Had it felt familiar to him? Had he gravitated toward it for a reason?

"I don't remember knowing your friend," Dom told Kiddo seriously. "He's a stranger to me."

Kiddo wearily pulled himself up and back to lean against the frame of the bed. "One day you might remember Tiny, and regret that you didn't get to pay your respects. But right now, at least you can appreciate that he was a warrior in the Raze cause."

Dom's gaze wandered around Kiddo's room. It lingered on Kiddo's ring – set on the bedside table. It touched on the framed photos on Kid's shelf; one showing Dom dipping Kiddo in front of the Ferris Wheel in Japan, and another being a selfie of Dom, Sparks and Kiddo.

"You're grieving the loss of more than just me, aren't you?" Dom asked after a pause. Sympathetic, and far away.

"You're not lost," Kiddo answered earnestly. "You're right here."

Dom's eyes returned to Kiddo, and he regarded Kid with a tilted head.

"You are a dream at the edge of my memory. A beautiful one. But still just a dream that has already slipped away." He reached into his pocket to withdraw a card, which he regarded without relish and also without distaste.

A Wolf card, used by The Hunt.

"I was only meant to come to deliver this," Dom explained unemotionally. "Yorak wrote an appointment date and a message on it."

He peered at what the Wolf's note to Kiddo said, and raised an eyebrow.

"Apparently he believes you need surgery to deal with those seizures. How poignant."

Kiddo scoffed, drawing his legs up and angrily hugging his knees. "Thanks," he muttered darkly.

Then he noticed that he couldn't feel any pants on his lower half anymore. Just the underwear.

Where'd those jeans get to? He cast his gaze around in search of them.

Had Dom ... removed and then folded his pants for him? Putting them away?

That was something Kiddo's Dom would have known

would be appreciated. Maybe that was how Dom had spotted the leather jacket.

Dom set the Wolf card beside the peacock brooch and leaned back with an impassive air.

"So, who was the older man you were hugging earlier?" Dom asked nonchalantly then.

That pulled Kiddo up short, as he wracked his brain to take his thoughts in such a new direction.

Narkon? Narkon had hugged him *much* earlier, on the work site for Kid's Place.

"How long exactly have you spent on delivering me that card?" Kiddo questioned in disbelief. "That was ages ago."

"That man is too old for you," Dom told him. Remaining as outwardly unbothered as ever.

Kiddo let out an involuntary gasp of laughter.

"It's not like that. He's straight. And … you don't even re-member being with me. So do you really get to say things like that?"

"I also don't remember us ever breaking up," Dom gave a faint smile in return. "Doesn't that give me a say?"

Kiddo shook his head incredulously, but not unhappily. And Dom shifted to lounge his long legs over the arm of Kiddo's chair before sighing.

"Another thing I can't remember," Dom went on in a low voice. "Is the woman with us in that photo on the shelf. But Sparks truly did sound like someone I would like."

Kiddo sank back against the bed again, as if the wind had been knocked out of him.

Dom had listened in on the Sparks story.

"You do. A lot. And it seems like you've gone back to your spying and eavesdropping ways," he commented without judgment – hoping that Dom really was doing his research again. "Air conditioning chutes?"

Dom winced. "Should've known that was how I did it before. And I should've changed it up."

"You really did take your time, with the Wolf card mission," Kiddo remarked. "To have caught the hug outside, the bedtime story, and my whole episode."

"Mmm. Been in your base all day," Dom admitted without shame.

"All day?" Kiddo gaped. "You need to be careful – the recruits ..."

"The sunburnt one who got my uppercut in the saferoom that time," Dom agreed. "He's been in here to check on you."

"Ugh," Kid huffed.

Jeffrey had probably been super proud of him, thinking Kiddo had finally been able to achieve a normal night's sleep.

"I could've murdered you, and all he'd know is that you're not abducted," Dom commented slyly. "But it's nice I've still got them on their toes enough to check in on you. I've got everyone on their toes."

Kiddo yawned. "You can't blame them. None of them know what to make of you. You're not with us, and you're heading back to Yorak every day, even after what you found out."

Dom stretched in the chair, draped over it comfortably, as if any wariness between them had never existed. But the fact that he was all the way over there meant that it still felt like any intimate closeness between them had also never existed.

"What do *you* make of me?" Dom asked curiously. "What's in that pretty head of yours?"

Kiddo smoothed the sheets around himself and sank down a little. "I trust you. You inspired a whole gang of Razes for a reason, and you've never lost your own moral compass or ideals. I trust in what you are."

Dom put his hands behind his head to lean back. "*But?*" he prompted.

"*But* … I don't trust who you're going to go home to after this. I hate knowing that you're with him. The fact that you brought his card here, telling me that he's going to force me into an unwanted procedure, is confusing."

Dom didn't deny that he was going to go straight back to Yorak after this, and didn't explain the plans in his own pretty head any further either.

He really would be sleeping in the Wolf's bed, rather than in the one in front of him.

Had Dom fallen in love with Yorak for real, because of the conditioning? Maybe he had somehow forgiven Yorak for the extreme things he'd done.

Dom just nodded in understanding. "I get it."

"And do you get how much I don't want you to go?" Kid asked.

"If it helps, I won't leave here right away," Dom answered slowly. "Even though it's late. Or early, at this point. I'll see if you can fall asleep without my assistance, and without more medical scares."

"I don't need any neck adjustments, thank you," Kiddo

assured him. Though he didn't tell Dom it was really completely safe for him to be left alone at this point.

"You're wide awake," Dom remarked. "How can you be sure you don't need help?"

Kiddo dragged himself down on the mattress, but hooked an arm under his pillow so that he could still see Dom easily enough.

"I could tell you a story, like you did for the baby snatcher," Dom mused. "But I don't have many sweet ones. And we're not close enough for confessions of love at the end."

"You and I got Rue out, before she became a snatcher," Kiddo informed him. "She's a baby Raze now."

Dom quirked a larger smile in surprise. He liked that.

"And I could be the one to tell *you* the sweet stories, if you've got none," Kiddo yawned again. "Though I suppose you should be careful of upsetting Yorak, if you're gone too much longer."

Dom's smile became more of a smirk. "He likes the game of never knowing when I'll be back, while feeling reassured that at some point I will be."

Dom huffed with a breath of short laughter.

"I see now that he must have been sending snatchers and … Hunters … to keep an eye on me when I headed out in the early days. But I kept killing anyone on my tail, and they eventually stopped coming. He doesn't know that I've realised they were his people."

"You … enjoy the game too?"

Dom's expression closed off again then in response. He shrugged.

"I've had a lot of thinking to do. I'm enjoying coming up with my own angles. My own games."

He cracked his knuckles.

"But now I want to know what story you could possibly tell me, that could get you out of my sleep specialty manoeuvre."

Kiddo gave a lopsided smile.

He could tell the story of Kiddo and Dom. Or of any of them. But it felt too soon to keep educating him about everyone else, when he was going to need to make his own mind up about them all first.

Kid decided on telling a story that was all Dom.

Dom had lost two years of himself, where some of the sweetest things had happened to help soften the first of the Razes.

"Close your eyes as you tell it, or you'll never drift off," Dom instructed.

A little sadly, Kiddo did as he was told. Knowing that Dom would not be there when they next opened.

"This is the story of how Raze found his grandmother," Kiddo began softly, smiling at the thought.

There was a moment's pause from the chair.

"I have a grandmother?"

"Mmm," Kiddo nodded. "She gave you that peacock brooch."

And as Kiddo gave Dom the tale of how he had met Miss Dorris, and how he had become her Raze and she his nanna, Kid himself felt lighter again.

He didn't notice when his words became slower, or as they began to peter out faintly.

And he didn't stir when Dom at last, reluctantly, made his silent exit from the room.

| 25 |

Twenty Five

"The Dires were sure they saw him," Hato's deep voice was saying as Kiddo descended the stairs to the kitchen. "But his bike was so quiet and fast, he disappeared before they could find out what he'd been up to."

Kiddo had Dom's jacket, and a piggy-backing Rue on his shoulders.

Hato was talking to Koa and Seethe, but as if Kiddo and Start had synchronised their stairway journeys, both of them entered the kitchen from their different levels at the same time.

Everyone wore black, ready for the service, though Hato was worried as well grief-stricken right now.

He rounded on Kiddo in concern. "You alright? Did they try drugs, or ..."

"I'm fine," Kiddo stated firmly. "All good. He hasn't been brainwashed again."

"So he *did* go to you?" Seethe asked agitatedly, running a hand through his mane of ice-blonde hair. "Why didn't you yell?" he asked in frustration.

Kiddo set Rue down, but she took his hand as if to stand in support of him, even though this was all news to her.

Her biggest hurdle for the morning had been matching white frilly socks to her black lacy dress without 'overdoing things on a serious day.'

"Dom came to give me the Wolf's card with a surgery date on it," Kiddo admitted, and the others groaned in horror. "But, he's been looking into how we operate again. Like the first time he found us. I think he wants to know he can definitely trust us."

"This time he's living with the enemy. We know for sure that he can report anything he learns about us straight back to the snatchers," Seethe growled. "To the *head* of all of the underworld."

"We haven't made any progress on our search for Jingle or the others," Kiddo answered unwaveringly. "We haven't had any bright ideas on how to strike at the Wolf. All he would have heard is day to day stuff, and funeral preparations."

"At the end of the day, he came to carry out the Wolf's will, and still returned to Yorak though, didn't he?" Koa laid out the facts. "It doesn't look good."

"Ahhhh, actually," Start cleared his throat. "I don't think he necessarily went *straight* back. I think he found me first."

Everyone stilled at that.

Kiddo even felt the colour drain from his own face.

"They're after our cleverest Raze again?" Rue moaned what everyone else was thinking. She smacked a dramatic hand to her head.

"I mean, it does make sense," she added. "Your re-sale

would rake in big bucks. Everyone wants a piece of your smarts," she told Start. "But it was just so much effort for all the normal people here to work out where you were the first time."

"Oh, no, no," Start cut in, waving his hands. "At least I hope not. I didn't even see Raze. I only noticed that I must have had a visitor because I haven't been back in my own bedroom for long, and only have a couple of things unpacked," he explained hurriedly.

"Map?" Seethe asked, already twisting a cap off a beer.

"Yes, a laminated map," Start acknowledged. "Along with markers. And when I woke this morning, there was something new written on that map."

"You got a surgery booked too?" Rue asked disconcertedly. "Why not just drop you a Wolf card?"

Start went on, undeterred. "There was a circle drawn around a street in the next city, and a musical note over the biggest property in that area."

"He crept into your room to draw you a musical note," Koa's face brightened. "You think he's found you –"

"Jingle," Start agreed delightedly, bobbing with excitement. "He may have become a double agent – in our favour!"

"Or he may be setting us a nice trap," Seethe scowled. He had chosen the 'expect the worst and avoid disappointment' strategy.

Kiddo realised he was clutching Rue's hand tightly.

If Dom was staying with Yorak for information, taking on the snatchers from the inside, it could turn the tides.

It would also mean that Dom wasn't just there out of a sense of indoctrinated love.

"We need to talk with him," Hato rumbled. "Try to get a feel for what's really going on."

"The Dires can never get him in time, and everyone else on guard yesterday had no idea he was even here," Seethe swilled his liquor unenthusiastically. "Don't think he'll accept any more Lotus drinks invites either."

"Well," Kiddo spoke up. "I did try to persuade him to come to the funeral. He might be there."

Seethe scowled at that too. "If he comes, he'll be showing Yorak that he's softened toward us and will blow his cover," he huffed. "If the double agent thing is even what he's doing."

"Dom told me last night that Yorak has become used to Dom coming and going with his many missions. And because Dom always returned, and too many snatchers were dying when Yorak sent people to watch him, he eventually stopped sending them," Kiddo informed the others. "Yorak might be getting comfortable."

"We could really use a break," Start said wistfully. "And not the kind of breaking that we've become used to."

Though he'd been lifted by the possibility that they had an inside man, Start's glasses were magnifying the fact that his eyes were already puffy from the night before.

If their guesses were wrong, and Dom was siding with the Wolf, it felt like they might as well *all* climb into their coffins now.

"I'll keep my eyes peeled at the service," Koa suggested. "You guys focus on what's most important at the moment."

Kiddo wished he could forget the real purpose of the morning.

How unreal the whole idea of it had felt last night.

"You're right," Hato told her. "Today is about Tiny. If Dominic is there or not, he'll only approach and speak if he wants to. So nobody push it. I'll tell the recruits and anyone watching not to make a move if they see him."

Rue sidled over to the fridge to check her diet plan. "Maybe Kid and I could make Tiny's favourite meals for everyone's dinner tonight," she pondered as she opened the fridge for some milk. "What did he like?"

Kiddo managed a sad grin. "Anything, if it had a good side of mashed potatoes."

"Chain smoking," Seethe added wryly. "So ... nicotine flavour."

"Or spearmint gum, every time he was giving it up," Hato sighed, downcast.

"I wish the others were here," Start confessed, trying not to become tearful. He lifted his glasses to rub at his eyes again. "Will they forgive us for doing this without them?"

Hato straightened. "They wouldn't have forgiven us for letting him go on like that. They'll appreciate us saying goodbye in a way he deserves."

Kid glanced around unhappily then, sinking down at the table. "I just hate that ... if we say goodbye ... it's real."

Tiny, the gruff, grumpy, surprisingly caring, stout tank of a person. Really gone.

Rue pushed an overly full bowl of cereal into Kiddo's hands so that he peered down at her.

She was coming to have the same effect on him as Teddy.

Warmth.

It helped.

"Say your I love yous instead," she advised knowingly. Lovingly.

She scooted in beside Kid with her own bowl.

"Cos that's real too."

| 26 |

Twenty Six

He'd slipped inside when everyone had already been seated – their attention forward.

He'd taken a seat at the back, and at the very end of the row. Distant, but present.

Nearest him were Madam Hellion and Sora, who had come to pay their respects. They made sure to studiously keep their eyes on the front.

And when it was over, he was gone before the coffin had been carried out on Hato, Kiddo, Start, Seethe, Flip and Frazzle's shoulders.

None of them had the energy to comment on what it could mean that Dom had chosen to be there, or how disappointing it was that they'd missed their chance to talk to him.

None of them had the energy to fully confront the fact that that had truly been Tiny's body in that box.

And no matter how much butter and salt Kiddo and Rue added to their mash, nothing could taste good at the end of such a day.

Trix and Blossom went to bed early. Start fell asleep with

his head on the table. Flip took a bike out to join the Dires. Koa left for her night shift. And Frazzle and Daleeah dozed hand in hand on the couch – more of Pash's most beautiful portraits currently showing on the TV screen.

It seemed the media were treating Pash as a tragic loss rather than a case to be solved now, and Kiddo rotated in his chair so that he didn't have to see the reel.

Instead he breathed in the scent of soap, and the ticklish bits of Rue's hair playing about his face. Her limbs dangled around him, slack with sleep, and her head was tucked under his chin as she dribbled on his chest.

Even though Seethe's reddened, fierce gaze made him look more dangerous than ever, Ryo considerately reached across the table to pass the fearsome Raze a tissue.

Seethe was sullenly leaning his chin on his clasped hands. But he accepted the tissue with a grunt. He couldn't seem to keep his inflamed eyes from watering with the angriest tears Kid had ever seen.

Hato, too, had remained quiet the whole evening. Staring dully in the direction of the stairs, and spread out in his kitchen chair like a defeated giant.

However, Kiddo noticed Hato's eyes widening now, and Kid followed the big man's gaze.

His heavy heart somehow managed to skip a beat.

"My condolences," Dom said in a low voice, leaning by the pantry.

He cast a glance at Kiddo, with Rue in his arms.

None of the sleepers in the room stirred. Except for Hato showing his surprise, Kiddo wouldn't have even noticed Dom's arrival.

"If you need your space in this time –" Dom went on.

"Dominic," Hato stopped him before Dom could suggest that he would leave. "Please stay."

Seethe was frozen. He hadn't thought that Dom would come to them, or out into the open while so outnumbered. But here he was, meeting them in the same room that he'd been tied up and confronted in so recently.

Despite his best efforts, he was regarding Dom with yearning, rather than suspicion.

Ryo appeared ready to rise from his seat, and Dom was aware of it – holding up a hand to stop any kind of moves. He appeared equally as ready to duck out of reach at a split second's notice if anyone were to try it.

"Raze ..." Ryo breathed sorrowfully as he took Dom's unyielding stance in. He needed to find the right words, but was struggling.

"Raze, Blossom and I are so very sorry to have used treachery against you. We had thought it was the only act of friendship we had left with which to help you. But, moushiwake nai. There are no excuses to justify making you feel betrayed in the process."

He shook his head in annoyance at himself, as if he wasn't capturing the gravity of what he really meant to convey. Then Ryo bent in the most respectful bow he could manage while seated at the table.

"Moushiwake Gozaimasen deshita," he apologised again, with a sincere formality and depth that somehow made Kiddo's skin prickle. And Dom closed his eyes to collect himself for a beat, as if it was too much for him to take.

Then Dom straightened from his position, moving cautiously and purposefully toward the head of the dining table. He got close enough to quietly draw the end chair back so that he could join them all in being seated, even if somewhat separately.

He regarded Ryo soberly, and visibly tried to remove any stiffness or steel from his expression.

"We've been through a great deal, tomodachi," he answered Ryo. "Shitsurei-shimashita. Pardon my behaviour. You were right. It was the fact that you and Blossom were willing to do that to me, that made me really think. Even when it hurt. But that was quite the test. And I need time."

"Sumimasen ..." Ryo's colour faded, though he nodded in understanding. "I'm grateful you are willing to see if time will heal this. Blossom and I can wait," he vowed.

His posture remained as straight as ever, but the energy had drained from him.

Rather than sending a tissue across the table to Ryo, Seethe deigned to push one of the beers he had lined up for himself to the dismayed Lotus apprentice.

Dom in turn inhaled deeply, addressing everyone at the table now.

"I'm here because I've become aware of the terrible losses your gang has suffered, today and in recent months. I've also begun to see that your gang truly are Raze," he granted in serious recognition, and with appreciation in his tone.

But he paused again guardedly when there was movement from Start.

Start simply stirred groggily from beside Hato, lifting his head.

He blinked around the quiet table slowly, until his gaze settled on Dom.

Then his mouth dropped, ready to exclaim in shock, before Dom lifted a lotus tattooed finger to his lips, and pointed at Rue, Dalee and Frazzle.

Start's exclamation fizzled down to a drawn out, low issuing sound of depleting air. But even as he reined his reaction in, he couldn't keep the hopefulness from dawning across his face.

"Do you …" Start licked his lips hesitantly. "Do you want to work with us again?" he whispered.

Dom regarded him unwaveringly. "It's my duty to help you," he answered with conviction. "We have the same ideals. So I will do what I can for you, whenever I get a chance."

Kiddo adjusted Rue's weight on his legs, unable to be as keen as Start just yet.

"Whenever you get the chance?" he asked Dom in a low voice, wanting, but also not wanting to clarify.

Dom gave a slight nod. He crossed his arms, as if putting up a barrier between himself and anyone else. Even those he was swearing to help, or to try to forgive.

"Brainwashed into the relationship or not, I have still been able to take down multiple bases and buyers while with the Wolf. It would be selfish for me to stop getting everything I can out of that … connection, just because I'm no longer obliviously comfortable with it."

The Wolf was using him.

He would use the Wolf right back.

"It's not healthy for you to be there with him like that," Hato frowned discontentedly. "And what if he realises?"

"What if he permanently zaps your mind?" Start uttered nervously. "He could decide that's better than losing you completely."

Dom lifted and dropped one unconcerned shoulder.

"He would only have caught on if I'd changed outwardly after learning the truth," he answered coolly. "But I went back to him, the same Raze he has come to expect."

He'd left their gang's intervention – inwardly shattered. And yet he had made sure not to show it. He'd made sure to be what Yorak *wanted* him to be.

Seethe rubbed his painfully bloodshot eyes aggressively, cussing under his breath.

"And he *has* been using his trigger words to wield control, now and then," Dom went on smoothly. As if it was really no big deal at all. "But it's a chance for me to get stronger. I'm working on self-training to get better at keeping a hold on myself when it happens."

"Then, you truly don't lose your recent memories again when he does it?" Start questioned tentatively. "That was just part of the conditioning process?"

Dom's expression hardened. "As you predicted, being able to recognise what is happening means I'm getting better at not letting him divert me totally to his will. There's still an effect on my body's reactions," he admitted. "But I'm at the stage where I'm aware of my own deeper thoughts. I need to keep it up."

"That is incredible progress, in such a short time," Start congratulated him with admiration. "Truly incredible."

"Is working out a weak chink in your armour worth staying there?" Seethe hissed. He was holding his frame as if he'd been hammer punched repeatedly all day, instead of attending a funeral, and instead of now finally speaking in a civil manner to someone he had missed.

Dom tilted his head, taking in everything about Seethe's prickly, wounded, aggressive exterior.

Maybe he was becoming aware of how Seethe showed care much more quickly than Kiddo had ever caught onto it.

"I don't like weak chinks," Dom smiled faintly. "But I'd say it's worth staying there while I find out everything I can about him. About the underworld. And about where on your clever Raze's maps I should draw little clues and tips as they come to me."

"But Raze what if you *are* caught, despite your best efforts?" Ryo asked gently. "What if he finds out you have been returning here, and does resort to extreme measures … to 'zap' your mind?"

"You'll all have hopefully got enough dirt to do something with it by then," Dom sighed. "And I'll either disappear out of everyone's reach before it gets that far, or become a useless symbol he can wave around if I don't get away." He flicked piercing blue eyes Kiddo's way again. "But I might be able to blame Kid if I'm spotted here on any quick tip-off trips. He does want me to keep getting into Kiddo's head."

"Instead of disappearing, instead of working on your armour, or working on the inside," Hato rumbled sombrely. "Why not really hurt the Wolf, and choose to just stay here with us? He said that a Raze's owner has to continually prove themselves worthy and able to keep hold of a Raze. To lose you would make him lose face in a massive way. We have many friends actively safeguarding this warehouse now, and it would be harder for him to reclaim you or his reputation."

Kiddo paused in rocking Rue.

Was that one a good enough argument to get Dom back here?

Dom raked a hand back through his hair and leaned forward on his knees, almost within Hato's touching range.

"The Wolf has already lost. He just doesn't know it. He's a dead man walking. But his destruction is going to have to be piece by piece. Careful and calculated. It's why I spent the last week searching out your Jingle, to execute Start's plans, at the same time as doing everything else on my gory to-do list."

Start shrugged sheepishly at them. "I actually do have a number of plans. I know what we can try, just not how to do it. We need Jingle. But not even General Wolder's sources were having luck finding her, when she's so close to under our noses. Without Dom's efforts, I don't know how long it would have taken us."

Hato lifted his arms, palms up.

"Alright," he accepted that grimly. "We needed your inside information to pinpoint Jingle. But once we have her, you can help us to find the other Razes, and to battle the Wolf from here," Hato went on, almost pleading with Dom.

"You can stay, Dominic. Stay with your family."

Dom was nearly motionless now.

The more they tried to reason, or to draw him in, the more closed off he seemed.

"I am sorry that I ever thought you were my enemy," Dom told Hato frankly – thinking back over their violent recent encounters with regret. "And perhaps deep down I knew that was wrong, and modified my attacks."

Seethe puffed a dark, low laugh at that.

"But if I have to disappear on the Wolf, I can't just come back here," Dom stated. Firm, and gentle at the same time. "If I stay with you, I'll be an easy and predictable target again." His voice became even softer, as if to make the next blow less awful. "It obviously happened last time."

Hato flinched with the truth of that. Dom making a home with them had made Raze accessible.

"I'll need to constantly be slipping out of the Wolf's reach, or it will be easy for him to get me back," Dom rationalised.

"But slipping out of our reach too?" Seethe said through his teeth. "You lost your covert lifestyle, but you gained an awful lot with us. How does losing your family leave you any better off?"

Dom winced, unable to hide the impact of that point. Especially coming from such an outwardly harsh, unloving person.

"It sounds so nice … to have this family you keep mentioning," Dom said honestly. "But … whatever bonding we did over the last couple of years," he shrugged helplessly. "I've lost it."

More punches seemed to keep landing against Seethe. He was pale and stony.

"We hardly had this kind of relationship when I was hero worshipping you at eight," Dom reminded him. "But I'll spend some time sorting myself out. I'll do what I can to help you all be your own Razes, and will work with you as I said."

He stood quietly, and placed the chair back at the head of the table.

"You don't have to worry and don't have to chase after me," he reassured them, as if any of this could really make them feel better. "I don't need saving, and I will come to you when I've got anything to offer."

"How can we not worry?" Hato asked in a voice knotted by emotion.

Ryo looked gutted. Seethe's eyes were burning all over again, and Start simply gaped.

"I know what I'm doing," Dom answered evenly. Certain of his path. "No fear."

"None?" Kiddo almost breathed the word in automatic despondence.

Dom's eyes connected with Kiddo's for a moment.

"None," he told him firmly.

Before he turned to descend the stairs.

| 27 |

Twenty Seven: Epilogue

The breeze from the docks was fresh, carrying the taste of the saltiness from the water lapping at the bay.

"Another late night?" Dom asked him, his eyes on the waves bobbing beyond the darkened merry-go-round.

He leaned against a war chariot – embodying the stillness of a warrior waiting in the calm between battles.

"Didn't think you'd go back straight away," Kiddo replied. "And thought I'd find you here."

He stepped onto the quiet carousel, and swung himself up to sit sideways on an eternally proud warhorse.

He rested his temple against the golden pole holding the horse in place.

"You here to try to trap me again?" Dom smirked, but without mirth.

"Mmm," Kiddo remembered the horrifying night, when he, Seethe and Hato had lost Dom to the Wolf. "Sorry about that."

Kid traced the extravagant mantle on his stallion's head. "You going to chop me in the neck again?"

"Ahh," Dom mused. "I recall getting in a few good jabs. And I'm sorry for that too."

He rotated, so that he could face Kiddo instead of the shore.

"I also recall being drawn here," he confessed. "And not knowing why finding a grand ride for children at this spot disappointed me so much."

Kiddo fidgeted with the leather strap that served as his horse's reins.

"You would have felt safer to find a row of derelict concrete pipes," Kiddo informed him. "Where we took shelter a few times."

Kiddo remembered the pouring rain, the beating of their shoes as they sprinted, the sound of the wire fence as they half flew up and over it. The first time he'd held Dom close, after a snatcher's blow to his head. The first time he'd realised that Dom had been guarding him from an ambush.

Dom laid himself back now, with his arms behind his head.

"I do like small, neglected spaces. And I love to hide," he drawled, gazing at the heavenly scenes painted in pastel colours on the carousel ceiling. "How romantic of me to share that with you."

"You *are* a romantic," Kiddo attested. "I was lucky that we shared a great deal."

Dom sighed. "It doesn't really sound like me," he commented listlessly. "But I can see how you might have made me want to try."

He rolled onto his side to lean on his elbow then – peering at Kiddo with an eyebrow raised.

"Did you come to tell me more stories about hiding and tunnels?" he asked inquiringly. "I'm still recovering from the story about my surprise grandmother."

Dom's expression was perturbed as he recalled the night before. "I'll have to come to terms with *that* at some point. As well as the fact that you've been left as a single father."

Kiddo shook his head.

"I'm not going to force you to come to terms with anything," he promised. "It's too much, and unfair."

Dom considered that, and hmmm'd quietly to himself in agreement.

"I've realised that one of the great things about you, and about Sparks," Kid began thoughtfully. "Was that you never pushed me before I was ready, except in ways I was open to." He grinned faintly when he saw Dom open his mouth to interject. "Even though you enjoy pushing people's boundaries."

Dom closed his mouth. It was exactly what he had been going to say.

"So I want you to know that I won't push you," Kiddo went on. "Except in ways that you are open to," he vowed.

"Slow and steady," Kiddo told him. "You're going to get to know me again. And I'm going to win you back."

Dom gave him a slow, curling smile.

"Fine …" he answered with a smouldering glint in his eyes. "So do it."

It was both consent, and a challenge.

Kiddo held his gaze.

"I will."

RECEIVE YOUR EXTRA RAZE WARFARE CHAPTER WHEN YOU SIGN UP FOR SHELLEY CASS' VIP LIST. GET YOUR BONUS HERE:

shelleycass.com/coming-soon-02

https://www.shelleycass.com/coming-soon-02

OTHER BOOKS BY SHELLEY CASS

The Raze Warfare Series
'A Fairy's Tale' Epic Fantasy Series:
Book One – 'The Last Larnaeradee'
Book Two – 'The Raiden'
Book Three – 'The Army for the World'
Dystopian Future:
'Awaken Dreamer'
Contemporary/Action/Fantasy/Erotica:
'Darkling'
The Sleep Sweet Series for children:
Book One – 'Little Pixie's Christmas'
Book Two – 'The case of the bored baby Ace'
Book Three – 'Mum and Me'
Book Four – 'The Cloud and the Flower'
Book Five – 'Hush'

Dear reader,
I would love to hear your feedback!
Please leave a review and feel free to visit my author Facebook page
or website (shelleycass.com).

ABOUT THE AUTHOR

I was an awkward, reserved year 8 student – totally in love with the escape and comfort offered by the novels I read. I could hear the voices of the authors' characters, I could tune out my stresses and uncertainties as I journeyed with each protagonist through their own troubles. And then one day I could hear the voices of characters who hadn't been written yet, in places that hadn't been created, and I decided to write my own worlds.

In the real world I became a high school teacher, and still face the epic battle of staying afloat in all the papers I must assess. And in the real world the magic has also sometimes been hard to find. Stress and disunity surface like cancer – making the nightly news too hard to watch on most days.

But in the real world there has also been inspiration – incredible students, loved ones, golden memories, growing up, warm hugs, big laughs and good people.

One of the greatest things achieved in my lifetime that I can remember, and that had a profound impact on me, was when Australia legalised equal marriage. I'd had this terrible sick fear that it wouldn't happen, and that I would have to face the fact that a majority of the people in my country do not want progress or equality. I would have to face the fact that some of my students and friends would not have the same rights or access to a future that I could choose to have. Teaching teens to reach for their dreams in a climate like that just seemed too hopeless. But instead, I remember sitting next to mum – happy tears streaming down her face – as something incredibly good was achieved. We proved that the majority of people appreciate love and the right to love in all forms. That love is love. Which is damn important in a world that can be so harsh.

So I wrote of the things that threaten the world, and of the big and small things that save it. I wish for a real world where the air is clean, the trees can grow without concrete borders, the darkness can be cured with the switch of a light, and the people can all have long days and happy lives.

ACKNOWLEDGMENTS

I am so thankful for the friends who understand me and embrace who I am.

I am so appreciative of my work family, for being my silver lining even on the most stressful days.

I am so appreciative of Wendy – the greatest neighbour to have ever lived, and Linda – the greatest mother to have ever lived. Your patience with reading my novels when they are still rough, clunky, colossal things is indescribably helpful.

I am so grateful for an extended family of extensive love: the bubbly and boisterous Brittinghams, Burkes and Rigbys, and the gracious, gorgeous Tangees, Lemmens and Plants. My grandparents too, though lost, are such a special part of me.

I am so thankful for Linda (mum) and Robert (dad), who would move heaven and earth to make us happy.

For my sisters and best friends, Melissa and Leigh.

For my brother in law, Andrew, and the lights of my life – Jack and Elyssia.

For the love of my life, my sunshine, Jarryd.

And for the little year eight version of me, who first picked up that pen to write.